SUSAN A JENNINGS

Second Chances

Lavender Cottage Book 4

SaRaKa InPrint

First published by SaRaKa InPrint 2021

Cover Image and author Photo SAJ Design

Interior author photo the late Doris Leightley

Shutterstock/Krakenimages.com Shutterstock/By Andrei Nekrassov

Shutterstock:ID: 717140545 By SasaStock - Golden Retrievers

Shuitterstock:ID: 280483640 by dezy Jack Russell Terrier

This book is written in Canadian style with Canadian spelling

First edition

ISBN: 978-1-989553-21-3

Editing by Meghan Negrijn

This book was professionally typeset on Reedsy.
Find out more at reedsy.com

I dedicate this book with gratitude to friends at
Manor Court, Barrow-upon-Trent, U.K.
for all their support and kindness
for my mother.

"A loving heart is the truest wisdom."

CHARLES DICKENS

Contents

Preface

What happened before *Second Chances* - Lavender Cottage Book 4

After a heartbreaking divorce Katie and her dog Buddy Boy move to Springsville, a quaint English village and narrowboat marina where she buys Lavender cottage and turns it into a B&B. She also meets the mysterious Dr. Piers Bannister, his dog Arthur and narrowboat *Tranquil Days.* The B&B is running smoothly. Daughter Melanie is married to Phil who discovers his estranged brother Tony. Son Ben is manager of a famous jazz band in America. Doris' the ghost of Adam, the live in handyman, lives on the veranda and guides Katie and Adam. Judy, Katie's best friend and her dogs, Lily and Sam support are featured in all the stories. The B&B is successful with regular guests like Sir Walter. Piers' partner Rick and wife Cindy. Various guests spend time and some have romantic episodes, and sometimes there are challenging times. All stories include the villagers and some focus a village resident as the main plot in the story. Mary, the cafe owner, Bob the marina owner appear in all stories as do Maisie owner of

Boater's Inn and son Stevie. Cyril owner of the Springsville Antique Shop and girlfriend Olivia frequently pop in and out of the Katie's stories.

Characters of Lavender Cottage

People:

- Katie Bannister ....Owner of Lavender Cottage
- Dr Piers Bannister......Katie's new husband
- John Saunders ....Katie's ex-husband
- Melanie & Ben ....Katie & John's adult children
- Phil Williams ....Melanie's husband
- Tony Williams ....Phil's brother
- Dr. Rick Larkin ....Piers' partner and friend
- Cindy Larkin ....Rick's wife
- Judy Clayton ....Katie's best friend
- Adam Cummings ....Previous owner and resident
- Doris Cummings ....The ghost of Adam's wife
- Lydia Dickson ....Maid at Lavender Cottage
- Sir Walter Rutherford. Guest and Adam's friend
- Bob Bingham ....Owner of Bob's Marina
- Mary Bingham ....Bob's wife Owner of the cafe
- Maisie Talbot ....Widow proprietress Boater's Inn
- Stevie Talbot ....Maisie's barman and adult son

- Cyril Winthrop ....Antique dealer
- Olivia Moreland ....Society lady, friend of Cyril's
- Dr George Duthie........Local GP & old friend
- Nancy Duthie...............Georges wife
- Pat..............................Clinic's nurse and receptionist
- Dr Stephanie Ward......New doctor at clinic

Dogs:

- Buddy-Boy ..... Katie's fluffy white bichon frisé
- Arthur ....Piers' brown and white terrier
- Lily and Sam ....Judy's golden retrievers

The Dogs of Lavender Cottage

Cruising Arthur | Protector Sam | Loving Lily | Laid-back Buddy Boy

Happily Ever After

N ever, in all her life had she been so happy, her insides tickled like champagne bubbles and made her laugh. Not in a million, trillion years could she imagine being so in love, every time she looked at Piers she thought she would burst and wondered why it had taken them so long to marry.

A summer boat accident and the threat of Piers dying or living with a brain injury had made them see sense. He had made a remarkably quick recovery, followed by the wedding, the move to Springsville and a new lifestyle. Deep down, below the champagne bubbles, she heard a whisper asking if it was too much, too fast.

Katie stood at the front door, waving to Piers as he turned off Marina Lane onto Main Street, his new routine. Piers left early to beat the traffic for his commute to Nottingham and a looming flu epidemic made his days longer as ill patients crowded the waiting room.

Buddy Boy, Katie's beloved bichon frise and Arthur, Piers' Jack Russell sat patiently at her feet. She watched the sky lighten into dawn and listened to the bare trees groan as the wind tried to bend the sturdy leafless branches and shake off the twittering birds perched on creaking twigs. Oblivious to the wind the trees settled in to rest until spring. *Spring* she thought *with Piers at my side. I will feel the brightness of spring for the rest of my life.* "Really, Katie," she said aloud with a giggle, "you are behaving like a love-struck teenager, rather than a mature woman with grown up kids."

The honeymoon aboard Piers' narrowboat *Tranquil Days* had been magical as the summer boaters had returned to the city leaving the canals quiet and perfect for newlyweds. Daytime cruising on bright days, stargazing on clear nights and early nights in the warm cabin to escape the October chill. *Not that we spent a lot of time out of the cabin*, she thought with a chuckle.

She gave a shiver and wrapped her arms around her midriff against the cold, suddenly realizing she was standing outside. Glancing down at the dogs she said, "Come on boys, let's get warm."

Katie returned to the kitchen, Buddy Boy and Arthur following with their paws clicking on the wooden floor. By the time she poured her second cup of coffee, the dogs were curled up by the Morning Room fire. They had started out with a doggie bed each, but as they only ever used one, and space was limited by the fireplace, Katie had moved the unused bed to the bedroom. She gave the fire a poke and with steaming coffee in hand, tucked her feet under her and settled in her favourite blue chair just as her mobile rang.

Reaching for her phone she guessed the caller was Judy,

2

her best friend of thirty years, also an early riser. Judy, an engineer in charge of massive construction projects, insisted on being on site when the contractors arrived in the morning. Her current project, a shopping precinct, was in the south somewhere near Guildford.

"Good morning Judy! I knew it was you, the only person who calls me at this hour of the day. How's the project going?"

"We're ahead of schedule. The first phase will be complete by the end of the week and that's why I'm calling. I'm in need of peace and tranquility at Lavender Cottage. The testosterone around here is getting to me." She laughed. "Men are such strange creatures. I've been an engineer for twenty-five years and a successful, senior project manager for ten of them and they still question my authority. One of the local contractors even called me 'babe' yesterday." Katie heard the frustration as Judy took a raspy breath, and imagined her balling her fist.

"Oh dear. Did you punch him?" Judy didn't answer. "I was joking. What did you do!?"

"No, I didn't touch him but he got a tongue lashing he'll never forget. I need some rest before I do something I regret."

"How soon can you get here? I'd love to see you. We haven't had time together since the wedding."

"Sunday. I have three days overtime due to me. I'll confirm tomorrow. I'm looking forward to long walks by the canal and coffee and scones at Mary's Cafe."

"That's perfect. The B&B is quiet during the week. We still get a few guests on the weekend but November is our slowest month. You can have the Daisy Den for as long as you want."

"I won't be intruding on the honeymooners?"

"Not at all. Piers is very busy at the clinic. He'll be home Sunday but he's on call next week and usually stays with Rick and Cindy. I'll be glad of the company."

"Terrific. I have to see my dad, pick up Sam and Lily on Saturday and I'll head to Springsville on Sunday."

They said their goodbyes and Katie put her phone down, leaning her head back on the chair and enjoying the quiet. At the same time the quiet felt almost odd. She was used to Adam buzzing around the kitchen making the morning tea and coffee for the guests, but there were no guests today and no Adam either.

She had bought the house from Adam, a widower having been persuaded to move out of his home and live unhappily with his son. Katie had guessed when she bought the cottage from him that he was unhappy and missed his garden and suggested he come and visit and help her with the garden. This led to him moving in permanently as the resident handyman and gardener, and friend to Katie. Although in his seventies, he was mostly fit and healthy, with arthritis occasionally slowing him down.

Sir Walter Rutherford was a regular guest at the B&B and having the same interests as Adam in gardening, especially roses, and playing darts, they had become close friends. The reason Adam was not at home was because Sir Walter had taken him on holiday to his house in Portugal, where it was warmer and not so damp as England.

Katie finished her coffee, stretched and said, "Time for a walk." Knowing that Buddy and Arthur would be on their feet in a micro second. "Give me five minutes to get dressed," she said patting each dog on the head.

Walking towards the marina, the damp air seemed to amplify the baking smells and coffee aroma coming from Mary's Cafe. But, having just finished a coffee, Katie resisted the urge to stop and chat with Mary. The dogs ran ahead, Buddy heading for the towpath and Arthur hesitating near *Tranquil Days*, still not completely understanding that his home was Lavender Cottage.

"Come, Arthur!" Katie called.

Bob, the owner of the marina, appeared from behind a boat, his face and hairless head red from tugging at a tarpaulin that had loosened in the wind, "Good morning, Katie!"

"Hi! Do you need some help?"

"Thanks, no! Just tightening the moorings and tarps." He spun his head around sniffed the air and added, "Storm's coming. Don't go far."

"Okay, thanks. We'd better get moving." She hurried the dogs along the towpath. Bob, a retired navy man, was never wrong about storms. He had a gruff exterior but a gentle heart that he kept hidden, except when he was with his wife, Mary.

Arthur and Buddy Boy ran ahead, occasionally glancing back to make sure Katie was still there. She laughed aloud at what seemed to be a competition between the dogs as they sniffed specific blades of grass or rocks, each raising a leg to mark the territory. When they reached the stile into the field, Katie sat on the wooden step and let the dogs run. As always, Buddy Boy searched for his friends, Sam and Lily, before running with Arthur. She, too, felt the stormy air, never doubting Bob. The stillness was expectant and heavy with moisture; the light growing dark as thick black clouds moved across the sky. She shivered, rubbing her hands and wished she'd brought gloves.

"Come, boys. We'd better get back."

The rain began as a drizzle and Katie clipped the leashes on the dogs. "No time for sniffing," she said and began running, glancing up at the heavy black cloud about to release its cargo of rain.

As she opened the gate to Lavender cottage, the rain hit them hard, making her run even faster through the front door. Dripping wet, she slammed the door and leaned against it. Buddy Boy and Arthur sprayed water everywhere as they shook the rain from their fur. Katie laughed, quickly grabbing towels and throwing them over the pair. The three sat wrapped in towels in front of the fire.

Katie glanced at the French doors leading to the rose garden. The rain, now being blown sideways by a howling wind, pounded on the glass and she thought about Piers driving into the city on the motorway. The spray from lorries and the heavy rain would make for an unpleasant drive. Despite their long talks about the commute, she had a strong feeling Piers wasn't one hundred percent comfortable with it. He had not said anything but she sensed it might become an issue.

The end of October and all of November were slow months giving her the opportunity to catch up and today she was preparing the budget for next year. The B&B had done very well since the renovations but the cottage was old and needed new triple glazed windows to match the ones in the extension. Planning for some big maintenance expenses was essential, as was the timing for big jobs so as not to interfere with the quiet and tranquility guests had come to expect at Lavender Cottage. It was rare for her to be completely alone in the cottage. Even Lydia, the young maid, finished early as there was little to do. During quiet times, she would wash curtains and deep clean. But the rain meant no drying outside. Katie was old-fashioned and still used a clothesline.

She stretched and eased her back from scrunching over the books before heading to the kitchen to start dinner for just the two of them. Piers had promised to be home early tonight. She hoped the rain wouldn't delay him or, as often happened, a busy surgery. But the wind and rain had kept up most of the day, prompting her to check the weather app on her phone. Flash flooding and downed trees were reported in Nottingham and South Derbyshire. Her mobile rang and Piers' private number flashed on the screen.

"Hello, it's just me." Katie felt her heart skip a beat, which happened every time she heard his voice but today, she was afraid he was calling to say he'd been delayed.

"Is everything all right?"

"Yes. I'm calling to let you know I'm on my way home. I can't wait to see you."

"See you soon. Take it easy on the roads. Lots of flooding and downed trees. We're okay here, other than a soaking I got this morning." Kate laughed. "I'll tell you when you get home. Love you."

"Love you more."

The rain continued for two more days, finally stopping on Thursday night, much to Katie's relief. Piers had looked tired this morning as though he hadn't slept well and was dreading the commute. His journeys to and from Nottingham had worsened every day as more roads closed and longer detours took him miles out of his way. But tonight he would be home for the weekend, leaving his partner Rick on call until Monday morning. Katie intended to pamper Piers all weekend. There were only three guests, a couple she had never met before celebrating their wedding anniversary, and Cyril Winthrop's girlfriend, Olivia Moreland. The weatherman's promise of no rain for the weekend pleased her, not just for Piers, but for her guests. If the weather was bad, Adam lit a fire in the big fireplace in the lounge, making it cozy for conversation and reading. She always felt bad for guests coming for a weekend of hiking or walking having to huddle under umbrellas and plod about in Wellington boots or stay shut inside. She hoped the warm lounge made up for the miserable weather.

Olivia arrived in the early afternoon. Katie watched her get out of Cyril's very ordinary Vauxhall car. It was quite a come down from the first time they'd met. She remembered the stuck-up, prickly lady, dressed in designer everything down to the crocodile shoes and handbag, who had stepped out of the taxi, flouncing an oversized cigarette holder and giving orders. That had not been a pleasant visit but things had changed for Olivia. A nasty divorce had stripped her of her children and her home, and perhaps most important to Olivia, her entitled life. Although Olivia had stayed at the B&B several times, and definitely was no long a mean conniving person, Katie still had a mixture of emotions and found herself being very cautious. Their initial encounter, full of Olivia's meanness and hurtfulness, was hard to forget, although she had certainly learned some lessons and changed. Katie actually felt sorry for her as the tables had turned and Olivia experienced horrible cruelty and lies during her divorce.

Katie watched Cyril take her suitcase from the car and give her a peck in the cheek. Olivia smiled and walked down the path, her high heels clicking on the crazy paving. Her Armani suit fit naturally on her slim frame, the cigarette holder, once her signature, was nowhere to be seen. The crocodile handbag that had hung queen-style from her arm had been replaced with an ordinary one, that might even have been good quality plastic, that hung elegantly from her shoulder. No matter how she was dressed, Olivia was a beautiful and striking woman.

Katie opened the front door to greet them. "Come in and welcome back, Olivia. Cyril, it's nice to see you."

"I am pleased to be here. I love your cottage, Katie and …" she paused, "your company."

Katie nodded, not quite sure what to make of the comment. "You'll be staying in the Lavender Suite, with a king-size bed and a sitting area, giving you lots of space. I wasn't sure if Cyril might like to join you." Olivia blushed and Cyril cleared his throat.

"Where's Adam?" Cyril said, looking at the suitcase.

"He's in Portugal with Sir Walter. He deserves a holiday. His arthritis is getting worse and Sir Walter thought the warmer climate would be good for him." Katie eyed Cyril, who could be demanding and also entitled, coming from a similar background to Olivia. There was a mystery attached to Cyril's past, perhaps at one time privileged but now he owned and managed The Springsville Antique Shop. Katie eyed him again. "I'm sure you can manage Olivia's suitcase. Or were you thinking I would carry it?"

"No, of course not. I was only enquiring about Adam as he is always here." Cyril's neck had a pink hue of embarrassment. Katie wanted to giggle. She and Cyril had a history of conflict but it was mostly harmless bantering.

One Crisis After Another

P iers arrived home tired and frustrated, the usual 50 -
60 minute drive had taken him over an hour and a half,
following detour after detour to skirt flooded roads.
Katie greeted him with a hug and cooked his favourite, lamb
chops. After dinner they walked to the marina with Buddy
Boy and Arthur to check on *Tranquil Days*.

That day the water had risen to only an inch below the
dock and ripples were splashing on the wooden surface. Piers
adjusted the fenders that hung along the side of the boat to
prevent the dock damaging the hull.

"Hello Piers and Katie," Bob called from the next dock. "I've
never seen the canal basin this high. If it gets any higher it
will flood."

"How come it's so high?" Piers asked. "I thought the canal
was supposed to stay the same."

"I called the authorities. They told me there is so much run
off from the waterlogged land it's difficult to keep it level. I

was warned that if we get any more of that torrential rain, or any rain for that matter, the marina is in danger of flooding."

Piers frowned as he lowered the fenders. "How do we secure the boats?"

"Same as now, maybe extra lines. These docks are secured in the canal basin. They aren't floating docks and even if we flood it's not like a river where you have rapid currents. The possibility of high wind concerns me more, blowing the boats against, or even on the docks."

Katie glanced up towards the dark unoccupied café, lit only by a security light. "What about the café and the gift shop? Will they flood? Can it reach Marina Lane?"

Bob shook his head. "The buildings are higher than the docks. They'll be fine and it would have to be a Noah's Ark flood to reach Marina Lane." He grinned at Katie. "Always the worrier."

Piers put his arm around her shoulder and spoke softly. "Everything will be okay. The weather forecast for the weekend is sunny. I bet the water will be down by Monday."

"I agree," Bob said, nodding his head up and down enthusiastically. "Mind you, I have to admit in all my twenty plus years here, I've never seen the basin this high. It has to be climate change."

Piers grabbed the side of *Tranquil Days* and stretched one of his long legs over the side of the boat and hauled himself on board. Opening the storage bin in the stern, he pulled out some heavy mooring lines and threw them on the dock, just missing Buddy Boy and Arthur. "Oh, sorry boys." He looked at Katie, expecting reprimand. "I didn't see them there. I'm going to attach an extra …" A sudden splash made them both turn to see Arthur in the water between the boat and the dock.

11

Katie screamed. "He'll get crushed. He's between the boat and the dock." Bob pushed Katie aside, attempting to grab Arthur before he disappeared under the dock. Katie, not paying attention, tripped on the ropes, almost falling in the water. Bob grabbed her with one arm until she got her balance and with his free arm he forced *Tranquil Days* away from the dock.

Piers yelled, panic in his voice, "Katie! Arthur!"

"I'm okay and so is Arthur. He's swimming to the shore." Katie ran down the dock, Buddy Boy close on her heels. She grabbed Arthur as his little legs struggled to climb up the slippery mudbank. Katie held him close to her, icy cold water pouring down her coat and soaking her jeans. Arthur gave her a look of 'what just happened' as Piers reached her side. "Oh Arthur, I'm so sorry. Are you okay?! Katie, take the dogs home. You are soaked to the skin. Bob will help with the moorings." He gave her a sheepish grin. "I am sorry."

"You're forgiven." She gave him a cheeky grin. "Maybe?"

Katie felt Arthur shivering from the cold and by the time she got to the cottage, the water dripping from Arthur, had soaked through her anorak. They shivered in unison. She filled the sink with warm water and gave Arthur, who was not impressed with a second dip in water, a good scrub. She wrapped him in a towel and rubbed his fur dry before giving the fire a poke. A hint of 'eau de canal' hit her nostrils and she pulled Arthur close to sniff his fur, but he smelled of fresh scented doggie shampoo. The smell was coming from Katie's wet jeans and discarded coat, now drying in the warmth of the Morning Room fire.

She turned her nose up at the odour and shivered from the coldness that had seeped into her body. Leaving Buddy Boy and Arthur in their bed by the fire, Katie ripped off her clothes and threw them in the washing machine before jumping into the hot shower. She sighed as the hot water warmed her body and the smell of eau de canal morphed to a floral scent from her body wash.

"Katie! I'm home," Piers called. She heard him talking to Arthur.

"In the shower!" Katie called, hearing the bedroom door open as she put on her thick terry robe. "I'll be out in a minute."

"Need any help?" Piers' head peered around the bathroom door. "Can I come in?" She was in his arms before she could answer. "I am so sorry. Are you alright? I see Arthur is bathed and no worse for wear."

"Yes, I'm fine. I was cold and smelled of canal water, that's all."

Piers pulled her close. "You smell delicious now." Taking a deep breath he added, "Umm … spring flowers floating in the breeze."

He kissed her neck, making her giggle. "Such flowery words. Do you have something in mind?"

Katie wrapped her arms around his neck while Piers stroked her cheek, her lips finding his. The towel on her head slipped to the floor, wet hair falling to her shoulders and making her tremble, or was it his touch?

"Perhaps the doctor should prescribe a warm massage for his beautiful wife."

"Oh yes, please." Gasping to catch her breath, she was hardly able to get the words out. "That would be lovely."

A noise coming from the lounge woke Katie. She glanced

at the illuminated numbers on the clock, 5:24. She listened
again. Someone was moving around. It was early for guests,
particularly Olivia as she slept until noon. The other couple
she didn't know but it was unlikely they were up as they had
ordered tea for 7:30. Could someone have broken in? She
crept out of bed, annoyed at having to get up. During the slow
season, especially when Piers was home, she slept until six.
Tying the belt on her robe, she tiptoed through the Morning
Room and put her ear to the door. Someone was definitely
in there. A low growl caught her attention. Buddy Boy and
Arthur were at her heels, their ears up and the hair on the
back of their necks standing on end, as did Katie's. She put
her finger to her lips, and whispered, "Shush." She took a deep
breath and slowly turned the door knob, opening the door
just enough to see who was there.

She let out a loud sigh and pushed the door fully open.
"Olivia, you gave me a fright."

Olivia was standing in front of the Keurig machine, frantically pressing buttons. "How do you work this damned
machine!" She waved exaggerated hands in the air and stared
at Katie accusingly. "There's not much point in offering coffee
when the machine doesn't work. Now I know why I stay in
five-star hotels with 24 hour room service."

Katie pulled as much air into her lungs as she could and
counted to ten to calm herself so as not to lose her temper.
"Here, let me do it for you. Tea or coffee?" Katie looked up,
shocked at Olivia's appearance. Her puffy red face was creased
with agony; her cheeks wet from crying. The way she looked,
Katie suspected she'd been up all night. "Olivia, what is wrong.
Are you alone? Cyril didn't stay?" Her annoyance had gone
and all she felt was concern for this sad woman.

Olivia didn't answer, but shook her head. Tears streamed down her face as she stared into nowhere. Katie guided her to the sofa, assuming the head shake meant Cyril had not stayed. "Take a seat. I'll light the fire and make some real coffee." Olivia sat down and Katie took the afghan blanket and covered her up, placing a box of Kleenex on the coffee table and lit the fire: thankful that Lydia had laid it ready. "I'll be back in a few minutes."

Katie, peeked into the bedroom to see Piers sleeping soundly. Both dogs escaping the drama, and not particularly fond of Olivia, were curled up on the bed. She pulled the door closed and left him to sleep, knowing how exhausted he was.

She carried a tray of coffee into the lounge. Olivia had not moved but she had stopped crying. Katie sat beside her and poured coffee.

"It sometimes helps to talk," Katie said, in a consoling tone. "I'm a good listener and nothing needs to go beyond these walls."

Olivia picked up her cup and sipped the coffee. With a weak smile she said, "This is good coffee, thank you." Katie saw her bottom lip tremble. "I'm not much good at making anything, even coffee out of a machine. I'm sorry I yelled at you."

"Apology accepted. You are very upset and I suspect you haven't had any sleep. And that machine? Well, you are not alone. Sir Walter hates that machine too but some guests, mostly younger, love it."

Distracted by the fire crackling in the big open fireplace, her mind wandered. *A crackling fire adds comfort to a room,* she thought. *I'm pleased I didn't allow the contractor to talk me into a wood stove or worse, an electric fireplace.* Katie enjoyed the warmth and stared at the bright flames reflected on the brass and mesh fire screen. The heat and flickering flames were comforting as they sat in silence

"He took everything," Olivia blurted out. "I didn't expect much from him but I expected justice from the courts. But then who was I kidding. Did you know Basil was appointed to the bench the same day our divorce was finalized?"

"No. So he's a judge now."

Olivia nodded. "He has everything he wanted; his judicial appointment, an heir and no wife."

Katie could find no words of reassurance.

"The court gobbled up his lies and awarded me a pittance in alimony but that's not the worst. The judge declared me an unfit mother with no income to support my children. Because of Basil's lies and innuendoes, the court deemed I was a danger to my children and a flight risk; in other words, at risk of kidnapping my own children. I can only see them under supervision for two hours, once a month." Tears flowed quietly and continuously as Olivia slid back into her thoughts.

"I am so sorry. Is there no way you can expose his lies? What does your solicitor say?"

She gave a sarcastic grunt. "Selected by Basil. Amy Anderson. I had met her at social functions; a nice person but no match for Basil and he knew it. I didn't have any money to hire my own. She assured me that she was bound by ethics to do the best for me. But after talking to Cyril, I realized she was afraid of reprisal from Basil. Even the judge questioned her lack of argument on my behalf." Olivia sniffed and pulled more tissues from the box, balling them up in her fist and dabbing her cheeks.

"It doesn't make any sense in this day and age. Assets are automatically divided between husband and wife. Child custody is almost always joint custody and, more often than not, it is the mother, not the father, who is favoured," Katie said, thinking of her own divorce. Child custody was not an issue as both Ben and Melanie were adults at the time of her divorce. Her ex-husband was a solicitor but that hadn't influenced their agreement. and the marital assets were split according to both party's wishes.

"I signed a prenuptial agreement without legal advice and until now I had no idea what I'd signed."

Katie poured more coffee and listened, occasionally shaking her head in disbelief at the injustice and cruelty of this horrible man. Olivia was not the most likeable of women but no one deserved to be treated this way.

Olivia related how she had married Basil on the rebound, after her family had forbidden her marriage to Cyril Winthrop, the man she really loved. Love alone was not enough for Olivia. She had wanted a life of leisure, prestige and money, which Cyril could not provide her at the time. She married Basil Moreland, Lord Thesleton, an older man but an aristocrat with a title and a large estate. He was ambitious and already a respected QC (Queens Counsel). Recently divorced, he wanted a young, beautiful trophy wife who would provide him with an heir. It took several years but eventually Olivia gave birth to a son, Jonathan. Basil was thrilled to have an heir but, as many aristocrats, he also wanted another son. Much to Basil's displeasure, Olivia gave birth to a daughter, Penelope.

Olivia dried her eyes and gave a weak smile. "And there you have it. Oh, I know I'm not the easiest of people and I have done and said some nasty things. I have many regrets but losing my children is more than I can bear. Perhaps this is my punishment." She glanced at Katie with a sheepish grin.

Katie didn't respond, remembering Olivia's accusations last Christmas. She had accused Lydia of stealing her necklace and, although it was resolved with a happy ending, it nearly ruined Christmas for everyone.

"I learned some lessons thanks to you and Cyril. I know I don't deserve Cyril after the way I treated him all those years ago but I never stopped loving him. I'd made a mistake marrying Basil. It never occurred to me that Cyril still loved me. I am grateful for him and he has found me a solicitor who thinks he can get a better agreement. We'll see. Basil is now a judge with even more influence than before."

"That sounds hopeful, doesn't it?" Katie asked with a frown. "Why are you so upset today? Did something happen?"

Olivia nodded. "Yesterday, I had my two hours with the children. I don't see them much because they are away at school but it is the half-term holidays." Olivia paused, her eyes overflowing with tears again. "At first, the visit seemed pleasant enough. I noticed a growing tension with Jonathan and asked him if anything was wrong. He muttered something under his breath. I asked him to speak up. He yelled at me, 'You're a whore and you threatened the family's reputation.'" Olivia's words screeched out above the sobs. "I asked him what he was talking about. He said, 'I asked my father why you divorced. He told me you slept with other men.'" Gasping for breath between sobs, Olivia couldn't speak. Katie waited for her to calm down. "He tried to slap me. My own son. He screamed, 'I hate you,' as he ran out of the room."

"Oh Olivia, that is awful. What about Penelope?"

"She is a sweet little girl, but sometimes very sad." Olivia smiled. "Poppy is my pet name for her. When she was little, she called herself Poppy, not being able to pronounce Penelope properly. Basil hated it but it stuck with me."

"That is cute. My Melanie had difficulty with her name too and called herself Melie, but when some neighbourhood kids thought it funny to put an 's' in front, John and I decided we needed to go back to Melanie before she started school. Did Penelope, Poppy, talk to you?"

A rich smile lit up Olivia's tired face. "She came over and hugged me and whispered in my ear, 'Don't cry, Mummy. I don't believe Daddy. You would never do anything like that.' She gave me a kiss." Olivia's fingers stroked her cheek, obviously remembering her daughter's touch. A worried frown suddenly creased her forehead. "Poppy whispered again as though afraid to be heard, 'I love you Mummy.' She glanced at the chaperone, one of Basil's staff, and lowered her voice. I could barely hear her. 'One day I'll come and live with you, but now I have to go or Daddy will be angry.' Katie, I saw fear in my little girl's eyes."

"But surely she would tell you if something was wrong?" Katie sensed Olivia's fear for her daughter.

"The chaperone is instructed to report everything that is said during my visits. Poppy is afraid to say anything." Olivia's tears began again.

"What about her school? Could you visit her in school? Maybe ask the teachers how she's doing. A mother inquiring about her daughter's progress is not unusual."

"No, he covered that too. The school has been told I'm a threat and I'm not to see the children without Basil or a chaperone being present."

"And the school believes him?" Katie's voice sounded exasperated.

"I'm allowed to accompany him to special events, like Sports

Day. There was a Parent's Day last month but he conveniently forgot to tell me about it. I doubt I would have gone, anyway. Basil would take pleasure in belittling me in front of the other parents and that would embarrass Penelope."

"Which school is it?"

"Hillcastle Academy." She gave a hesitant chuckle. "Believe it or not they resisted, changing to a co-ed school. The name used to be Hillcastle School for Delicate Young Ladies. It is old-fashioned but I don't mind that. Good old-fashioned rules, etiquette and ethics; a firm grounding for girls."

"I'm not sure about that." Katie raised an eyebrow. "Girls need to be raised to be assertive and confident to compete with men in this modern world."

Olivia stared at her, looking puzzled. "Why would she want to compete with men?"

Katie shook her head at the women's naivety, which also explained the passivity and lack of drive to fight for her kids. She wanted to reprimand her and say, *It's a pity you don't use your entitled voice and behaviour towards Basil and the school instead of people around you who don't deserve your disdain when your ex and the school do.*

Contentment

Katie delivered tea to the anniversary couple and began preparing breakfast, glad that Olivia had gone back to her room to rest. She suspected she would sleep most of the day. Although a heartbreaking story, she couldn't help wondering if Olivia's grief was real, having experienced her drama in the past. Katie couldn't imagine what it was like being declared an unfit mother. Perhaps it was real this time. Normally a very empathetic person, Olivia always managed to rub Katie the wrong way. She suddenly felt sorry for Poppy, being raised to be like her mother in an era that had long passed, instead of allowing her to be whomever she wanted. She thought of her own daughter, a confident, strong woman, a scientist and university professor. She laughed and said aloud, "Melanie is certainly not a 'delicate lady'." *But,* she thought, *that doesn't stop her being a loving, caring person.* Katie remembered how kind she was when her own life was falling apart and how supportive she was with her husband Phil when he searched for his lost brother. It was hard to think of Olivia in the same sentence, as none of these qualities applied to her, but her daughter, Poppy, seemed different, showing concern for her mother and not believing her father's lies. Poppy had learned to be loving and caring. Had that come from Olivia? Perhaps the hardness in Olivia had come from events in her early life.

She didn't hear Piers come into the kitchen but she felt his warm arms wrap around her waist then his whisper on her neck. "Good morning, my darling." She turned to kiss him.

"Um! I had no idea married life would bring such lovely morning greetings. You were up early." Piers hugged her, resting his chin on her head.

"I heard a noise and thought someone had broken in. I got up to investigate."

"You did what?!" He moved her to arm's length and stared. "Why didn't you wake me?"

"There was no need. It was only Olivia trying to make coffee." Katie gave a sarcastic chuckle. "She couldn't work the coffee machine."

"What if it had been a burglar?"

"Well, it wasn't. I don't need protecting. I managed okay before we were married."

Piers dropped his arms to his side, pushed his bottom lip out, and gave her a hurt look. "I'm crushed. Are you saying I'm not needed? I can't rescue my damsel in distress?"

Katie gave him a playful punch on his arm. "I've had enough of damsels in distress listening to Olivia this morning. But I will always need you." She stood on tiptoe and kissed him.

Piers placed his hand on his heart with drama. "Phew! That

is such a relief. What's wrong with Duchess Olivia?"

"It's a long story but Judge Moreland is a nasty man and left her with nothing, even taking her kids away."

"That's sad but she's not the easiest person." He hesitated. "I don't know what Cyril sees in her, beyond her striking beauty."

"I think Olivia is learning some hard lessons and she loves Cyril. He seems besotted. Changing the subject, what are your plans today?"

"I'm heading to the marina to check on *Tranquil Days* and I'll see if Bob needs any help. I'm worried about the water level. Hopefully it's gone down."

"If you wait until I've served breakfast, we can take the dogs for a walk."

"A morning walk sounds good. Any of that breakfast for me? I'll eat and get a shower. Oops, I guess we shouldn't have said w.a.l.k." Arthur and Buddy Boy were waiting expectantly by the door. Piers opened it. "Okay, guys. Go for a run in the garden while we get ready."

Katie stared out of the kitchen window watching the dogs chase each other around the garden. "I think those two are very happy dogs. Living in the same house suits them."

"Can you blame them? My darling Katie, I could not be happier. Being with you in this lovely place, life doesn't get any better. And I get to kiss you any time I want. Come here." He gently pulled her close. She looked into his eyes and they shared a long sensual kiss.

Katie pulled away, fanning herself and giggling. "Oh my goodness, Dr. Bannister. You make a young lady blush."

"I'd like to do that again, fair lady."

"I think not. I have work to do." She giggled again and winked. "Maybe later?"

Piers shifted uncomfortably. "On that note, I will get a shower, a very cold shower." They both laughed.

Buddy Boy and Arthur ran side by side to the marina. Arthur was delighted that they were heading towards *Tranquil Days* and sat on the dock, waiting for everyone to catch up. Bob waved from the other end of the marina. Piers adjusted the fenders on his boat, noting the water had dropped several inches. He waved to Bob and walked over to chat.

"Do you need any help?" Piers asked. "I see the water has gone down."

"Thanks, but I'm okay. I just finished adjusting the moorings. Yes, the water dropped dramatically. It'll be back to normal by tonight at this rate. I suspect some of the owners will be out later today to check their boats. Thanks for the offer. You enjoy your weekend."

Katie and Piers walked along the towpath, hand in hand. "It's a totally different view walking instead of cruising down the canal. I like it."

"I find myself listening for the putt-putt of *Tranquil Days*. You always caught up with me somewhere near the bridge."

"And I always waited, or slowed down, hoping to see you. Oh, Katie, it took us a long time but I couldn't be happier."

"You waited for me? And, I thought it was all coincidence. That is so sweet. I couldn't be happier either. It did take us a long time but it's definitely worth it."

"The only thing..." Piers paused. "The commute to and from Nottingham."

Katie felt a twinge of panic. He'd never mentioned the commute before and if they were to stay in Springsville he had no choice but to make the daily journey to Nottingham.

"But there's nothing we can do except," Katie hesitated afraid to say the words. "Piers, I can't move closer to Nottingham. I can't give up all…" He put his finger to her lips to stop her talking.

"Shush, no, no! That thought never crossed my mind. I love living in Springsville. Katie, I would never ask you to give up the B&B. I thought about getting a small studio flat near the office. Cindy and Rick are kind but I feel as though I'm imposing."

"No!" Katie snapped the word, remembering how John her ex had had a trendy loft flat. The circumstances were very different but the thought of Piers in a flat away from her hit all the wrong buttons.

Piers stopped walking and stared, her reaction surprising him. "Why not?" He waited for an answer and when she said nothing, he added, "I don't understand. Why does the idea of me having a flat upset you? If it's the cost, don't worry, I have it covered."

"No, it's not that. I'm afraid history will repeat itself. John had a fancy flat and …" Her words tailed off. She was being unreasonable and knew it but the fear was real.

"Katie, I'm not John. I will never hurt you and I'm sorry. I had no idea it would upset you. Okay, no flat. It won't be so bad when the floods go down. It's just been a tough week with all the detours. Normally it's not an issue and I always look forward to coming home to my Katie."

She smiled, aware that she had overreacted, but at the same time realized just how much she hated being apart. She really wanted Piers home every night. She was trying to hide it even from herself, but she felt the resentment building. "I want you home as much as possible and Cindy and Rick don't mind. It's only the floods and the threat of winter. Most of the year it's okay." She slipped her hand in his. "Isn't it?"

"Of course. I'm on call next week so I'll be staying in town at Rick's most of the week. I won't have to worry about driving around flooded roads."

"Speaking of water." Piers stopped as they approached a large puddle, a dip in the path where the canal water had found a small breach.

"Arthur, don't you dare!" Piers words were still on his lips as Arthur splashed into a puddle much deeper than he expected. He jumped out, shaking muddy canal water from his coat. Piers laughed. "I told you not to go in. I bet that was cold on your belly. Come!" Arthur ran to Piers and then down the path, Buddy Boy on his tail.

"Buddy hates water so I never worry about him. See how he jumps over even small puddles?" She shook her head, laughing. "Now, Judy's dogs, Sam and Lily, would be rolling in that puddle and rinsing off with a swim in the canal. I almost forgot. Judy is back from Surrey. She's desperately in need of a break. She'll be here for dinner tomorrow so you'll get to see her and I'll have company while you're in Nottingham."

Piers and Katie tied the dog leashes up to the Dog Moorings outside Mary's Café and went in for a mid-morning coffee.

"Hello, love birds!" Mary called from behind the counter, carrying a tray of steaming hot scones. "I'll be with you in a minute. Katie, Bob wants to talk to you."

Bob sat at the back table, where he always was, unless the café was full. His large, calloused and chapped hands were wrapped around a steaming mug of tea. "Come join me. Katie, Abe Shapiro is looking for you. He wants to book a room for tonight. His boat *Bluebell* has a leak. The rain seeped in and soaked the bedding and he has nowhere to stay while he does some caulking on the cabin roof."

"Not a problem. It's quiet at this time of the year so there's lots of room. Send him over."

Piers and Katie sat with Bob while they drank their coffee. Katie had declined her favourite scones, having not long had breakfast, but bought half a dozen to take home. They left the café; Katie going home to wait for Abe Shapiro and Piers walking with Bob back to the marina.

It was early morning and the cottage felt still and peaceful, no one but Katie stirring. She gazed out of the kitchen window, the last of the moonlight twinkling on the frost covered lawn. Katie wrapped herself in the afghan from her blue chair and quietly opened the back door to the verandah. Sitting in one of the rocking chairs she watched the dark night sky shift to midnight blue and the stars disappear as the dawn approached. Glancing at Doris' rocking chair, it stood as still as the air. Doris, Adam's deceased wife, lived on the verandah, having chosen not to cross over, but to wait for Adam, which would be a long time. Katie knew when she was there as a breeze would waft pass her cheeks and the chair would rock to and fro. Doris kept a watchful eye on Adam and, during her visits, she would impart words of wisdom to Katie. She hadn't heard Doris since Adam and Sir Walter had left for Europe. *I guess ghosts can go wherever they want and Doris would be with Adam.* She sighed. *Such a beautiful love story.*

She missed Doris' comforting words and Adam's presence. He was a father figure and a friend. At this time of the morning,

27

he would be puttering in the kitchen, getting the trays ready for the guests' morning tea and coffee. The church bell gave a sombre toll, calling its parishioners to early morning service. She shivered. Even with the afghan it was too cold to stay outside and she needed to get busy with morning tea.

She took out two trays. Olivia, exhausted from her grieving, usually slept until noon so never had morning tea. The anniversary couple enjoyed the luxury and the new guest was impressed with the offer. Abe was a nice man and very handsome, with an athletic build, probably from working out at the gym. He had a thick head of steel-grey hair that flopped sexily on to his forehead and a smile that would melt the largest iceberg in the Arctic. She knocked on his door and waited for direction but the door opened and he stood in front her in navy-blue silk pyjamas, the top open and showing his bare chest. *Oh, yes* she thought *he definitely works out at the gym.* He took the tray and thanked her. Katie ran down the stairs, smiling and feeling guilty. *I'm a married woman and crazy in love but he is some gorgeous eye candy.*

Katie opened the morning room door and stared affection-ally at Piers pouring himself coffee. His dark hair, flecked with grey, was tousled from sleep and he wore red tartan pyjama bottoms with an out of shape T-shirt. *No silk pjs here,* she thought, *and I wouldn't change it to for the world.* She wrapped her arms around his neck and kissed him, whispering, "I love you."

"Um, nice. But what was that for? Not that I'm complaining."

"Because it's a lovely Sunday morning and you are home with me. Now, give me a hand with breakfast. We have three, plus you and me. I doubt Olivia will eat. She'll have something later."

"What time did Judy say she was coming today?" Piers asked. "I'd like us to take the boat out."

"That would be nice. Let's go after breakfast, have lunch at Mary's and be back for when Judy arrives this afternoon."

Buddy Boy and Arthur sat on the deck at the bow in guard mode, as they always did when *Tranquil Days* cruised along the Trent and Mersey Canals. The boat moved slowly so as not to make too much wake as the water was high for the canal. Piers noted a few spots where the canal had spilled onto the towpath.

"How long is Judy staying?" Piers asked.

"Until Wednesday, I think. Are you off on Wednesday?"

"I'll be home Wednesday night and back on duty Thursday night, but I have patients booked Thursday afternoon. I wanted to cancel the afternoon but flu is beginning to get a hold. My nurse, Pat, said she couldn't re-schedule them all. I can't get it into people's heads to get the vaccination early, before flu starts."

"I'll miss you but I know it's part of the package so we can live in Springsville. I'm getting used to every second week. And there is lots to do. As soon as Adam gets back, we need to do some decorating. The original rooms haven't been done since I moved in."

Piers steered the boat back into the marina, moored it and pulled a tarp over the stern. They walked to Mary's Cafe and Piers tied the dogs to the Dog Moorings and motioned to Katie to go inside. "You go ahead and order the chicken special. I'll go report to Bob how high the water is so he can warn boaters."

After lunch, they sauntered along the dock but even before they turned onto Marina Lane, Arthur and Buddy Boy ran full speed up the lane, tails wagging.

"How do they know?" Katie shook her head, pointing to Judy's car. "Judy is here but those dogs knew before we even saw her car." Piers nodded his agreement.

Katie opened the front door and Sam and Lily bounded towards her, Arthur and Buddy running through their legs.

"Hi Judy," Piers said, tripping over Arthur and opening the door. "I think I'll let the dogs have their greeting in the garden."

Katie hugged Judy. "It is good to see you. How did you get in?"

"I met this nice man by the gate. He said he was a guest here and I explained who I was and he let me in on the condition I offered him coffee." Judy leaned in and whispered, "Where did you find him? He's gorgeous."

Katie stepped back, raised an eyebrow, and gave Judy a puzzled look. "Did you find the coffee?"

"Oh, I just used the machine."

"Ah," Katie nodded. It was out of character for Judy to comment on a handsome man and even more out of character to make coffee for him. She was surprised that she had even condescended to use the machine. In fact, Katie had never seen Judy so starry-eyed.

Tension is Building

"Hello!" Piers reached over to shake Abe's hand. "How are the repairs coming along?"

"Okay. It was just the caulking that had dried up over the summer and the rain managed to find its way in." Abe gave a shrug.

"Water has a way of doing that. Did much get in the cabin?"

"Not a lot but enough to soak one of the bunks, blankets, mattress and all." Abe turned to Katie. "Katie, can I book the room for one more night?" He glanced towards Judy adding, "I'd like to make sure the caulking has dried and sealed properly."

"Of course. That room is vacant until Friday." Katie winked at Piers and they both smiled, noticing that Abe had not taken his eyes off Judy. She grinned, amused to see a blush on Judy's cheeks and the self-assured woman disappear for a second or two.

Catching Katie's eye, Judy cleared her throat awkwardly and

said, "I hope it's okay, I dumped my things in the Daisy Den."

"The room is always yours, except in the summer when I'm fully booked."

"Thanks." Judy picked up the dogs' leashes. "I'll take Sam and Lily for a run in the field. I'm guessing you just came back and won't be joining me."

"You're right. I have a few things to do here."

Abe jumped up from the sofa. "I'll walk out with you. I need to get that caulking finished."

Arthur and Buddy Boy sat on their haunches next to Sam and Lily with a puzzled look as Katie made no attempt to leash them. Arthur gave a bark.

Judy ruffled Arthur's head. "Alright. You two can come too but no canal. It's the field today."

Piers had his arm around Katie's shoulder as they watched Judy, Abe and four dogs walk down Marina Lane. "Is something going on between those two?" Piers asked with a frown.

"I don't know. Judy has never shown the slightest interest in a man since her divorce twenty years ago. But there was definitely some chemistry going on there. Do you know him?"

"Not well. Only as a neighbour boater. He's friendly enough but I sense he's a bit of a loner. I've never seen anyone else on the boat with him but he's not been there long. July maybe?"

Katie's phone rang and she glanced at the screen. "It's Melanie."

"Hello, what's up?"

"Phil and I wondered if you were free for dinner tonight?" Melanie replied.

Katie looked up at Piers. "Are we free for dinner tonight? Melanie is asking." Piers smiled and nodded.

"That would be a yes. Oh, I forgot. Judy is here."

"Bring her along. I'd love to see Judy," Melanie said without hesitation.

"What time?" Katie nodded. "Six is fine. See you then."

Judy returned with four exhausted dogs and declined the invitation to Melanie's, saying she was tired and would stay at Lavender Cottage.

Arthur and Buddy Boy jumped into the back of Piers' BMW. Katie buckled her seatbelt and frowned. It wasn't like Judy to be tired. Melanie would be disappointed. Judy had known Melanie since the day she was a toddler and treated her like the daughter she'd never had. Katie and Judy's friendship had emerged when they were both young mothers. Melanie and Ben had grown up with Judy's sons. The more she thought about it, the odder it seemed.

"Penny for them?" Piers asked. "You look worried."

"Don't you think it's odd that Judy didn't come with us?"

"I hadn't thought about it. I expect she needs a rest."

"You're right. She did say the last few weeks had been busy and she needed some rest-and-relaxation." Katie's voice trailed off into thought, suspecting something was wrong.

Piers drove the car down Autumn Lane and into Melanie's driveway. Katie gave a cursory glance at number 23, the house she and her ex, John, had lived and raised Melanie and Ben in. It pleased Katie to look at the house with no regrets or even sadness. That was all in the past and now it was just another house.

Phil opened the front door and walked to the car, opening the rear door to let the dogs out. Buddy Boy hesitated, recognizing his old neighbourhood and then, like Katie he seemed to dismiss it and ran to Melanie.

"Come on in." Melanie looked behind Katie towards the car. "Where's Judy?"

"She's exhausted and decided not to come. She sends her love." Katie shrugged her shoulders at Melanie's frown. "I know it's not like her, but I think this last project on the shopping precinct has been a challenge. She's staying until Wednesday so I'm sure she'll tell me what's up. Why don't you come by after class on Monday?"

Melanie gave a cursory nod, somewhat pre-occupied. She headed towards the kitchen, talking over her shoulder. "Sorry, dinner's a little late. I was marking the last of the mid-term papers. There are always stragglers that can't get their papers in on time. I lost track of time. Phil, pour everyone a glass of wine. I won't be long."

"Need any help?" Katie called into the kitchen.

"No, everything's under control. You sit and relax," Melanie replied, filling a saucepan with broccoli. "I just need to put the veggies on and then I'll join you."

Laughter and chatter filled the living room. Phil and Melanie, both university professors, related excuse stories students came up with when assignments were late. Katie smiled at the competitive but loving bantering between the couple.

Phil cleared his throat and tried to keep a straight face. "This is the best yet. A first year student stood in my office and I kid you not, he said, 'I had to fly home to see my dying grandma in Ireland. I managed to finish the paper and I was just checking it over on the plane coming home and the papers just flew out of the plane.'" Phil was laughing so hard he had trouble continuing. "'You see, sir, there was no chance of catching the papers at 35,000 feet.' And, that's not the best. Being sarcastic and figuring this kid was being flippant I asked him how come the dropping cabin pressure had not sucked out the passengers along with the papers." Phil took a deep breath. "I suddenly realized he was quite serious as he replied, 'Oh, the window was only open enough to catch the papers.' Can you believe he was a science major?" Phil rubbed the tears of laughter from his face. "Honestly, I don't know how some of these kids get into uni. This one I failed. I suggested he might do well at Macdonald's as a drive thru clerk if he liked little windows. Harsh perhaps, and I'm usually the first to help someone learn, but some kids just don't get it."

Everyone was laughing so hard they didn't hear the doorbell. A voice shouted over the laughter. "Hello, what's so funny?"

Phil jumped up. "Tony, what a surprise. Come in and sit down. Sorry I didn't hear the doorbell. We were laughing about the silly excuses students make."

"It sure sounded funny. I'm glad it wasn't at my expense." Tony's voice sounded bitter and the laughter turned into an awkward silence. Melanie got up and went into the kitchen.

Phil slapped Tony on his back. "No, of course not, little brother. Have you eaten? Mel has cooked a roast of beef."

Melanie called from the kitchen. "It's ready! Tony, I assume you're staying. I set a place next to Mum."

Katie took Tony's elbow and pulled the chair out before he could say a word. "Old habits die hard. I always sit in the same place. It's good to see you. How are you doing?"

"Good. Really busy at work. The flood waters have damaged a lot of the trucks." Tony gave Katie a sheepish smile. She patted his arm knowing he often spoke without thinking and underneath all that paranoia and anger was a kind young man trying to find his way. Phil and Tony had been orphaned and sent to a foster home. The family adopted Phil but not Tony. The boys found the separation difficult and Tony had been bounced around from one foster home to another, making him angry and bitter, especially with Phil. Katie understood that Tony was afraid to reach out, keeping everyone at a distance except Katie.

While she and Melanie cleared away the dishes and made coffee in the kitchen, the guys guiltily snuck off into the living room. Phil did give a half-hearted attempt. "Need any help, Mel?"

"I'll let you off the hook just this once. Mum and I will do this. You can empty the dishwasher later." Melanie flipped the dishcloth at Phil. "Go on. I want to talk to Mum."

Katie grinned. "I wondered why you were letting the guys off so easily. What's up?"

Melanie peered around the kitchen doorway and waited for the men to get settled in conversation. In a low voice she said, "I'm worried about Tony. He's so, what shall I say, sarcastic, constantly making comments like he did today. Accusing Phil of not caring. We can't get him to understand that Phil had no idea the Coopers were stopping him seeing Tony or that Tony was in such a bad home."

"I thought he'd come to terms with Phil," Katie said.

"It is better than it was, but he hurts Phil with nasty remarks or losing his temper over the silliest of things. Mum, I hate to say this but I don't trust him and there are times I'm afraid of him. His temper…" Melanie paused. "He started dropping by, like today. At first, we thought it a good thing that he felt welcome and Phil embraced it, admittedly, more than I did."

"So what is wrong?" Katie frowned. It wasn't like her daughter to be suspicious.

"He came round unannounced on Monday, and that's not the first time. But this time he was threatening and Phil wasn't home from work yet. Tony said he'd come to see me. He wanted to know how I liked living in *his* house. I repeated what he already knew. That Phil had bought his share of the house, which their parents had bequeathed to the boys."

Katie interrupted, "But he knows the solicitor put Tony's portion of the estate and house in a trust fund."

Melanie nodded, adding, "He got very angry and said I had stolen his house." Melanie hesitated, moving her gaze from her mother to the kitchen window. "Mum, I thought he was going to hit me. If Phil hadn't opened the front door at that moment, I think he would have."

"What did Phil say?"

"I didn't tell him. By the time Phil got into the kitchen, Tony had stepped back and smiled at his brother."

"I thought the solicitor had paid Tony out."

"We all thought that but there was some legal stuff associated with the trust account, which has now been settled. You know lawyers. They take their own sweet time and Tony is not the most patient person in the world. They finally paid him on Friday."

"It's going to take Tony a long time to trust again. Underneath all that anger is a man not dissimilar to Phil. But you need to tell Phil about the attack. Melanie, you should be afraid if his anger is out of control and it's not fair to Phil to keep this from him."

"When you ladies have stopped nattering …" Phil stopped, his teasing smile turning into a frown. "What's wrong?"

"Nothing. Just mother and daughter talk. Here, you can carry the tray. I'll carry the chocolate mints." Katie gave a chuckle. "Not that I don't trust you but I do remember that Minty Thins are one of your favourites."

Katie sat in the rocking chair on the verandah; the mid-day sun shone in a blue sky, rare in November, taking away the chill. Judy had gone back to work and Piers had not made it home for over a week. The surgery was flooded with sick patients and those too sick to come to the office received house calls. Rick could not manage on his own as flu ravaged the community. An epidemic was imminent. Katie hated her own selfish thoughts as she resented Piers staying in Nottingham. She leaned back, feeling the sun on her face and then the familiar breeze and the squeak of wooden rockers on Doris' chair.

"Doris! Is that you?"

"Yes. Adam is on his way home. I sense anxiety, dear Katie."

"Doris, it is so good to have you back. I miss you and Adam. It is weird being in the house all alone and Piers is working so hard I never see him. He has promised to come home on Friday but, he can't stay for the weekend."

"He's a doctor, Katie, and flu season is bad this year. I'm seeing many new faces here in the heavens. What is worrying you?"

"Oh nothing." Katie heard a sigh and was pretty sure if she could see Doris, she would have an eyebrow raised. "All right, I resent Piers spending all his time in Nottingham. He's making no attempt to come home and he talked about getting a small flat so he didn't have to commute. There, I've said it and I feel terrible." Katie felt her lips pout.

"I can't help you, my dear. But I suggest you ask yourself

a question. What are you afraid of? I think you know the answer. Time for me to go."

Katie felt the breeze on her cheeks and the rocking chair went still. The sun disappeared into a bleak grey November sky. Too cold to stay outside, she went into her office and opened her laptop. As she expected, there was an email from Adam.

> *Hi Katie,*
>
> *We travelled by train, first class no less, to Lisbon today and are staying in a very posh hotel. Travelling with Walter has some pretty nice perks. We have a flight booked from Lisbon Airport tomorrow morning. Sir Walter's chauffeur is picking us up at Heathrow and driving us to Springsville. I'll be home sometime in the afternoon. Sir Walter needs to get back to the estate so he will continue on after he's dropped me off.*
>
> *See you soon,*
> *Adam*

Katie smiled, happy that Adam was on his way home. He was always good company, especially when Piers was on call. When she and Piers had discussed the commute before they were married, Katie hadn't realized it would be as difficult. He was hardly ever home and, with partner Rick, they decided to alternate weeks and weekends but Katie found the week Piers stayed in Nottingham, lonely. The week Piers was home, commuting to the office daily, was hard on him. Every second weekend was okay and they paid a locum to ease the burden mid-week but it wasn't working. "I wonder if Rick and Piers did every second day instead of week," she said aloud counting the days on her fingers. "Yes, that would work."

Katie picked up the phone, excited to tell Piers her new idea but he was out on calls. The receptionist put her through to his nurse, Pat. Instead of sharing her exciting news, Pat gave her the bad news that he wouldn't be home again tonight. There was a new outbreak of flu in one of the nursing homes and both doctors were working around the clock.

The First Quarrel

K atie stared through the kitchen window, barely able to see through the sheets of rain pounding into the glass. Great rivulets of water slid into pools on the wooden frame already soft from age, confirming they needed replacing. The glass actually moved as a gust of wind whipped across the verandah, the noise from the delicate wind chimes sounding more like a freight train. A loud crack made her jump back, half expecting to see broken glass. Instead, she witnessed a massive branch split from the sycamore tree. Fascinated, she watched as the bark of the trunk slowly opened up a great gash, showing white pulp, as it released the heavy branch that dropped to the ground with an almighty thud.

Adam came running into the kitchen as the ground shook. "What was that?!"

"The old sycamore tree. The wind ripped off that branch." Katie pointed into the garden.

"Wow!" Adam shook his head in disbelief. "That's half the

tree! If it doesn't stop, these old trees will be uprooted.

Katie frowned with worry. She crossed her arms around her midriff. The storm had unnerved her and she shuddered. *Where is Piers? Something is wrong.* Then, suddenly, as if the wind had heard Adam's comment, the chimes went quiet and the rain reduced to a gentle patter.

"It's stopped," Katie said, glancing towards Adam. "That was scary. The branch just pulled away as if it was a twig."

Adam put an arm around her shoulder. "I suspect that wind was a microburst. It was too strong to be a gust of wind. They are short lived but can do a lot of damage." Adam leaned into the window and looked left and right. "I don't see any other damage." He took a deep breath, "Hm! Something smells good."

"I made Piers' favourite but he's late. I'm afraid dinner is very late tonight"

"I'll go and check that there's no other damage while I wait." Adam put on a heavy rain coat and yellow sou'wester. "I won't be long!"

Katie opened the oven door again. The leg of lamb was drying out. She covered it with foil and turned the temperature dial to warm. Piers should have been home an hour ago. She'd phoned his mobile, only to get voice mail. She tried calling the office again but the phones were switched through to the answering service. It was two hours since she had spoken to the office. Pat said he was late leaving but he was on his way.

She called Rick's house to see if he was there. Cindy answered.

"Hi Cindy, do you know where Piers is? He said he'd be home around six. I spoke to Pat earlier and she thought he was on his way home."

"No, I don't. Rick was called out to the nursing home again. He's not here. He's never here."

"You sound frustrated too. Piers should have been home hours ago."

"I don't know what to say. Piers told me he was going home tonight so he must be on his way. I hardly ever see either of them other than sometimes at breakfast. I leave cold meals in the fridge. They come and go at all hours. The phone never stops and now Molly is sick." Katie heard the frustration in Cindy's voice and a little voice calling 'mummy' in the back ground.

"I'm sorry Cindy, you have your hands full. I hope Molly is soon better."

"I have to go." Cindy hung up without saying goodbye.

Piers struggled to see the road. The windshield wipers slapped from side to side, useless against the torrents of rain. He squinted, leaning forward and trying to see through the water, his knuckles white from hanging on to the steering wheel as the wind shook the BMW. He felt the car lift and in seconds he was in the ditch. He took a deep breath, rubbed his head where it hit the mirror, thankful the car was at least upright. He pushed the car door open, which took little effort as the wind flung it wide. Grasping the car door, he stepped on to the grass verge, bracing against the wind and inspecting the car. The far front wheel was in muddy water but one of the back wheels was still on the tarmac. With any luck, it would let him reverse back onto the road. Suddenly the wind dropped as fast as it had started and the rain eased to a heavy drizzle. He looked ahead and was grateful to see the lights of Springsville.

He wasn't far from home.

He knew Katie would be worried and smiled, surprised she hadn't called. He regretted stopping to help Rick at the nursing home. If he'd left earlier, he wouldn't be in the ditch. But two patients had died and matron had called to say she had several new cases. It was a really good nursing home and they needed help so Piers joined Rick. It didn't take long so he hadn't called Katie, not realizing the kind of journey ahead. *But,* he thought, *I'm almost home* and jumped into the driver's seat. He started the engine, put the gear shift into reverse and slowly felt the back tires grip the road and the car move a few inches before stopping. He gently pressed the accelerator pedal and it moved a few more inches. Holding his breath, he pressed again. The engine roared and wheels spun ferociously but the car did not move. He tried again, feeling the front wheel sinking into the mud. Pushing the door open with difficulty this time he found the car had shifted to an awkward angle. He stood and stared at the vehicle, willing it to move. Muttering to himself, he leaned in and grabbed his brief case, slammed the door shut and kicked the tire. Pulling his collar up around his neck, he walked towards the village. A light shone from The Springsville Antique Shop. *Perhaps Cyril will give me a lift,* he thought but when he looked in the window it was only a security light. He stretched to look up to the flat above but it was in complete darkness. Even the Boater's Inn was quiet. He hesitated, tempted to go in and warm up. He shook his head and thought better of it, aware that his late hours were causing friction between him and Katie. He didn't like worrying Katie any more than he liked the long commute.

Katie heard the front door open and frowned, annoyed that Adam would use the front door in muddy boots and dripping rainwear. She heard scuffling and her heart missed a beat as she called out, "Who's there?"

"It's me!" Piers replied.

Katie ran to the front. "Piers, I was so worried. What…" She stopped, staring at him.

He was bent forward, literally dripping and trying to pull his water soaked shoes from his feet. "My shoes are muddy and I'm wet and cold." He gave Katie a grin. "The car is in the ditch. I had to walk home from the main road."

"Oh Piers! Are you hurt? You have a cut on your forehead."

"No, I'm fine. Just cold and wet." He put his hand to his head. "Ouch, that's sore. I didn't realize. The wind blew me off the road. I've never seen anything like it."

"Never mind. You're home now. I'll get a towel."

Piers stripped off his wet clothes and wrapped himself in the towel. "Something smells good. I'm hungry but I'll get a hot shower first."

Adam came in through the back door, leaving his raincoat and boots on the verandah. He frowned, watching Katie slice the lamb and pour gravy on it to moisten it. "Piers' car is not there. Is he staying in town?"

"No, he's home, very wet and very cold. Getting a hot shower. The car is in the ditch up on the main road."

"What happened? Did Piers get caught in that microburst?"

"So that's what it was," Piers said, coming out of the bedroom. "Hello, Adam. It was weird. The car just lifted off the road and I was in the ditch. I'll need your help to get it out. But let's eat first."

"I'll be back in a minute. I need to wash up," Adam waved

his dirty hands in the air.

Piers wrapped his arms around Katie's waist, "I love you, Katie, and miss you so much." Katie turned around, resting her face on his shoulder. She breathed in his scent, clean and masculine fresh. "I miss you more. Stop scaring me." She punched him playfully on the chest. He cupped her chin and their lips met, warm and hungry for more than food.

Rubbing his hands and clearing his throat Adam said, with a whimsical laugh, "I hate to break up the love birds but dinner is getting cold."

Katie blushed, pushed Piers away and placed the plates on the table. "Bon appetite!"

"This looks good. My favourite." Piers took a large fork full of lamb and frowned. "Not your best, Katie. The lamb is very dry. Can I have some more gravy."

"*You* were more than two hours late for dinner. And you didn't have the courtesy to call," Katie snapped. Piers never criticized her and the hurt stabbed her inside.

"Sorry, but getting stuck in a ditch was not planned."

Adam took a breath. "Now you two, you are both tired. Katie, the meal is lovely and Piers, don't worry, we'll get the car later tonight."

Katie and Piers glared at each other for the rest of the meal, the atmosphere mixed with anger, hurt and regret.

"I'll go fetch Bob and we'll get your car." Adam got up from the table, obviously glad to be out of the atmosphere. Neither Piers nor Katie spoke until he had closed the door.

"Why didn't you call or answer my calls? Have you any idea how much I worried, wondering where you were, imagining you in a ditch somewhere?"

Piers laughed, not a jovial laugh but one full of sarcasm.

46

"Well, as it happens I *was* in a ditch. How soon you forget! And I didn't get any calls from you."

"You still haven't answered my question. Why didn't you call me?"

"I had sick patients to attend to at the nursing home. I'm a doctor, remember! I had no idea it would take me so long to get to Springsville. It is a long commute at the best of times. You don't seem to understand that, Katie. I give up a lot for you. A little understanding would help."

Adam called from the front door. "Bob's here. Let's get going."

"Okay!" Piers picked up his rain coat, pulled on rubber boots and stomped out of the cottage, slamming the door. Katie couldn't answer. Her throat was tight with tears waiting to burst.

She loaded the dishwasher and tidied the kitchen, trying hard not to cry. But as she nursed the hurt of Piers' angry words and realized they had just had their first quarrel, the tears began to flow. She flopped into her blue chair, Buddy Boy and Arthur jumping on her lap. "At least you two still love me." She stroked their heads, relishing the comfort of two warm trusting bodies and stopped crying.

Arthur jumped off her knee and ran to the door. Katie listened as Piers' car pulled into the driveway. A few minutes later he and Adam stood on the verandah, shaking off wet rainwear.

Piers gave Katie a sheepish look. She rubbed her eyes, hoping they weren't too red from crying. Adam came in behind him. "I'll put the kettle on. We could do with a cup of tea. Piers, can you put a log on the fire, please?"

"How's the car?" Katie asked in a sheepish whisper.

"Muddy, but no worse for wear. Bob's truck easily pulled it out of the ditch." Piers poked the fire and added another log.

Adam placed a tray on the coffee table and poured tea, talking as he handed each of them a cup and saucer. "Now, you two, I have something to say. I loved my Doris and still do. But, at times, we quarrelled, often silly arguments over dried lamb or missed phone calls and that's normal. This may be the first quarrel you've had but it won't be the last. In all the years I was married to Doris, we had plenty of arguments but we always made up and we never went to bed angry. So, heed my words and sort this out, kiss and make up before you go to bed." Adam finished his tea and put the cup and saucer on the tray. "I'm off to bed."

They sat silently watching each other, each waiting for the other to speak until they both took a breath at the same time and giggled. Piers pressed his finger to her lips and said, "Me first. Katie, I am sorry for criticizing the lamb. I know you made it specially for me and I was the reason it was dry. I should have called but I honestly thought I would be home in time for dinner." He pulled his phone from his pocket. "No wonder I didn't get your calls. I'm sorry. I had put it on silent when I was at the nursing home. I shouldn't have gone to the nursing home. If I'd headed home from the office, I would have missed the bad weather and been home on time. But Rick needed help. There were two deaths and four new cases of flu. I couldn't just leave him on his own and Matron was beside herself. She needed the support. I am sorry. Am I forgiven?"

Katie nodded. "Of course. I'm sorry for reacting. I know it might not seem like it but I do understand. Sick patients come first and that commute is a problem. I miss you and want to be with you."

Piers pulled her onto his knee, sending Buddy Boy and Arthur flying. "Oh sorry, guys, but I really need to kiss my wife."

Katie snuggled on his lap. "What are we going to do?"

Piers rested his chin on Katie's head. "I think I have an idea. What if Rick and I did every second day instead of every second week on week days and still doing every second weekend?"

"Hey, great minds think alike. I was going to suggest that. I even called you to tell you but you weren't in the office. Do you think Rick will agree?" Katie snuggled her head on his shoulder.

"Yes, Rick will be okay with that routine. Cindy's been complaining about the long weeks with Rick never home, especially now when the kids are sick with colds."

"I talked to her earlier and she sounded quite frazzled," Katie said, frowning. "But what can we do about the commute?"

Piers nodded thoughtfully. "What if I change my office hours? I'll start early and finish early."

Katie frowned. "But you already leave early to beat the traffic."

"I was thinking of leaving even earlier when there is no traffic. You are always up at five. I'll get up with you get to the office at six, do paperwork and see patients by seven. That will help and those patients who don't want to take time off work, can come by before work. If I do the paperwork in the mornings, it allows me to leave the office by three and I'll miss all the traffic. And if Rick works regular hours, the office will be covered for a longer period of time, offering better service to our patients."

"That's a brilliant idea. Do you think Rick will go for it?"

Piers nodded. "Absolutely. It will solve his problem too." Piers yawned. "I'm too tired to talk anymore."

"Are you ready for bed?" Katie raised an eyebrow. "Kiss and make up? Adam said never to go to bed angry. We have some making up to do, or are you too tired?" Katie took his hand and they giggled as she pulled him into the bedroom.

Life's Struggles

❧

K atie woke up still in Piers' arms. She listened to him breathe. Feeling his breath flutter in her hair, she snuggled closer, loving him more with every breath. The argument last night had frightened her. She wanted everything to be perfect. Piers' angry words hurt and she regretted her own. She hated conflict and hated arguing with Piers even more. But as she thought about it, she was relieved that they could work things out. Her heart filled with gratitude for the perfect Adam and Doris advice; an example of true romance and a long happy marriage, which had continued even after Doris died. Such devotion was rare these days. Was it too much to hope that she and Piers would have such happiness

Piers stirred, holding her tighter as he woke up and kissed her head. "Good morning, my darling," he whispered, sending shivers down her spine. She rolled over and kissed him. "I hope you're not starting the early morning routine today."

"No, I'll talk to Rick first. I have far too much loving to do this morning." He pulled her even closer.

"Funny about that. I feel the same way. I'm in need of more kisses."

"And kisses you shall have." Piers kissed her all over, making her giggle as they nestled into each other's arms and made love.

The smell of fresh coffee filtered into the bedroom. Katie looked at the clock. It was way past her usual getting up time but today it didn't matter as there were no guests to feed this morning and Piers didn't have patients until 10 a.m. Lots of time for a leisurely breakfast. She stretched and leaped out of bed, heading for the Morning Room and leaving Piers to snooze a little longer.

"Good morning, Adam! We're a bit late today."

"Coffee's made. I slept late too. I woke very early and then went back to sleep. It's always nice to be back in one's own bed." Adam put his head to one side and added, "How are you and Piers?"

Katie blushed. "All is well. We took your advice and we apologized and we may have found a solution to Piers' commute."

Adam handed her a coffee. "That's good to hear. Now, tell me what has been happening while I was in Portugal?"

"Not much. Olivia was here, visiting Cyril. She's having a difficult time with the custody battle with Basil. He is such a nasty man. We haven't had many guests, just a nice anniversary couple and a few regulars but that's about it. How was Portugal?"

"Portugal is beautiful, well in the southern parts. We didn't go north and we only saw Lisbon from the airport." Adam sat down with his coffee, his expression almost euphoric as he continued. "Walter's house is perched on the top of a cliff overlooking the Atlantic Ocean, only a few miles north of the Algarve. The view of the ocean from my bedroom was stunning. The cliffs are a golden colour and the tide comes in and out around rocks and caves and the beach is gold against the blue water. The weather was perfect, warm and comfortable with a gentle sea breeze all the time and lots of sun. My arthritis didn't bug me once. Pedro and Marisa live there all year and look after the place. Pedro is a keen gardener. I suspect that's why Walter hired him. The flowers were abundant, every kind and every colour imaginable. Some I've never seen before. There was a walled in vegetable garden and ..." he gave a chuckle. "Marisa ruled the vegetable garden as strictly as the kitchen. Every vegetable we ate came from the garden and can she cook? Oh, the food was out of this world." He patted his belly. "As you can see."

Katie smiled at Adam as he prattled on about the holiday. "A few extra pounds looks good on you. Doris will be pleased. You were getting a bit too thin."

"Doris came with me. She didn't appear much but I knew she was there."

"I know because she left here the same day you left and I only saw her the day you came back. I'm glad you had a good time. Back to reality, I'm afraid. There's no gardener here and we have a few winter projects. The old part of the cottage needs painting." She grimaced at the thought of the upheaval.

"There are some winter jobs in the garden. I need to prune the roses and clear the debris from the vegetable garden. I don't mind winter chores as long as I'm busy but I will miss the warm sun." Adam gave a little shiver. "I can go into town and get the paint if you like?"

"Hold on. We can't start painting until the windows are done but there are a few other things that need doing. Let's do a tour of the house after Piers leaves and decide what needs doing first. There are no guests today but we have a full house on Thursday night as Cyril has an auction Friday morning and a few, including Olivia, are staying for the weekend."

"I can get the gardening done first. When are they doing the windows?"

"Next week, I hope," Katie said, showing crossed fingers to Adam. "You know contractors. I'm making breakfast for Piers. Do you want anything?"

"No thanks. My usual toast and marmalade will be sufficient." Adam picked up his coffee mug and, walking to the French doors, he added, "I need to check out my rose garden."

Piers emerged showered and dressed ready for the office. "Hm, something smells good."

"So do you." Katie giggled as Piers pulled her close and she gave a shudder, feeling his breath on her neck. "Perhaps we should eat breakfast and not each other or you'll never get to work."

Friday morning the breakfast table at Lavender cottage was full of antique dealers excited about Cyril's auction. An old estate had been liquidated for taxes and death duties, with some valuable furniture and paintings up for auction.

Katie and Adam fried eggs and several pounds of bacon, hash brown potatoes and mountains of toast. As fast as she served coffee, the pot ran dry and the machine couldn't cope. They were a jovial crowd but Katie couldn't help noticing the posturing and competitiveness. She smiled to herself, thinking it would be a very interesting and lively auction. She'd only seen Cyril in action once but he was a brilliant auctioneer.

Olivia appeared at the bottom of the stairs, looking over-whelmed. Mornings were not Olivia's best time of the day and the rowdy guests made her step back.

"Olivia, good morning!" Katie said as she placed plates of eggs and bacon on the table. "Would you like to come into the Morning Room and I'll get you some coffee?"

"Thank you. That would be lovely. I'm not up to all this noise in the morning. I'm beginning to regret offering to help Cyril today."

"Follow me." Katie pushed the door open. "Sit by the fire and I'll get you a cup of coffee. Would you like a croissant, scone or some toast? I don't think you are a cooked breakfast person."

Olivia shook her head. "Cooked breakfast? Oh no, how revolting. A croissant will do, as long as they are fresh."

"Fresh this morning from Mary's Café." Katie gave a wry smile. As vulnerable as she was, Olivia had to dig at something.

The bulk of the cooking done, Katie poured herself a coffee and joined Olivia by the fire.

"How are you? Have there been any developments regarding the children?"

"Some. Cyril found me a new lawyer, John Saunders." Katie froze. John Saunders was her ex-husband. He'd been through some hard times and was almost disbarred. What was he doing defending someone like Olivia in a child custody battle against powerful evil Basil, Lord Thesleton no less, and his army of top-notch lawyers? She frowned. *Why would Cyril hire him? I guess he doesn't know the history.* John had certainly changed since his recovery from cocaine addiction. He used to be an excellent solicitor but this seemed out of his league.

"Katie? Is everything all right?"

"Oh yes, sorry, I was miles away." She tried to brush her inattention away with a laugh.

"Do you know John Saunders?"

Katie thought for a moment. Obviously, Olivia had not connected the last name and since Katie had married Piers, she was more often called Bannister than Saunders. "Actually, I do. He is an excellent solicitor and works hard for his clients." She took a deep breath and decided to be honest. "John is my ex-husband."

"Of course. Katie Saunders. I hadn't made the connection. I'm not sure he's the right person for me. He didn't treat you too well."

"Olivia, he was a good husband and father for most of our married life. Mid-life hit him hard and he did some stupid things, which resulted in our divorce. I can assure you, he's a good solicitor and a kind man. He loved his children and they are who they are because of the home he made for us. You already know this is a difficult case. Lord Thesleton is a tough, vindictive man and ..." she paused, "there are few solicitors who would go to court against him and his high-powered legal team."

Olivia nodded, looking almost contrite, as she brushed an escaped tear from her cheek, unable to speak. Katie wondered if the tears were for her children or the fact that she couldn't afford a high-powered lawyer herself. Whatever the reason, Katie felt sorry for her. Her privileged upbringing had taught her nothing about the real world and, unable to express her true feelings, she was floundering.

"I know John, and I know he will fight to bitter end for you and your children." Katie took a gulp of her coffee hoping she was correct. Before John had gone off the rails she believed it, but she wasn't one hundred percent sure since the divorce. Melanie was close to her dad and had looked after him during those dark days. That was a long time ago. He'd moved into a new apartment and was working with a new legal firm, Bryant & Bryant, and doing well. Melanie went as far as to say he was his normal self again and Katie wanted to trust Melanie's word.

"I will assume you are correct. I realize I don't have much choice in the matter and I trust Cyril's judgment. Now, I must get ready. Cyril is picking me up early. He's teaching me…" she paused, "*skills* to assist at the auctions."

Katie tried not to show her amusement, wondering what *skills* Cyril was teaching her or indeed what she would be willing to learn. She said goodbye to Olivia and waved to Cyril.

Pleased the morning rush was over, Katie went into her office, leaving Lydia to clear up the breakfast things while waiting for the guests to vacate the rooms. That would be early as the auction started at ten. Everyone was leaving, except Olivia who was booked for the weekend.

Adam popped his head around the office door. "Is there anything else you want done this morning? If not, I'm off to prune the roses."

"No, Lydia is here and I have office work to do. Namely, getting a firm date about the new windows so we can plan the decorating."

She smiled, acknowledging Adam's nod. She felt comforted

that Adam was home, a fatherly figure in her often chaotic life.

She glanced at the clock, deciding whether to call Piers. She was surprised he hadn't phoned. Rick had happily agreed to the new weekday schedule since it suited both doctors. The weekends hadn't changed and he was working this weekend. He should have been off last night but the surgery was backed up and Piers decided to stay in Nottingham. Katie was busy welcoming the antique dealers so didn't pay much attention to the change of plan. But this morning she couldn't help wondering if Piers' new system was in words only. She brushed it away, rationalizing. Firstly, it wasn't really scheduled to start until Monday and all doctors were facing a busy cold and flu season. Katie jumped and slapped her chest when the house phone rang. "Oh Piers, I was just thinking about you."

"Hello Mum. Not Piers, I'm afraid. Just your daughter."

"Melanie, sorry. Piers hasn't called this morning and I thought…never mind. It's lovely to hear from you."

"Do you have time for lunch today?"

"I certainly do. I would love that. What time and where?"

"I'd like to try the new seafood place on Derby Road. Phil said they serve an amazing shrimp dish." She laughed. "Of course, he can't remember the name of the dish, but I'm sure we can figure it out. Is 12:30 okay for you?"

"My mouth is watering already. I'll see you then." Katie put the phone down, excited to be seeing her daughter when her mobile rang. This time it was Piers.

"Hello, darling. I missed you last night. Sorry I had to bail, but it looks as though we might have a potential measles outbreak."

"Measles! I thought the vaccination had more or less eliminated it."

"Unfortunately, not all parents agree with vaccinations. I had a case in the surgery yesterday. I quickly sent them home but it means more house calls. I have a busy weekend ahead of me but with our new system I will be home on Monday."

"Let's hope it works," Katie said, her tone decidedly sarcastic. She felt the resentment creeping in.

"It will work, I promise. So, what are you doing this weekend?" Piers voice was cheery and she noticed he had ignored her sarcasm.

"Melanie called and we're going for lunch today. Olivia is our only guest for the weekend. She's having a difficult time. I nearly forgot. Guess who is defending her? John!"

"Really! You can tell me all about it on Monday. Pat just gave me the nod. My next patient is ready. Love you!"

"Love you more!"

Love All Around

It was a miserable, dull November day. A light rain drizzled, making the windshield wipers squeal with not quite enough water for a smooth swipe. Katie shut them off until she couldn't see clearly and flipped them back on again. Pleased to see Melanie's car already in the parking lot, she pulled in beside her. They hugged and walked together towards the entrance of *Seafood Supreme*, the babble of a full house greeting them as Melanie opened the door.

"A popular place," Katie said, realizing Melanie had had the foresight to make a reservation. They followed the hostess to a table for two overlooking a pretty courtyard. "It looks as though they serve al fresco when the weather is nice."

Melanie nodded. "It's pretty and that would be lovely on a warm sunny day. Certainly not today. I find November depressing."

The waiter handed them the menu and they quickly found the shrimp dish, the house specialty called simply, Shrimp

Supreme. Melanie laughed. "How could someone not remember Shrimp Supreme?" She looked up at the waiter. "Two of the house specials and two glasses of Pinot Gris." She glanced at Katie. "My treat today."

"Thank you. What is the occasion?"

"Nothing. Just wanting to spend time with my mum."

"I know that tone. What's wrong?" Katie gave her the 'mum' stare. "Has Tony done something?"

"No, not really, but that chip on his shoulder gets very annoying and Phil placates him all the time. But that's not it." Melanie hesitated and fiddled with her fork, avoiding eye contact.

"Melanie, it can't be that bad. Tell me?"

She took a deep breath. "It's Dad?"

"Your dad! What's happened?" Katie frowned, waiting for the reply and wondering if he'd had a relapse.

"As you know, he was doing really well after Bryant & Bryant hired him. He was back in court and doing a great job. There was no sign of substance abuse. I was so proud of him."

"So what changed?"

"Probably nothing and maybe I'm overreacting. Mr. Bryant, Sr. acknowledges Dad's brilliant legal mind and that is good. Dad needed a confidence boost."

The wrinkles on Katie's forehead tightened. "Isn't this a good sign? He's back to his old self and he was an excellent, tenacious and very clever lawyer before …the addiction."

"You're right. He sounds and acts like my dad, the dad I remember growing up. But I'm not sure he's ready for high profile cases. Mum, I'm afraid the stress will tip him over the edge and he'll start drinking or using again. The psychologist warned us of this."

Sitting back in her chair, Katie mulled over Melanie's concerns and easily figured out that the case was Olivia's child custody. Melanie's concern was valid but before she mentioned this she needed to find out if John was committed to his life-long recovery. The waiter interrupted her thoughts and placed two glasses of wine on the table, followed by two steaming plates of Shrimp Supreme.

Katie raised her glass. "To us!" Melanie followed and smiled. "Let's eat."

They ate the delicious meal in silence. The food taking their minds off the subject allowed Katie to gather her thoughts. She had to tell Melanie what she knew but she didn't want to frighten her. The key was whether or not John was able to take the stress of a big case. Katie frowned, deep in thought. *Why would a medium sized legal firm like Bryant & Bryant assign such a high profile case to John? Surely they were aware of his past?*

"Mum, you're frowning. It can't be the food. This is a gastronomic delight. Phil was right and we will be coming often. What's wrong?"

"I know about the case your dad is working on. Talk about coincidence. Olivia Moreland is staying at the B&B. Cyril had an auction today. You'll laugh at this. Cyril has asked Olivia to assist with the auction. She said he was teaching her 'skills'."

"That is funny. I can't imagine what useful skills Olivia brings to an auction." Melanie gave her mother a quizzical look. "And I fail to see what it has to do with Dad."

"First, let's make an assessment on your dad's health. Remember these days you know him much better than I do. Is he still seeing his psychologist and does the psychologist understand the stress of a high profile legal case? Second, is he attending AA meetings? He would have to tell his sponsor about the changes. Third, have you seen any changes in his demeanour, habits, attitude? I remember Piers telling me the tell-tale signs that someone was using."

"We talked yesterday and his therapist is supportive, assuming he was honest with him. He's definitely attending AA meetings and I can't say I've seen any behavioural changes. He's just happy. He loves his work and appreciates the chance Mr. Bryant has given him. He hasn't said much about this latest case but then he often can't talk about cases. If I'm honest, it's boosted his confidence and I should be happy for him. I just can't help worrying. What if this is too much?"

"Is his happiness euphoric one minute and miserably depressed the next?"

Melanie shook her head. "No, just a normal life-is-treating-him-well kind of happy and I haven't seen him depressed since he was at his worst, one, two years ago."

"I am no doctor or psychologist but from what you are telling me, I think he's okay. You should call the psychologist and give him a heads up. He might already know but if he doesn't, he needs to."

"That's a good idea. Dr Fred makes me laugh. He insists his patients call him doctor with his first name. A combination of respect and familiarity, I guess. Anyway, I can call him anytime." Melanie gave Katie a quizzical stare, her head slightly to one side. A thoughtful frown creased her forehead. "Mum, your concern about Dad surprises me."

"Oh, don't get any ideas. My feelings for your father ended a long time ago. It doesn't mean I don't care about him. I do. I raised a family with him and we spent many happy years together. What he did is water under the bridge. The hurts heal over time. And, if I wasn't divorced, I would never have met Piers and be as happy as I am now."

"I hear what you're saying and I suppose you are right. Everything has a silver lining. But," Melanie added, "you still haven't told me what Olivia has to do with this."

Katie glanced around the restaurant, thankful that most diners had left and there was no one within earshot. She then went on to tell Melanie what Olivia had told her.

"Wow!" Melanie said, falling back in her chair and letting out a big sigh. "You can't get much higher profile than that. Not only does he not stand a chance but the media will be all over it." Melanie screwed up her nose, a habit she'd had since childhood when something didn't seem right. "Why would Bryant assign a case like this to Dad or even take this case on in the first place?"

"I thought the same thing and I don't like it. The chances of anyone winning against Lord Thesleton's legal team, Morton-Smith, Widdicomb whatever and more double-barrelled names on the shingle than you can count, is dodgy at best. They are as brutal as Basil. I'm surprised Bryant agreed to take it. Unless …" Katie paused. "They might think that, win or lose, it will be great publicity. If they win, it will bring the crème de la crème clientele. If they lose, it will be poor John Saunders who will take the fall. The firm will gain from the notoriety."

Melanie put her hand over her mouth to quell a gasp. "Do you think they would do that to Dad? You're right, they would. Putting his health issues to one side, is Dad good enough?"

Nodding, Katie said, "There was a time I would have said yes without hesitation. Your dad loved a challenge and hated to lose. If he can keep it together, maybe he can pull it off.

I suspect Bryant would put a strong team together so he wouldn't be doing it alone. But as lead counsel, his name would be front and centre. A child custody case would be judge only. No jury and, because it's for minors, the press would be barred from court. But outside court the paparazzi would have a field day."

"I'll talk to Dad. He's coming over tomorrow. Not much more we can do for now. I thought we'd finished with dad drama but I guess not."

Katie ordered coffee and a large tiramisu with two forks, smiling guilty. "I think we deserve a treat. Let's talk about something else. How's university?"

"My desk is covered from end to end with papers waiting to be marked and I'm always listening to excuses about why papers are late. Pretty boring really. Phil is in the same situation so we either work late or bring stuff home and sit at the dining room table staring at each other."

"And how's Tony?"

"Well, there's not much brotherly love on his part. He blames Phil for not being adopted by the Coopers and feels abandoned. It wasn't Phil's fault. He was just a kid and had no idea the Coopers stopped the visits." Melanie shrugged her shoulders.

"I thought he was getting better. He seemed quite cordial after he received his portion of the inheritance and realized Phil had put it in a trust fund and not stolen it."

"You're right," Melanie said. "He's actually grateful and it did build some trust between them but the abandonment chip on his shoulder is more like a boulder. Mum, I've tried everything and have come to the conclusion that Tony wants to stay a victim."

Katie gave her daughter an understanding tap on her arm. "You're doing your best. Tony will come around eventually. I can't imagine what it's like to lose your parents and be put into foster homes. Phil was lucky getting adopted and Tony was shafted, mostly because he was a difficult kid and the system let him down." Katie gave a long sigh. "Sad, very sad."

"I agree, but he's not a kid anymore." Melanie sighed, not with sadness but frustration. "Let's change the subject. The most exciting thing in my world is my lab assistant who is pregnant. The whole department is baby crazy." Melanie wagged her finger, catching her mother's look. Shaking her head she added, "And, *no*, Phil and I are not ready for babies yet."

"Just wondering when I might be a granny, although I'd prefer to be called Nanan. Ben certainly isn't going to give me grandchildren."

"I wouldn't be too sure about that. My little brother is in love."

"Really! He hasn't said anything to me."

"He's dating Chloe Nightingale. The last email indicated this might be serious."

"She's the lead singer in the band, a beautiful voice and very pretty." Katie frowned. "Do you think it's a good thing?"

"If Ben is happy, I certainly do. You know, Mum, Ben isn't the wild kid he used to be. He's a strong man and an amazing manager. That band would not be where they are today without Ben."

"I know that. I never doubted him and I'm very proud of him. Hum, my Ben in love!" Katie added wistfully. "Love's a wonderful thing. I never thought I'd find love again but I did and so did you. I have Piers and you have Phil and now Ben."

Katie paused. "I almost forgot Judy!"

"Really Mum? Ball-busting Judy is in love? Sorry! I'm not insulting your friend but Judy's opinion of the male gender is not very complimentary. I wondered if she was gay."

Katie ignored the last comment, mostly because she wasn't sure herself about her friend. "Abe Shapiro owns a boat in the marina. Piers knows him as a quiet sort, keeps to himself. He had a leak in his boat and stayed at Lavender Cottage while he repaired it and Judy happened to be there that weekend. There was definitely chemistry going on." Katie sighed. "Love all around. Well, on that happy note, it's time for me to go home." Katie hugged her daughter and Melanie returned it with an amused expression, shaking her head as they walked to their cars.

"My mum, always the romantic. It's early days for Ben. And Judy? Wow, that is a surprise. See you soon. Bye!"

The first thing Katie did when she got home was email Ben. She didn't mention Chloe but she had learned that an email usually prompted a phone call and if he had good internet, depending on where he was in the world, it was sometimes a video call. The thought of Ben settled with a wife filled her with joy, except she couldn't help wondering if a singer was a good choice. Rock stars had a reputation for passionate flings and nasty divorces. Having experienced divorce, she did not want that for Ben. The band was a traditional jazz, not rock, band. She took comfort in noting they were more sophisticated than fly-by-night rock or pop stars and, from the videos, Chloe seemed nice.

She picked up her mobile as it trilled Katie's one of a kind ring. It was Ben.

"Hello stranger," she said, smiling as Ben's face appeared on the screen. "You must be back in New York with decent internet. I love video calls. You look tired. Are you all right?"

Ben gave a warm laugh. "Always the worrier. I'm fine, just jet lagged and tired. We got back from New Zealand yesterday. How's life in Springsville? And how's Piers?"

"It couldn't be better. I love it here. Piers is good but finding the commute a bit long, mostly because we've had some awful weather. The wind blew his car in the ditch the other night. He was not pleased about that, but he's started a new routine and we think that will help. How was the tour?" Katie desperately wanted to ask him about Chloe but decided to be cool about it.

"Was the car damaged? And what about Piers, is he all right?"

"Both are fine, so how was the tour?" Katie asked again.

Ben hesitated with a broad grin on his face. "The tour was great. We rest for a couple of months and start a North American tour in late January." He grinned again, teasing. "Chloe did exceptionally well. The crowds loved her."

"Oh, that's nice." Katie tried to sound casual.

"Mum, I'm teasing you. I read your email and you had lunch with Melanie so I'm assuming she told you about Chloe."

"Well, she did mention it. Dare I ask if this is serious?"

"We've been friends ever since she joined the band. I'm not sure how serious so don't go planning a wedding. But I like her a lot and we are dating. You'll love her Mum, she's amazing." He paused in thought and then added, "I have to be sure."

"She looks lovely on the videos and she has a beautiful voice. I'm glad you're happy, son. Does your father know?" The air went cold. Even at a distance, Katie could feel the disdain Ben

68

had for his father. "He's changed, you know."

"I know but I can't forgive the way he hurt you and, frankly, you are better off without him. In some ways I'm glad it happened because Piers is a wonderful man and I'm so glad you found happiness." Katie stared at Ben's face, taught with anger, even anguish.

"Ben, he wasn't always like that. He was a good dad when you were little."

His face lightened into a smile. "I remember but that is no excuse. Doing what he did is unforgivable. I know he's better now and Melanie keeps me up to date."

"I'm sorry, dear. You have to forgive or it will eat you up. Now, tell me about Chloe?"

"She's beautiful, born and bred in New York. She still lives with her parents, except when we're on tour. Her father is a pianist and her mother is a music teacher. I've met them a few times at concerts here in New York."

"Ah, meeting the girl's parents is a sure sign…"

Ben cut her off. "No Mum, we are not that serious. Mum, I have to go. Take care and look after yourself."

"Love you and promise to call more often."

"I will. Bye!"

Katie gave a wave at the phone as the screen went blank. She was excited for Ben, certain he was in love but holding back. At first she thought he was holding back from her. She did get a bit intense at times. Suddenly it occurred to her that she was not the issue, it was his father. He was afraid he'd be like his father. "Oh no, Ben, you would never be like your father." *But*, she thought, *he is like his father in many ways.* It crossed her mind that celebrities were prone to addiction. She never understood how John changed or what caused him to turn to drugs and alcohol. Would Ben give in to temptation? She shook her head "Never!" But then she would never have expected John to seek the high life and Ben was already in it just by the nature of his work. Perhaps his disgust with his father's behaviour would be a good reminder.

Legal Drama Brewing

❧❦❧

Buddy Boy's eyes snapped open as the doorbell chimed, followed by Arthur's sharp bark, making Katie jump and slap her chest. "I wish you wouldn't do that, Arthur."

Only guests ring the doorbell and there were no guests. A greeting of 'hello, anyone home' sufficed from the neighbours, usually after they walked in; something that had taken Katie a while to get used to. She peered through the window before opening the door for Cyril, the only villager who remained formal.

"Cyril, please come in. Do you need some bookings? Another auction?" Cyril maneuvered around the dogs. He didn't particularly like them and they knew it and taunted him by sniffing around his legs rather more than necessary.

Katie muffled a smile, thrusting an arm towards the door. "Arthur, Buddy, into your bed!" The pair slunk off into the Morning Room.

Cyril gave Katie a sheepish smile. "No, not bookings for an auction. The next one is already booked for the end of the month. But I would like to book a room for Olivia this weekend …" He hesitated and cleared his throat.

"Okay," Katie said slowly, wondering why Cyril had not phoned. Coming to the cottage to make a booking was unusual.

"Katie, could I speak with you about a rather delicate subject?" His eyes wandered around the room, glancing at the stairs and the open Morning Room door. "Actually, it is rather private."

Katie frowned. "Goodness! Cyril, this sounds serious. Of course, you can talk to me …" She paused, following Cyril's gaze. "We are alone. Adam is out and there are no guests." Pointing to the sofa, she added, "Take a seat. Can I offer you tea or coffee?"

"Thank you, that's awfully kind but no, I can't stay long." Cyril sat down, his arm across the back of the sofa in a confident pose, but Katie saw worry in his eyes. She sat opposite in one of the big easy chairs.

Katie waited. Cyril cleared his throat again, rubbed his chin, took a breath to speak but then his words barely squeaked out. He blushed and cleared his throat one more time. "Katie, it may have come to your attention that I am rather fond of Olivia." He blushed more and rubbed his chin, his five o'clock stubble sounding like fine sandpaper on his rough hands.

"I had noticed and there's nothing to be embarrassed about." Katie reassured him with a smile.

"Olivia has a way about her that frequently upsets people and…" He paused and smiled. "I know that is an understatement and there is no excuse for the rude, even vindictive, behaviour she has displayed in the past, but underneath all that is a very different person."

Katie nodded in agreement. Leaning her head to one side she said, "Accusing Lydia of stealing was a terrible thing to do but she did put things right in the end. Her actions were more about fear. Not excusable, but she is terrified of her husband, or should I say ex-husband."

He nodded and took another breath. "Olivia wasn't always like that. She was a privileged, spoiled woman, demanding her own way but she used to be kind and a lot of fun. Her parents divorced when she was young and her step-mother was not the nurturing type. As a result, she was allowed to run wild with no boundaries."

"You knew each other as kids?" Katie thought for a minute, remembering there was a family connection. Cousins perhaps?

"Cousins," Cyril nodded agreement, adding quickly, "But not blood related. Olivia's step-mother is a distant cousin of my father's. Aristocratic families cling to distant cousins. Perhaps because their numbers are declining but they need numbers for balls and entertaining. That's how we knew each other as kids and teenagers. I had an awful crush on Olivia when I was sixteen, my last year in boarding school. I'd go back after hols and swoon over her." He laughed at the memory.

"Is this what you wanted to talk to me about?" Katie raised an eyebrow.

"No, but it is relevant to my problem. Olivia and I fell in love." Cyril blushed. "Olivia was a debutante, presented at court and all that with expectation of a 'good match'. One would think the eldest son of an earl with a large estate would be a 'good match'. Not so. Rumours of my father's debts, shameful gambling and womanizing did not suit Lady Felicia, Olivia's stepmother. Nor did they suit Olivia at the time. She had her heart set on being a society lady. She didn't marry Lord Thesleton. She married his money, title and position in society."

"I'm sorry, Cyril. That must have been very hard for you. You never found anyone else?"

"No. Shortly after Olivia married Basil, Lord Thesleton, my mother died, sending my father into the worst spiral of alcoholism imaginable, resulting in the estate being sold and he falling into the arms of a chorus girl. Mortified, I ran away to France to my maternal uncle's family. I haven't seen my father in twenty years." Cyril gave Katie a sheepish grin. "I'm not sure why I'm telling you all this. You are easy to talk to."

"So I've been told. I'm sorry, Cyril. You lost the woman you loved and your family all at the same time and you were so young. How did you manage?"

"My uncle collected antiques and the whole antique business fascinated me. Having learned so much from him, I discovered I loved the challenge of the business. After buying and selling for my uncle, my reputation preceded me. His friends and associates asked me to find paintings and rare artifacts. I earned myself an excellent living and a reputation for finding the impossible and began buying and selling for wealthy collectors all over Europe. I found the challenge exhilarating and lucrative. But, after fifteen years of travelling and kowtowing to extremely difficult, and on occasion unpleasant, people, the challenge became a chore. I had made my fortune and decided to settle down. I happened to drive by Springsville. The store was up for sale. It was just a junky second-hand store at the time and, on impulse, I bought it."

He gave her a sideways glance that held a hint of intimacy. "I'm a very private man. You are the only person who knows my story."

Katie saw his demeanour change with regret at having spoken so candidly. She stayed silent, waiting for him to continue.

"I've said too much and my reason for coming was to talk about Olivia, not me." He took yet another rather raspy breath, his fingers worrying the back of the sofa. "I have persuaded Olivia to fight for custody of her children. I am appalled at how Basil and the legal system has treated her. The divorce was bad enough but to deny access to her children is cruel."

Katie watched his face redden and his anxiety turn to anger as she listened more intently. "I was afraid for her when she married him, full of charm but a very cruel man. He accused his first wife of unfounded infidelity so he could divorce her. The real reason? She couldn't provide him with an heir. And his reason for marrying Olivia, a young woman twenty years his junior, was to have a son. Now he has a both a son and a daughter. He divorced Olivia, again claiming infidelity, also untrue, but he has clever solicitors. He then went on to charge her as an unfit mother and claimed sole custody of Penelope and Jonathan. She challenged the allegations and reported his abuse. He denied and retaliated by threatening to refuse any kind of visiting rights to the children. Olivia backed off, when she realized how far Basil would go. He told so many lies that the court believed she abused the children and denied, not just custody, but access to her children except under supervision." Cyril was wiping the sweat from his brow and Katie saw his eyes moisten. Her heart went out to this very private and stoic aristocratic man struggling to hold his emotions in check.

"What a cruel man!" Katie said. "It must be very hard for you." Cyril's story had moved her but she couldn't help thinking about John and what he'd got himself into.

"Cyril, would you like a brandy?" She didn't wait for an answer and got up to get the decanter and two glasses from the Morning Room. Buddy and Arthur, pleased to be let out, bounded into the lounge, but stopped short at sniffing around Cyril. Sensing he was upset, they sat demurely by the hearth, hoping that Katie would not banish them again.

Katie handed Cyril a brandy and said, "How can I help?"

His eyes followed the golden liquid as he swirled it around the glass and sighed. "Thank you, I needed this." He raised his glass towards Katie, "One of my clients, an avid antique collector, is the senior partner in a legal firm Bryant & Bryant." He gulped his drink, visibly enjoying the sensation as he swallowed. Katie watched him, anticipating his words.

"I asked Mr. Bryant for his opinion on Olivia's situation. Long story short, he agreed to take the case and assigned it to a new, but experienced, lawyer in his firm."

Katie interrupted. "John Saunders."

Cyril frowned. "How did you know? Have you talked to him? He's your ex, right? I seem to remember there was some trouble a few years ago."

"Actually, Olivia told me and yes we were married for thirty-five years."

"It seems to have taken me a long time to get around to my question. To put it bluntly, is John any good? Could he win Olivia's case?"

Katie gathered her thoughts. "John did have some problems around the time we divorced but he has resolved his issues. He's an excellent lawyer and fights for his clients to the bitter end. If anyone can win the case for Olivia, it would be John. But the stakes are very high and I don't have a crystal ball." She smiled, raising her eyebrows. "I can only say Olivia is in good hands." Katie felt like crossing her fingers. The John she knew ten years ago would have taken the challenge, ignoring the odds. But today she wasn't so sure he was ready and the odds were against him.

"Thank you, Katie. That's what I wanted to know." Cyril drained his brandy glass. "Thanks for the brandy. I'd better scarper and get some work done. I almost forgot Olivia will arrive after dinner on Friday."

Katie closed the door and leaned on it, letting out a big sigh just as she heard the back door open.

"Hello! Katie?"

Katie ran to the Morning Room. "Piers, what are you doing home early?"

Piers laughed. "Not quite the greeting I was expecting. New schedule? Remember?"

"Sorry. I thought you were too busy to start the new schedule but I am very happy to have you home."

"Pat has rearranged my appointments and I decided to leave the paperwork until tomorrow morning and spend the afternoon with my wife." He pulled her towards him. She stood on tiptoes and kissed him.

"Umm… I'm going to like coming home early." He frowned and held her at arm's length. "Do I smell brandy?"

Katie nodded. "Yes, Cyril was here. He came to talk about John defending Olivia in the child custody case. You know Cyril, the perfect aristocrat not expected to get emotional, which he did. I gave him a brandy and had one myself." She giggled and punched Piers playfully on the arm. "Are you checking up on your wife, the secret drinker?" They both laughed.

"It's a lovely afternoon. Can I persuade you to come on the boat for a cruise? I'll buy you dinner at the Ragley Inn."

"That's a great idea."

Piers changed into more casual clothes and Katie grabbed her Aran sweater. Hand in hand, they walk to the marina, Arthur and Buddy Boy running ahead. By the time they reached *Tranquil Days*, Arthur was on the deck. Buddy Boy sat on the dock, patiently waiting for Katie to lift him onto the boat. Laid-back Buddy didn't do much leaping. Somewhat chubby, he had learned that trying to leap onto the deck could result in a dip in the water and he hated the water.

"There you go, big fellow. We might have to reduce your kibble," Katie said tickling his tummy. Ignoring her comment, Buddy ran to sit beside Arthur at the bow.

Piers started the engine while Katie untied the boat and they putt-putted into the canal basin. She leaned back and stared up at the blue sky, watching fluffy white clouds drift slowly by. She glanced at Piers, concentrating on steering *Tranquil Days* out of the marina. He looked so handsome, she wondered what she had done to deserve such a wonderful man and to be so in love. She thought about Olivia and the cruelty she'd had to bear. Certainly, a difficult women but no one deserved such treatment. Would Cyril's love be enough for her? Her thoughts drifted to John. Would he be able to get her children back? She wondered what kind of a mother she was and found herself doubting Olivia's ability to be a good parent. She was self-centred and even narcissistic. Lord Thesleton would use whatever he could to keep his children. Not because he loved them, but because he wanted to spite Olivia and mold his heir to be a bully like himself. She sighed. *John sure has his hands full with this case.*

"Penny for your thoughts?" Piers said, as he maneuvered the boat along the canal.

"I was thinking about Olivia and the custody battle and how John will cope."

"Is that what Cyril wanted to talk about? He's crazy in love with Olivia." Piers reached out and touched her hand. "Not my kind of woman, very high maintenance and harsh."

Katie nodded with agreement. "True, but I've seen a different side of her. For all her privileges, she's had a hard life, which has made her afraid and unable to trust. Underneath is a kinder gentler woman. I think Cyril brings that out in her. Maybe she'll change."

"Perhaps. I just want to enjoy being with my beautiful, loving wife." Piers leaned over the tiller and kissed Katie. "Come sit next to me before I steer the boat into the bank." He laughed as he pulled the tiller to straighten the boat as it moved under the stone bridge. Katie sat beside him. With his free arm around her shoulder, she rested her head against his chest. The boat veered towards an inlet where the canal widened.

"Let's stop here for a while and have a glass of wine."

Piers moored the boat and Katie poured them wine. They sat in silence, the only noise chirping birds, buzzing insects and a dog barking in the distance. As though in unison, they turned and kissed with the passion of newlyweds so much in love. No words were spoken as Piers led her into the cabin.

By the time they emerged from the cabin, the sun had set,

leaving an orange-red glow along the horizon. Piers started the engine and untied the moorings. Katie sighed, feeling the breeze on her warm cheeks as Piers steered *Tranquil Days* into the mainstream of the canal, just minutes away from the Ragley Inn. Buddy Boy and Arthur jumped up, tails wagging as Piers moored at the Ragley dock.

"Sorry, boys, it's dinner in the cabin for you tonight. It's too cold to eat outside." Katie gave each dog a head pat and pointed to the cabin. With tails down, they slowly curled up on the cabin floor. "Ah, don't look at me like that. I'll bring a treat."

Katie closed the cabin door, took Piers' hand and stepped onto the dock. It felt almost eerie. They were the only narrowboat at Ragley's dock. Few boaters ventured out after Harvest Festival. Most were wrapped in tarps and unused. The great expanse of lawn leading to the pub with unoccupied picnic tables gave her a spooky feeling in the half light. Piers' arm wrapped tightly around her so he could kiss her, making them walk awkwardly towards the inn; much later than originally intended.

She giggled as Piers opened the pub door, frowning with his hand on his stomach.

Katie giggled again and said, "Hungry?"

"Starving!"

Unknowns

P iers kissed Katie as she handed him a travelling mug full of hot coffee and watched his dark shadow walk to his car. It was still pitch dark and the engine sounded very loud at 5 a.m. She hoped the noise hadn't woken anyone. She glanced towards her neighbour but their lights were already on. Bob came towards the window and waved. Mary would be at the café, baking bread. She gave one last wave to the car brake lights as Piers turned off Marina Lane to the main road. "I hope this works," she said to Buddy Boy and Arthur, looking puzzled at this new early morning activity.

Katie settled in her blue chair, her feet tucked under her, with a dog on each side and her hands wrapped around her coffee mug. The warmth tingled into her cold fingers. She wanted this early morning routine to be a success but deep down she suspected it would be no better for Piers. It would be better for her, and Cindy would like having Rick home on alternate days. If she was honest, the commute was the root of the problem and the new routine would actually increase Piers' time on the road, albeit not at rush hour. She felt guilty as he was doing this for her. If they lived in Nottingham, there would be no long commute. But the B&B was her life now. Could she give it up and would she have to make a choice between Piers and the B&B? She shook her head and yelled, "No." Arthur and Buddy Boy sprang from sleep. She patted them both and directed her speech to them. "I never want to have to make that choice. I have to find an alternative. Until then, this must work."

"Is that stubbornness or determination?" Adam said, walking into the kitchen. "Sorry. I couldn't help but overhear. You know Piers would never expect you to give up Lavender Cottage. He loves it here as much as you do." He turned to face her. "Katie, everything will be okay."

"Always wise words from you, Adam. Thank you. I can't help feeling there are a lot of unknowns and it's going to be a hard winter."

"Maybe, but you'll weather the storm." He lifted his coffee cup in the air as he opened the backdoor. "I'm going to have a word with Doris."

"Okay. Give her my love. I'm off to get dressed and start my day. Put your jacket on or you'll catch cold. It'll be chilly on the verandah this morning." Katie smiled as her instructions fell on deaf ears and she heard the unison rhythm of the rocking chairs.

Two minutes later, Adam came in, blowing into his cupped hands. "It's cold. Doris sent me to get my coat before I caught my death." He gave an endearing laugh. "She chuckled at saying 'death' and told me to mind my ways. It wasn't time for me to join her yet. And, she said to listen to you. I guess she heard you tell me to wear a jacket."

Katie smiled, putting her head to one side. "I guess it would be mean to say I told you so."

He nodded as he grabbed his coat and a pair of gloves. "But well deserved."

"Don't forget *Ingram Windows and Doors* is coming at 10 this morning to give us an estimate about replacing the windows," Katie called as a blast of cool air filled the kitchen.

"I didn't forget," Adam replied, closing the back door.

Showered and dressed, warmer for the hot shower, Katie sat at her desk feeling overwhelmed. The window frames were rotten in places and last winter's heating bill had sky-rocketed. She knew the windows would be expensive but it had to be done. But what about the guests? Normally the winter season, November to March, was quiet but between Cyril's auctions and seniors avoiding the busy season, there was barely a night without at least one guest. Closing down for a week would be a loss of revenue she wasn't sure she could afford. The new roof and renovations, although essential, had depleted the contingency fund. The bank manager was eager to give her a low interest loan. She chuckled. More money in the bank's pocket and another expense she didn't want at the moment. A loan was something she needed to discuss with Piers. She knew she was being stubborn but her independence was vital to her and Piers would offer her the money. After all, it was his home too. She felt a twinge of guilt, knowing that as a result of her ex-husband's handling of money, there was a small part of her that didn't quite trust Piers. That was both unfair and unwarranted.

She almost jumped out of her skin when the phone rang. Taking a breath, she answered. "Lavender Cottage B&B, Katie speaking!"

"Good morning. Why so formal this morning?" Judy's voice answered.

"Oh, Judy, it is so good to hear from you. Sorry, I was deep in thought when the phone rang. Anyway, you usually call on my mobile."

"I figured you'd be in the office at this time of the day. What's up? You sound stressed."

"Nothing. I'm figuring out finances. I think I told you we need new windows. So, are you heading our way?"

"Unfortunately not. My plans just changed. I'm at my dad's place and he's not well so I'm going to stay with him until he's feeling better. Not how I planned to spend my days off but I'm worried about him."

"Oh dear. Is it serious?"

"I don't think so. A head cold but he has a hacking cough. I'm taking him to the doctor this afternoon. I'll let you know what the doc says. I doubt I'll make it on Sunday."

"Stay with your dad. It's a good thing you had some time off. We can catch up later."

As Katie put the phone down, she felt disappointed. She could really do with Judy's advice. Judy was the down to earth part of the friendship. She had a knack of looking at situations without the clouding of emotions. Katie was the opposite.

Adam knocked on the office doorframe. "The window man is here."

"He's early but that's good. Let's see what he has to say."

Derrick, the window man, was Ingram's son. Katie liked dealing with a family business and Derrick was thorough and knowledgeable. He confirmed Katie's thoughts that all the old windows needed replacing, except for the more recent addition of the French doors going to the rose garden. Two hours later, Derrick left with measurements, promising a quote by the end of the week. His estimate of time needed was much longer than she had expected, ten to twelve days in addition to that several days for painting and decorating. It was a problem. She couldn't close the B&B for three weeks this month. Cyril had two auctions booked and, apart from the fact that it would be too cold in December to change windows, she always had a full house over Christmas. Letting out a long sigh, she decided to wait until she had the quote. Perhaps with planning and using the extension that already had new windows, they could manage.

"I'm not looking forward to that quote," Katie said, glancing at the ledger on her desk. "Adam, what's your opinion on the time frame?"

"It might take a bit of planning but if he can get the windows in around our guest bookings, I could always do the painting early December before the Christmas rush. The window frames are PVC so they don't need painting. The kitchen, morning room and lounge could wait until the new year. We rarely have guests in January."

"I agree. Thanks, Adam. Let's hope he can start right away."

Buddy Boy gave a woof and both dogs sat expectantly at Katie's feet. "I didn't forget you. We're going now." Katie clipped the leashes onto the dogs and called, "I'm taking the boys for a run. See you later."

Katie pulled the collar up on her jacket and pushed her hands in the pockets. It was dull and cold, typical November but she was as glad as the dogs to be outside. As soon as they reached the towpath, she unleashed them and let them run. As always, the dogs stopped at the wooden stile, waiting to see whether Sam and Lily were in the field. Judy's dogs loved swimming so they were not allowed on the tow path near the smelly canal water.

Katie shook her head. "Go ahead, boys. Judy's not here today." She whispered, "I wish she was. I could do with a listener. How am I going to pay for the windows?" She looked back at the wooden stile, wishing she had stopped and sat down. She needed to think. Instead, she kept walking. *I wonder if Ingram would accept payments. I estimated £8,000 but after talking with Derrick he indicated £6000. A deposit of £3000 and I have that put aside, and if he would accept £1,500 next month and the rest after Christmas I could cover it all without a loan.*

Katie turned around, called the dogs and sprinted back to the marina. The aroma of Mary's coffee reminded her that she'd skipped breakfast. One of Mary's scones sounded inviting.

She tied the dogs to the Dog Moorings, the appropriate name always made her smile and watched as they lapped thirstily at the bowl of water. The familiar bell jangled as she opened the door and a voice from the back called, "I'll be right with you!" Mary only had staff on the weekends during the winter so she was baker, cook, waitress and coffee maker all in one.

"It's just me, Katie. A coffee and scone. Take your time, I'm in no rush!"

Mary appeared carrying a tray of just-out-of-the-oven scones, steaming with mouth-watering aroma. "Hello Katie, good to see you. You certainly timed that right. Couldn't be fresher." Mary put the tray down and slid the scones into the display basket. Taking one out for Katie, she poured two coffees.

"I'll join you. I'm ready for a break. It's been quiet for the last couple of days." Mary got up from the table and filled a brown paper grocery bag. "Here, before I forget. Some bread and scones, leftover from yesterday's afternoon bake."

"Thank you. That's unusual for you to have leftovers."

"I know, it's such a waste. Old Mrs Higgins came by as I was closing yesterday." Mary laughed. "She's always looking for a bargain. I'm not quite sure if she's frugal or poor. I suspect her husband spends most of their money at the pub."

"I don't know either of them, other than her reputation as the village gossip."

"Sometimes the gossip is useful. She told me the General Store was closed. The Johnsons have the flu and Mr. Johnson was taken off in an ambulance. I hear flu is rampant in Derby and has spread to Willington and Barrow. I think that's why business is down."

"You could be right. Piers is busy and he said the flu season had started early. There's an epidemic in one of the nursing homes in Nottingham."

"Is that why Piers was driving off at five this morning?" Mary chuckled. "Not that I'm prying. Bob mentioned it."

Katie smiled, knowing Mary was curious out of concern. "We're trying a new routine. His long hours and the rush hour commute are causing a little friction between us." Katie sighed. "I'm not convinced it will work, especially if he's dealing with a flu epidemic."

Mary gave Katie's hand an affectionate tap. "Marriage has its ups and downs. You of all people should know that."

"I do and I trust Piers but some of the old wounds from the

break-up with John niggle at me. I know Piers isn't like that and I get mad at myself even thinking about it. But I'm not always as considerate as I should be. We had our first fight the other day."

"Fights are good as long as you made up before you went to bed."

"Adam said the same thing and yes we did make up." Katie blushed as the bell jangled and the bakery door opened. "Saved by the bell," she said, laughing.

"You and Piers are made for each other. Stop worrying. Now, I'd better get back to work." Katie slipped the bag of goodies under her arm and collected Buddy Boy and Arthur.

A loud chime came from her pocket. She always set her mobile on the highest setting so she wouldn't miss calls but the chances of getting this one was remote as she juggled two dogs and a bag of bread while opening the gate to Lavender Cottage. The phone kept ringing so she dropped the dog leashes and answered.

"Hello, Katie! It's John."

John? Why is he calling me? Darn! I should have checked before answering.

"Hello? Are you there, Katie?"

"John, what a surprise! I have my hands full. Can you hold on while I get into the house?"

"Sure," John replied slowly. Katie heard disappointment. *Why is he calling?* She was glad of the hold to gather her thoughts. She dropped the bag of bread on the kitchen counter and walked into her office.

Taking a deep breath and sounding more enthusiastic than she felt, she pressed speaker. "Sorry about that. I just returned from walking the dogs and picking up bread from Mary's. So, how are you? I'm surprised to hear from you. Is something wrong?"

"I'm well, thank you. In fact, more than well. I have been assigned a high profile case. It feels good to be back in the saddle."

"I heard. I had lunch with Melanie." Katie frowned, not sure what to say. "I'm pleased for you John, but …"

John interrupted before she could finish. "I guess old habits die hard. I wanted to share it with someone who knew me from the old days." He paused. "You were always my best cheerleader. Like mother, like daughter, Melanie has been a saint. Although I think she has misgivings about whether or not I can handle this case. Definitely misguided concern. I can do this." He paused again and Katie heard the anxiety in his voice. She surmised his bravado was for him as much as others.

"Katie, are you still there?"

"Yes, yes, I'm here. I remember how hard you fought for your clients. It's good to hear you are back but do be careful." She hoped her words sounded supportive. She was not entirely convinced he was ready and she worried about Olivia and the price she might pay if John wasn't up to it.

"What do you mean, be careful?" His words sounded hurt.

"You've been through a lot and I know you are better now but I can't help wondering why Bryant and Bryant have even taken on this case. Lord Thesleton is a brutal man, both personally and on the bench."

"I'm not stupid, Katie. Old man Bryant knows that win or lose, this case will put the firm on the map. I also realize I'm being used as a scapegoat. But if I win, my legal career will be made for life and I can put my past behind me."

"And if you lose?"

"I won't lose. Bryant has underestimated my tenacity. I'm back. I'm the lawyer I once was, maybe even better."

"I'm pleased to hear that, but why are you telling me this?"

"Two reasons. I need your support and Melanie tells me you know my client. Before you say it, I honestly want to share with you. I still miss you and this is not just a ploy for information."

Katie let out a long breath. The hurt he had inflicted on her in the past still stung at times, even though they were divorced and she had married Piers. She couldn't deny John seemed like his old self and, if nothing else, by helping John, she would be helping Olivia get her children back.

"I'm not sure how I can help but Olivia stays at the B&B from time to time and she told me about how Basil treated her. As long as I'm not breaking any confidences, I'll tell you what I know. Olivia is staying here this weekend. If she's okay with me talking to you, and I'm sure she will be, give me a call early next week." Seeing Adam standing in the doorway and holding up a piece of paper, Katie said, "John, I have to go."

Adam's face creased around his eyes. "Was that John?"

"Yes, long story. What do you have there?"

"Ingram just called with the window quote. Less than we thought. £5,500. The windows are in stock and he can start on Monday."

"Cyril has the rooms booked next Friday for the auction."

"I mentioned that. He said he can work around the bookings. Shall I tell him to go ahead?"

Katie nodded.

Drama, Big and Small

L avender Cottage experienced a busy weekend with several drop-in guests, unusual for November. Katie wasn't complaining. The extra revenue was welcome but it meant she hadn't been able to chat with Olivia until she was leaving on Sunday night.

"Olivia, can I have a word?"

"Of course. Is something wrong?" Olivia had one hand on the front door. She turned to look at Katie.

"No, nothing's wrong. It's just that John, John Saunders, called me the other day. He told me he was representing you in the child custody appeal. Of course, you had already informed me that John was your solicitor. He was asking me questions about you and Basil. I wasn't comfortable answering them without your consent."

"Oh. What I told you about Basil's bullying, I haven't told anyone else." Olivia's eyes filled with shame as she dropped her gaze to the floor.

"Olivia, there is nothing to be ashamed of. Anything you tell your solicitor is confidential but he needs to know everything. Basil's bullying, I suspect, will be key to the case. What if he hurts Poppy or Jonathan?"

"It's obvious, isn't it? Jonathan is mimicking his father's behaviour. Poppy is scared of him, but I don't think he'd hurt her." Olivia's eyes widened. "Would he?"

"It's hard to say and until you can speak with Poppy alone, you can't be certain one way or the other. Do you mind if I tell John what I know?"

"No, I don't mind. I know you'll do what's best. Katie, I am so worried about the case, about my children and you are correct, I don't want to believe Basil is bullying the children but I have my suspicions." A car horn beeped. "I must go. Cyril is waiting for me. I'm meeting John and Mr. Bryant on Tuesday."

"I'll speak with John tonight. I'll see you on Friday for the auction."

Lydia, the maid, breezed in at 6:45 on Monday morning, as cheerful as ever. She took the dust sheets from the linen cupboard and, with Adam's help, moved the furniture and spread the dust sheets to protect the bed. Katie watched, wishing she had Lydia's energy, but she hadn't slept well and was tired. She poured her second coffee, hoping it would wake her up. She had barely finished her drink when Derrick and his crew pulled up to Lavender Cottage.

"Mrs Bannister, we are all set to start. We'll do the bedrooms at the back of the house first."

"Okay. Do you need me for anything?"

Derrick shook his head as he ordered his crew to get started. Katie was amazed at the efficiency and disappeared into her office, firmly closing the Morning Room door. Neither Arthur nor Buddy were happy with the chaos, and strangers banging around the house put them on guard with low growls and warning barks to the intruders.

She checked the weekend bookings. A full house on Friday night for Cyril's auction participants and she was pleased to see several guests had booked Saturday too. Then she remembered she'd forgotten to call John last night and made the call. Pleased that his attitude was suitably business like, she repeated Olivia's account of Basil's behaviour and suggested he ask Olivia for details about the bullying. He couldn't discuss the case but was grateful for Katie's input. Olivia had not made him aware of Lord Thesleton's behaviour. Katie, having once been married to John, understood his momentary silence indicated his legal mind was already forming a case around this information. She would have to talk to Olivia for updates but hoped the case would go well for everyone's sake.

"Knock, knock! Is this a bad time?" Two large Golden Retrievers bounced into the office. Buddy Boy and Arthur ran through their legs, almost knocking Judy over. "What's going on?"

"Judy, what a lovely surprise and so early in the morning. Is everything okay?" Katie frowned. "How's your dad?"

"Everything is fine. Dad is much better and I just needed to get away. Just a sec. Is it okay to let them in the back garden?"

"Make sure the back gate is closed. The window crew are here replacing the back windows."

"That explains the construction," Judy said, peering into the garden. "It's closed. Dad's fine. The doc gave him antibiotics.

I went home last night but woke up early and here I am. I was hoping to crash here for a couple of nights but you have your hands full."

"New windows! I'm not sure how restful it will be with all the banging. Hopefully the Daisy Room will be finished by tonight. Otherwise, it will be the couch or bunking in with me."

"Where's Piers?"

"Working!"

"I thought you had worked out a new system so he was home more."

"Well, we had one great day. He was on call this weekend and I was crazy busy here so I haven't talked to him but he should be home this afternoon if the new schedule is working."

As if on cue, Katie's mobile jangled. "Speak of the devil." She pressed answer. "How was the weekend?" Katie nodded with a few aha's and hung up. "He sounds terrible. Piers was up all night with a patient at the nursing home and Rick was called out to deliver a baby." She smiled. "A doctor's life, the beginning and the end. Rick's taking the morning surgery and Piers is getting a couple of hours shut-eye and will take the afternoon surgery. He said he'd call when he's finished. I doubt he'll make it home tonight."

"So, the new schedule isn't working so well." Judy patted Katie's shoulder. "I'm sorry, Katie. I know you were hoping this would work."

"Oh, I knew what I was getting into when I married Piers and we both knew the commute might be difficult." She hesitated. "But it is harder than I expected."

"A good long walk will cheer you up. Sam and Lily could do with some exercise. Looking after Dad, our walks were short."

"Good idea! How about breakfast at Mary's? Mary is struggling as business is slow. It seems there's a lot of flu around, keeping people at home. Although there was no evidence of flu this weekend. She must have been as busy as the B&B."

All four dogs were leashed as they walked along the towpath. Sam and Lily straining to get into the canal, Arthur and Buddy Boy sulking as they were never leashed. Neither liked water, unless it was a muddy puddle, but it wasn't fair to the retrievers for them to be loose. As soon as they reached the wooden stile, all four bounded into the field, unleashed. Buddy's short legs and robust body looked comical as he tried to keep up with the long legged retrievers. Arthur, as short as Buddy, but skinny and agile, ran under their bellies. Judy and Katie linked arms and laughed at the antics, enjoying their friendship. By the time they reached Mary's Café, the dogs were exhausted and, after emptying the big water bowl, they happily flopped down at the Dog Moorings. Katie picked up the bowl and went into the Café for a refill.

Mary took the bowl and leaned into Katie, whispering, "I think she needs some help." Katie followed Mary's gaze and was surprised to see Olivia staring into a cup of coffee, tears streaming down her face. "I'll take this out for the dogs. Do you want coffee?"

"Yes please, two. And two eggs and bacon with scones and jam. Judy is with me. I'll go and sit with Olivia."

Approaching the table, Olivia looked up and gave Katie a watery smile. "Hello."

"Olivia, can I help? What happened?"

"I'm not sure I can get through this, Katie." She leaned down

95

for her handbag and handed Katie a piece of writing paper. "This was on my doorstep this morning. I think Basil found out I had a meeting with my solicitor today. I can't believe he'd use his own son this way."

Katie watched the tears pour down Olivia's cheeks and she felt the embossed Thesleton crest as she unfolded the expensive linen paper.

Mother,

I don't know why you are pursuing Father and trying to wreck his career, but as your son I am asking you to stop this nonsense immediately. The court made its decision. You are not a fit mother and justice has been served. I am happy with Father and I do not want you to have custody of me or my sister. Father says you are a bad influence on Penelope.

You know Father will win and if you continue with this charade, I will never see or speak to you ever again.

Your estranged son,
Jonathan

Katie lifted her eyes from the letter, wet with tears for Olivia. She couldn't speak. What could she say? The hurt was something a mother should never ever feel from her child.

Olivia spoke haltingly, trying to stop the tears. "I didn't know where to turn. I drove to Cyril's but I'd forgotten he's in Nottingham picking up furniture for Friday's auction."

"Olivia, I don't know what to say, except I doubt your son, a ten-year-old boy, wrote this without help from his father. I agree Basil knows you are seeing John tomorrow and wants to stop you."

"How would he know? I haven't told anyone except you and Cyril."

"A loose lipped law clerk? It's hard to say but this is intimidation. He dare not write it himself but coming from your son, he can plead innocence. On the bright side, this could mean he's afraid of what might come out during the appeal."

"How can I be sure?" Olivia began crying again. "I meant what I said. I can't go through with it."

Katie took her hand. "Yes you can. You have friends to help this time."

"Maybe."

"Do you mind if Judy joins us? We came by for breakfast," Katie said beckoning to Judy standing discreetly by the counter, talking to Mary.

"I would appreciate the company but I'd rather not talk about this." Olivia took the letter and stuffed it into her handbag.

"Don't hide from this, Olivia. Promise me you will show it to John."

Olivia nodded affirmative as Judy leaned on the back of a chair and said, "Mary asked me to ask you if you'd like breakfast. She's making eggs and bacon and scones for us."

"Thank you. No to breakfast, but one of Mary's scones would be lovely. And coffee, this has gone cold."

Judy nodded to Mary who was plating the breakfast and repeated, "Two bacon and eggs, three scones and three coffees coming up."

Katie gave a satisfied sigh as she finished her breakfast and, buttering a hot scone, she looked at her friends and said, "Ladies, as I am neither a lady of leisure nor on holiday, I have to get back to work after this. Olivia, you are welcome to come to Lavender Cottage and wait for Cyril, but the place is an awful mess."

Judy nodded. "That is true. New windows and lots of hammering. Olivia, would you like to come shopping with me? I have to pick up a new hard hat. Mine had an argument with a steel beam."

"What! You never told me," Katie screamed. "Were you hurt?"

"No. That's why we wear hard hats on construction sites, although I did have a headache for a couple days." Judy gave a clucking noise. "Katie, I'm fine. Now back to shopping. The place I need to go is at the back of Madam Couture's and close to Debenhams Department store."

Olivia and Judy stared at Katie, who was laughing hysterically. "I never thought I would hear the words 'hardhat and Madame Couture' in the same breath." Seeing the funny side of it, Judy and Olivia joined in with more laughter.

"That would be delightful, Judy, thank you. I can no longer afford Madam Couture but I love to shop and browsing through Debenhams sounds very therapeutic."

Katie gave Judy a warm, understanding smile. Judy, although a kind person, was not good with tearful people and she hated shopping, especially browsing. This was her way of helping Olivia and, she suspected, staying out of the construction noise.

Katie waved to Judy and Olivia as they drove off and she returned to her office, accompanied by four dogs. The first thing she did was phone John to tell him about the letter and make sure Olivia showed it to him. He thanked her, acknowledging this was a great piece of evidence and possibly a big mistake on Lord Thesleton's part, especially if he could prove the boy had been coerced. It amused Katie that John had slipped into his old habit of confiding in her. Suddenly aware he may have said too much, he made Katie swear she would not discuss this with anyone. She willingly agreed, knowing that the element of surprise was key. She suggested he be careful with his own clerks as there was a possibility someone had told Basil that Olivia had engaged a legal team and the timing of the letter implied Basil was aware of the upcoming meeting.

The hammering coming from the second floor made it impossible for Katie to concentrate and she wished she gone shopping with Judy and Olivia. She smiled at Judy's kindness and worried about her nonchalance at having a steel beam drop on her head. She also knew that even if she was hurt, she'd say nothing for fear of appearing weak. Women engineers were still a minority and a woman project manager on a major construction site rare and barely tolerated by some male workers. But Judy managed her team well.

Breaking Glass

K atie sat at her desk, trying to think while trying to ignore the hammering. Suddenly an enormous crash jolted her out of her thoughts. Adam ran in from the rose garden.

"What was that?"

Without answering, Katie ran up the stairs with Adam and four dogs at her heels. She came to a halt at the Daisy Room door. Derrick stood, holding a window frame and surrounded by shattered glass, with blood dripping from his hand. Adam brushed past Katie and went to help Derrick.

Katie yelled "Sit!" to the dogs and then ordered them downstairs away from the glass. She secured them safely in the Morning Room and returned to the disaster.

"I am so sorry, Mrs Bannister. The frame slipped on the window sill. I tried to catch it." He moved his bleeding hand forward.

"Are you alright? You've cut your hand."

"I'm fine, just embarrassed. This has never happened before. My dad won't be pleased."

Katie looked at the blood pooling on the floor, grateful Lydia had spread a dust sheet over the carpet. She flipped the wardrobe door open, pleased to see a neatly folded towel on the shelf. Grabbing it, she wrapped it around Derrick's hand as his concerned crew of two gathered at the bedroom door.

"I'm okay, guys. Back to work."

Katie glanced at his pale face. "Come downstairs so I can clean that cut."

The dogs all sat up expectantly when Katie opened the Morning Room door. "Stay," she commanded, and motioned to Derrick to sit by the kitchen table. Lydia was already in the kitchen and had placed the First Aid kit on the table.

"Thank you, Lydia. Would you make some tea? Derrick needs a sweet cup of tea for the shock."

Carefully unwrapping the towel, Katie almost gasped at the size of the cut and wished Piers was home or easily contacted. But he would have an office full of patients and was at least an hour's drive away. She panicked as the wound was bleeding profusely and wondered if the glass had hit an artery.

"Derrick, I'm going to tie this bandage very tight on your arm to make a tourniquet to slow the bleeding. You may have nicked an artery. You need to go to the hospital. I'll have Adam drive you."

"No!" Derrick shouted. "It's too far. It'll be okay. Can you put a plaster on it?"

"Derrick, this needs medical attention."

"Is there a clinic in the village?" Derrick asked.

"There's a doctor on the Willington Road. Sorry, I didn't

mean to interrupt," Lydia said as she tossed teabags in the teapot. "Dr Duthie. My dad goes there sometimes. I've got his number if you like."

"Lydia, thank you. I'll call him now. Lydia, would you mind going upstairs to clean up the glass? And, please be careful. Ask Adam to help you."

Katie dialled the number and listened to it ring for a long time. She was about to hang up when an efficient sounding voice said, "Dr Duthie's Surgery."

"Hello, my name is Katie Bannister from Lavender Cottage B&B. I would like to see the doctor as soon as possible. I have an emergency."

"Dr Duthie is out on calls. This is his answering service. Can I take a message?"

Katie gave the answering service the details, resigned to a long wait and wondering if she should call Piers or insist Adam take him to the hospital. Derrick was whiter than the proverbial sheet.

The tourniquet had slowed the bleeding so she cleaned the wound, placing a large piece of gauze over the cut and wrapped a tight dressing around his hand, trying close the cut.

Derrick looked up at her. "Thank you. I've had cuts before but this really turned my stomach. I need to call my dad and tell him what happened and to order a new window. He's going to be some pissed."

Katie poured two teas and stirred several spoons of sugar in before handing Derrick the sweet beverage. "Drink this. It'll make you feel better. Don't move your hand. I'll dial your dad's number and you can talk to him on speaker phone. Don't look so worried. He'll be concerned for you."

The ring, ring sounded and a gruff voice answered, "Ingram

Windows and Doors."

"Dad, it's me Derrick. I'm at Lavender Cottage and I had an accident."

"What!? Are you hurt, Son?"

"A cut hand. Mrs Bannister is looking after it but the window is smashed. Can you order another one? It's the B4 PVC - 4.5 model. I'm sorry Dad, it just slipped on the window sill."

"Don't worry about the window. I'll see to that. Do you need to go to the hospital? Stay there, I'm coming to get you."

"Its ..." Derrick shrugged and said, "He hung up."

"I told you, he's more worried about you than the window," Katie said, patting him on the shoulder. "Maybe your dad can persuade you to go to the hospital."

Lydia peeked around the Morning Room door. "Katie, Dr Duthie is here."

"Really. Wow that was fast. Show him in."

A tall, thin man with a paunch and a tired, sagging face walked into the Morning Room. All four dogs eyed the doctor with suspicion. Sam, the protector, gave a low growl.

"Dr Duthie, this is a surprise. I didn't expect a house call." Seeing the doctor's fearful eyes glance at the dogs, Katie opened the back door and sent them in the garden. "They are friendly but four are intimidating and Sam considers himself a guard dog." The good doctor did not look amused so Katie stopped talking.

"Mrs Bannister, I assume. My office called to say you had an emergency. I happened to be in Springsville visiting the Johnsons. Mr Johnson came out of hospital yesterday." He gave Katie a warm smile. "I'm old fashioned and still do house calls. Are you the patient?" He frowned as it was obvious

Katie was fit and healthy.

"No, not me." Katie tapped Derrick on the shoulder. "Derrick Ingram. He was replacing my windows and one slipped and smashed. There's a deep cut on his left hand." Katie pointed to the bandage which had turned red with blood.

Dr Duthie put his black bag on the table, pulled up a chair to face Derrick and gently unwound the bandage. "Um … that is a nasty cut. I see you used a tourniquet. Very wise. It's definitely bleeding but it missed the artery. It needs stitching."

"I don't want to go to the hospital. Can you just bandage it?" Derrick's words pleaded and Katie wondered why the hospital frightened him.

"One of the good things about being an old fashioned doctor is that I do everything myself." His mouth turned upwards into a reassuring smile and Katie noticed an endearing twinkle in his eyes. "I'm quite accomplished in needlework. I've sewn everything from cut chins to severed toes and you won't feel a thing. To answer your question, no hospital for you today. I will fix you up right here at the kitchen table." The doctor opened his bag, taking out a white package with the words 'Suture Kit - *Sterile until the seal is broken.*'

He pulled on latex gloves and snapped them into place. "Are you Dan Ingram's son?" Derrick nodded. "Your father built the surgery extension when I set up my practice. Ah … that must be thirty years ago. So you work with your dad? He must be proud of you following in his footsteps. Do you like the work?"

Derrick nodded enthusiastically. "I do, most of the time. He's probably mad with me today."

"You tell him from me, he's lucky to have a son who will work with him. My boy followed me into medicine but not my practice. Family practice is too mundane for him. He's training to be a surgeon. I'd rather he do that and be happy than do as I want and be miserable." Dr Duthie worked at the wound as he talked. Katie liked his manner and Derrick hardly noticed as he skillfully stitched the cut and wound a fresh bandage around his hand, placing it upright next to his chest. "Keep your hand elevated for a day or two. All done!" Dr Duthie pulled a prescription pad from his pocket and scribbled. "I want you to take these three times a day for five days to ward off any infection. Have you had a Tetanus shot recently?"

"Yes. My dad insists we keep that up to date because of our line of work."

"Excellent. Now you need to rest. You're going to be fine. Come by the surgery in about a week and I'll take the stitches out."

"Derrick," Katie said. "Why don't you lie down on the couch in the sitting room and wait for your dad? You'll feel better after a rest."

"Thanks, I do feel woozy." Katie propped him up with cushions and a blanket, making sure this hand was upright before returning to the kitchen.

"Doctor, would you like a cup of tea?"

"Oh, that would be lovely, my dear. Milk, no sugar." Katie poured the tea and added a plate of Mary's scones to the table. "From Mary's café?" he asked. "My wife picks them up occasionally. Since she started working at the retirement home, she doesn't pass by Springsville anymore and this little village stays healthy, so I'm not here often. My wife mentioned a new B&B in Springsville. I'm surprised I haven't had a call before."

"My guests seem to be healthy and my husband is a GP."

He rubbed his chin and thought for a minute. "Dr Bannister. You are his new bride. I'm sorry I only just made the connection."

"You know my husband?"

"We're acquainted through boating. My wife and I were keen boaters at one time, and met Piers and Julianne through boating friends. I don't think they owned a boat at that time." He paused, looking at Katie. She smiled to reassure him it was okay to talk about Julianne. "It got too much for us. We sold our boat a couple of years ago. We exchanged narrowboats and canals for cruise ships and oceans and enjoy being pampered." Dr Duthie frowned. "Does your husband practice near here?"

"No, he is in partnership with Rick Larkin. They have a clinic in Nottingham."

"Now I remember. Piers bought a boat just as we sold ours. Julianne's death was tragic and he became quite reclusive. I haven't spoken to him in years. You live here all year?"

"Yes. I met Piers when I bought the cottage and turned it into a B&B. After we married, Piers sold his house moved in here."

"I'm glad he found someone but that daily commute must be difficult."

Katie gave him a resigned look. "It is causing some friction. We're trying to work it out. He stays in town when he's on call." Katie took a breath to say more but decided against it.

"Well, I had better be on my way. It was a pleasure meeting you. Please give my regards to Piers. It would be nice to see him sometime."

"Perhaps you and your wife would like to come for dinner

one night?"

"I would like that very much. Call in the evenings and speak with my wife, Nancy." He handed her a card. "That's our private number."

Katie walked to the front door and bumped into Judy coming in. "Doctor, this is my friend, Judy. She's staying here for a few days."

"Doctor! Is something wrong?" Judy asked.

"Long story. Go ahead and I'll be with you in a minute."

Katie closed the front door and checked on Derrick before joining Judy.

"You're back early. Where is Olivia?"

"She got hold of Cyril and he picked her up. Saved by the boyfriend. I really do hate shopping but it was a distraction for Olivia. It looks as though I missed some excitement here."

"It has been quite a day," Katie began to update Judy on the morning's events when the doorbell rang. "What now!?"

Dan Ingram stood at the front door, holding a window and frame against the wall. "Dan, come in. Derrick is sleeping. Dr Duthie came and patched him up. I don't think he'll be working for a few days."

"So he doesn't need to go to A&E?"

"A nasty, deep cut on his hand required stitches but the doctor said it hasn't done any other damage. I wanted to take him to the hospital but he was adamant." Katie hesitated. "Even frightened."

"Derrick had a bad experience at A&E when he was a kid. I'm grateful you found a local doctor."

Katie waited for more explanation, but Dan changed the subject, pointing to the window. "I was passing the supplier and it seemed silly not to pick it up. That's why I'm later than

I intended. I wouldn't have stopped if I'd known the cut was serious."

"He'll be okay and I'm pleased you picked up the window as I have a bunch of B&B bookings for Friday. I was worried about the delay."

"No need to worry. I'll fill in for Derrick. He can stay in the office for a day or two. We'll be finished on time." He leaned over the sofa and smiled. "Even as a little kid, he could always sleep anywhere. I'll take Derrick home but I'll be back this afternoon to finish that window and the crew will be back tomorrow and Wednesday for the rest of upstairs. Is it okay if we do downstairs next week?"

"Absolutely. I'll leave you to it. Can you show yourself out?"

Dan nodded as he tapped Derrick on the shoulder to wake him.

Katie pushed the Morning Room door open and let out a long, relieved sigh. "Judy, it looks as though you can have the Daisy Den tonight after all. It's not painted but you're not exposed to the elements. So tell me, how's your dad?"

"Much better. He went to the Legion to play cards this afternoon, so I decided if he was well enough to meet his cronies, he didn't need me hanging around and here I am. I'll give him a call later and make sure he's okay." Judy frowned. "Are you sure I'm not in the way?"

"Positive. It was a crazy morning but everything is under control and there's not much I can do. Piers should be home for dinner tonight. I emphasize 'should.' We started a new schedule but I'm not sure it will work."

Judy's eyebrows creased together, a habit she had when she was confused or thinking hard. "What's up?"

"Oh, nothing." Katie shrugged adding, "Just me being silly."

Judy gave a tut with a determined stare. "Katie, I've known you a long time. Something is bothering you and I'm pretty certain it has to do with Piers."

"Really. I'm being silly."

"Tell me anyway."

"Piers is finding the commute difficult. We had our first fight, all because he was late, having been delayed at the nursing home, followed by a terrible journey home in a thunderstorm. I was unreasonably resentful. I want my husband home. Is that too much to ask? Now I feel guilty because Piers agreed to sell his house and move to Springsville. We both knew the commute would not be easy and I was aware before we married that his patients come first."

"Be patient. I'm sure the new schedule will work out.

"I guess so, but honestly, Judy, I don't think it will. He needs to be close to the practice and that means staying Nottingham. I never mentioned this but some time ago he suggested renting a small flat."

"That sounds like a great idea but I thought he stayed at Rick and Cindy's."

"He does but he thinks he's imposing. I know Cindy is as frustrated as me about the hours they keep but she's always made Piers welcome. He doesn't need a flat. I don't want him in a flat. His home is here."

Judy gave Katie a knowing stare and stayed silent.

"What!?" Katie snapped.

"The idea of a flat in the city seems to be a sore point, Katie. Piers is not John. The circumstances are very different."

"How did you guess? It was like a slap in the face when John spent all our money on that fancy flat to entertain his girlfriends. I couldn't bear Piers doing anything like that."

"And he won't." Judy took Katie by the shoulders. "Look at me. You have to get past this. Piers adores you and if it is better for his well-being to have somewhere to stay in town, it might be a good solution to the problem."

"You see, I am being silly. I'll give it some thought. So, how's the project going?"

Judy laughed. "Nice subtle subject change. Good. Ahead of schedule but this has not been an easy crew to work with, a chauvinistic bunch, need I say more.

New Schedule

P iers opened the door slowly and smiled at Judy sitting by the fire, reading. He pressed his finger to his lips and crept across the room towards Katie, intent on layering pasta in a lasagna dish. He wrapped his arms around Katie, kissing her before she could say a word. Releasing his grip, he said, "Ah, I'm glad to come home to such a lovely domestic scene. Judy relaxed and reading and my beautiful wife slaving over a hot stove just for me…and our guest of course."

Kate took a deep breath and whipped the tea towel across his arm. "You scared me half to death. I didn't hear you come in. And we might have to talk about the 'slaving over a hot stove' part. But you are forgiven. I'm so glad you made it."

"Our new schedule. Don't you remember? I know I'm a little late, but with Pat's help, she shooed me out of the surgery and I left my paperwork for the morning. Here I am."

Katie flipped the tea towel around his neck and pulled him

towards her, smacking a kiss on his cheek and another on his lips.

"Ah! Would you two like me to leave?" Judy said, laughing.

"No, not at all." Piers said, adding, "Let's have a glass of wine to celebrate." He spun around, looking at the floor. "Something is missing from this domestic scene. Where are the dogs?"

Right on cue, four heads appeared at the French doors, tails wagging as they desperately tried to get in to greet Piers. He opened the door and frowned as the dogs bounded in, jumping with excitement. "Why are the dogs outside?"

"The window people only just left and we had some drama here today. Pour the wine and I'll tell you all about it. Dinner will be a while yet. I suggest we go into the lounge. There are no guests and I think Adam lit a fire."

Adam held the door open. "I thought we might need more room. Wine! What are we celebrating?"

"Piers' new schedule of coming home early alternate days and weekends." Katie raised her glass. "To the new schedule!"

Judy grinned at Katie with an I-told-you-so look as she raised her glass. Katie nodded understanding as she slipped her arm around Piers.

Piers furrowed his brow, looking puzzled and asked, "What was the drama today?"

Katie told the story of Derrick's accident and meeting the local doctor.

"Wow! I did miss some drama. I remember Dr Duthie … um …George and Nancy. It was before I bought *Tranquil Days* and Julianne's cancer." Piers hesitated and cleared his throat several times, glancing at Katie. "Julianne wasn't much for boating but we occasionally rented a narrowboat on weekends.

112

George and Nancy had a lovely boat and were keen boaters back then. I haven't seen him on the canal for years. He's old. I thought he would have retired by now."

"No, he still has his practice and does house calls. He made a big deal of how he's an old fashioned practitioner. I liked him and I suggested he and his wife come for dinner."

"Katie that would be lovely. You don't mind?"

"Of course not."

"Did you tell him who you were?"

"I didn't need to. He knew about Julianne and he called me Dr Bannister's new bride. He also said what a tragedy it was for you to lose Julianne. He gave me his card with his private number. It's over there on the mantlepiece."

Piers picked up the card and pulled his mobile from his pocket. "I'll call him now. What about Saturday?"

"That won't work. Cyril has an auction this weekend and I have a full house. Too many people milling around for a quiet dinner here at the cottage." Katie hated bursting his bubble. She had never seen him this keen to entertain and it would be nice to make friends with people in the medical world.

"The boat, *Tranquil Days!*" Piers blurted out.

"The boat?" Katie repeated.

"Saturday afternoon. A cruise up to Swarkeston and back, drinks and snacks on board. It might be better than dinner for the first time. What do you think?"

"Dr Duthie certainly spoke fondly about his boating days, although he did mention their preference was cruise ships these days. But that sounds like a good idea. I won't have time to make dinner but I can put a few hors d'oeuvres together. Just one thing. The weather. It is November."

"It'll be okay. Excuse me, folks."

Katie raised an eyebrow, somewhat puzzled by Piers' reaction. The smell of burning drew her back into the kitchen. Fortunately, the burning was only spilled sauce from the lasagna and maybe the garlic bread was a touch browner than it should be.

Piers helped Katie serve dinner while telling her the Duthies were thrilled by the boating invitation and it was all arranged for three o'clock on Saturday.

Mellowed by wine and satisfied by a good meal, the animated chatter slowed down and everyone elected to have an early night.

Piers and Katie cleaned up the kitchen, glad of some time alone. Curious about Piers' reaction to the Duthies she said, "I'm pleased the Duthies are coming but I have to say, I don't remember you ever being so enthusiastic. Is there something you're not telling me?" Katie slipped her arm around his waist and looked up into his hazy blue eyes.

"I'm not quite sure how to explain this. I don't think I really know myself. But here goes. Even after five years, I still find the memories of Julianne painful." He pulled Katie closer to him. "It has nothing to do with us or how I feel about you." He kissed the top of her head. "My memories of being with Julianne when we met Nancy and George are very happy ones. They are kind, generous people and, although we didn't see a lot of them, when we did the time seemed special." Tears brushed his eyelashes. "It's so nice to have something of Julianne that isn't painful. It's happy and it feels really good."

"Dearest Piers, hold on to that memory." She took his hand. "Now, let's get some shut eye. We have an early start. By the way, how's this working with the patients and practice?"

"Very good. I think we have solved the commute problem."

"Good news indeed."

Buddy Boy's ears perked up and he opened one eye when Katie crept into the kitchen to make coffee. The look was fleeting and Arthur twitched but barely opened one eye. Katie made some toast while the coffee gurgled and sat at the table, scrolling through messages on her phone. Her finger stopped when she saw Olivia's name. It was a long message so she scrolled past it. She'd read it later.

Fully dressed in his suit and smelling delightfully of musky aftershave, Piers yawned as he joined Katie and kissed her cheek. "Good morning! I envy the dogs all snug in their beds." He grinned. "I think Arthur has disowned me. No greeting for me today, sleepyhead?" Hearing Piers' voice, the little dog scampered towards him. "Hey, that's better." Piers tickled Arthur's ears before picking up his black bag and walking to the door. "See you Friday afternoon. We have the weekend together."

Katie kissed his cheek and handed him his travelling mug of coffee plus a small package containing toast; a ritual every morning. She waved him off with a happy sigh.

Katie topped up her coffee mug and settled in her blue chair, her feet up on the ottoman with two sleepy dogs on her lap. She returned to her phone messages, searching for the text from Olivia. Seeing it was sent at 2 a.m., she sighed, feeling sorry for Olivia, worried and not able to sleep.

I met with John and Mr. Bryant senior this afternoon and I gave them the official go ahead to start proceedings to get my children back. John was enthusiastic and positive. I see what you mean. He's a fighter. Mr. Bryant was considerably more cautious. Perhaps to be expected as he has known Basil most of his legal career and is aware of his tactics. You were right about the letter from Jonathan. Even Mr Bryant gave a wry grin as he read it, commenting that Basil had made a big mistake. I can't thank you enough for persuading me to show them the letter. It also led to questions about Basil's abusive behaviour. You'd be proud of me, Katie. For the first time, I told them the truth. Mr Bryant was not surprised. He's seen Basil use nasty bullying tactics in court. He went as far as to say Basil should never have been appointed to the bench. Sorry for the long text. I couldn't sleep. Can we talk some more on Friday?

Katie's thumbs clicked away in reply.

So pleased you were honest with John and Mr Bryant and I am proud of you. I would love to chat on Friday. Why don't you come early before the dealers arrive? Cyril will be busy getting ready for the auction. Piers will be home later on Friday afternoon but the two of us could have an early lunch at Mary's. That is if you have time. Are you helping Cyril this time?

Katie hit send as Adam called "Good morning," followed by two Golden retrievers and one sleepy Judy. Katie let the dogs into the garden.

"Morning, Judy. Help yourself to coffee. I'm just warning you the window guys will be here in an hour. I'm off to get dressed."

"I'll make us breakfast. Bacon and eggs okay? We should have time to eat before Dan's crew arrives," Adam said.

"Sounds good!" Katie and Judy chorused.

Katie's phone pinged. She glanced down to see a text from Olivia.

> *Early lunch on Friday is perfect. I am helping Cyril, but not until after 2 p.m. I'll meet you at noon. Looking forward to seeing you.*

Katie took a breath, finding it hard to believe the change in Olivia, and even harder to imagine they could ever be friends. But the harsh, inconsiderate, jealous, unkind and demanding woman that had arrived at the B&B a year ago had all but disappeared. Although she was still demanding with an air of entitlement, Olivia had a soft side to her and desperately needed a friend as she battled against her bullying ex-husband.

Dan, and one of the young guys from the day before, arrived at seven sharp. Derrick had been grounded in the office until his hand healed. Katie noticed that Dan seemed to be enjoying being on the job again. She left them to it and settled in the office, scheduling the Christmas bookings and ordering supplies. It was hard to believe Christmas was only a few weeks away. Judy had returned from taking the dogs for a long run to tire them out and was at the kitchen table, organizing her next project somewhere in Cornwall for the new year. Katie missed Judy when she was on an out-of-town job and Cornwall meant she would be gone a long time.

The back door slammed and Adam clattered into the kitchen, dropping cans of paint, scrapers and brushes on the floor. Katie checked out the paint colours: a soft yellow with white trim for the Daisy Den and a trendy pink and white for the Rose Suite.

She grinned at Adam. "The yellow is perfect but I'm not sure about that pink. Trendy or not, it looks too bright. What do you think, Judy?"

"I like it. It might be too much for the whole room, though. What about a feature wall?"

Adam nodded. "I can do that. One wall full colour and I can mix it with white for a lighter colour for the other walls and do white trim, same as the Daisy Den."

"That's a great idea but the windows have not been installed yet. Can we start with the Daisy Den? Judy, do you mind if Adam paints the trim today?"

"No, go ahead. Will it be dry by tonight? I was only thinking about the dogs leaning on it. Lily likes to lie with her back against the wall."

"It is quick drying paint," Adam said thoughtfully. "But it might be sticky."

"Lily and Sam can sleep down here with Buddy Boy and Arthur. They do that when you're not here." Katie giggled and pink flushed her cheeks. "Since Piers moved in, the dogs are not always allowed on the bed at night."

"That's fine with me. Do you need help? I'm a good painter and I'd like something to do," Judy said.

"I'd like that." Adam looked at Katie for approval. "I'm not so good on top of ladders these days."

"Of course, it's okay. Adam, you should have told me. I'm sorry, I should have had someone help you." Katie felt bad because Adam was not a young man and his arthritis was often painful. She made a note to get help. She'd ask Maisie, owner of the Boater's Inn, if her son, Stevie, could help.

118

The next few days were a hive of activity. Dan finished the upstairs windows ahead of schedule, leaving downstairs until early December. Katie was pleased she'd made that choice as Cyril had booked all the rooms for the auction on Friday and the following weekend for a special private auction.

Adam was grateful for Judy's help and Judy relished getting her hands dirty and enjoyed the physical work. Katie was thrilled that both rooms were finished and ready to receive guests.

"Thank so much, Judy. I'm not sure what we'd have done without you. I was remiss not to realize that, as willing as Adam is, the work is too much for him.

"I'm happy to help but it will be some time before I get more time off other than Christmas."

"Don't worry. I'll make sure I hire some help. When do you go back to work?"

"Monday. I'll drop in and check on Dad on my way home. I have a pile of work waiting for me and much of the paperwork I'll be doing this weekend, but it was good to be here and have a break." Judy opened the car doors, threw her backpack on the front passenger seat and motioned to Sam and Lily to get into the back.

"It's a busy weekend for both of us. At least Piers will be home this weekend," Katie said as she hugged Judy.

Judy gave her a stern look. "Speaking of Piers. I hope you are convinced of how much he loves you and how committed he is. No more silly talk!"

Katie laughed. "I promise. Cross my heart."

Changes for the Better

⟨ornament⟩

L ydia arrived early as she always did on Fridays to prepare for the weekend guests, especially with a full house.

"Good morning, Lydia! Lots to do today so I'll give you a hand this morning. Can you start by opening the windows of both the Rose Suite and the Daisy Den? I want to make sure any residual paint smell has completely gone before the guests arrive. I'll help you clean the windows. I noticed a few finger marks on the new ones."

"I'd like that. I don't like hanging out of the windows to clean the outside but really I'm okay to do the rest." Lydia said with a reassuring tone.

"I know you can, Lydia. It is no reflection on your work. I recognize there is a lot to do and I have to leave at 11:30 for a luncheon meeting. Would you mind staying until I return? Just in case we have any early check-ins. So, you see, I'm helping you so you can help me."

Katie wasn't too keen on hanging out of the windows either and was hoping Dan's sales pitch about the hinged windows for cleaning was actually correct.

Lydia collected her cleaning stuff from the broom cupboard and Katie followed her into the Daisy Den.

"Woo … look at this?" Lydia gave the window a twist and she easily put her hand around the outside of the window. "I don't need no 'elp. I'll 'ave these done in a jiffy. I'm okay, Katie."

"Dan said they were easy to clean but I didn't realize how easy. I'll strip the bed. This duvet needs a wash. I'll use the dryer since there's no time to hang it outside."

Katie checked the Rose Suite and admired the paint. It was pretty, a rich deep pink on the wall behind the bed and delicate pink on the others. The bedding was clean so other than cleaning the new window and a vacuum, this room didn't need anything. *As much as I like to be hands-on,* she thought, *I really don't need to be here. Lydia can cope and, to be honest, she probably thinks I'm interfering.*

"Lydia, I'll leave you to it." She pointed to the duvet "I'll put this in the washer on my way downstairs."

Lydia's head popped around the door. "I'll have it all spick and span before you know it."

"I know you'll do a better job with me out of the way."

Katie surveyed the lounge. She had yet to choose a colour. The furniture was boring beige, as Cyril would call it, but she liked it. Preferring to use accent colours in cushions and other nick knacks, she realized that she'd never replaced the rather drab, worn cushions that age had bleached of colour. This room definitely needed a face lift. The walls would remain plain to show off the dark wooden beams.

There were two windows to be replaced, a small one by the front door and one large bow window looking onto Marina Lane. The bow window had a window seat below it. She'd noticed guests liked to sit there but had never paid much attention. She sat down and curled her legs underneath her, leaning against the wall. She could see the water through the trees and the view of the garden was pretty. She cranked the window open and the scent of the lavender bushes wafted in, urging her to closed her eyes and feel peacefulness; lavender was known for its calming qualities. She tried to relax but started wiggling, aware the wall was digging in her back and the hardness of the wooden window seat distracted her from the moment of serenity. *I need to fix this.* Katie determined that the window seat needed a thick custom-made cushion to sit on and nice big cushions on each side to lean on. *Why didn't I see that before?* And, once again, surveying the lounge, she added a new, bright area rug on the wooden floor with an assortment of big, bright coloured cushions for the sofa and chairs. Her mobile jolted her from her thoughts.

"Piers. A nice surprise."

"I have a moment between patients. Lots of coughs and running noses and some quite serious flu-like symptoms. It is the season." Piers sighed. "What are you up to?"

"I've decided to give the lounge a face lift. It needs brightening up. What do you think of cushions in the window seat?"

"We have a window seat?"

Katie laughed. "Yes we do and the view is lovely so I'm going to make it comfortable."

"That sounds great. I have to go. Duty calls. I love you!"

"Love you more! Bye!"

Katie did her best thinking when she was walking and she

had almost an hour before meeting Olivia. She abandoned all thoughts of office work. Removing the duvet from the washer, she called to Lydia, "The duvet is in the dryer. I'm taking the dogs for a walk, followed by lunch. I have my mobile if you need me. I'll be back around two."

"Okay!" Lydia replied.

The word 'walk' had not escaped Buddy Boy or Arthur. Katie smiled, seeing them waiting expectantly by the door. She put on her raincoat. The clouds looked heavy with rain, but one could never tell in November as the skies always seemed grey.

The dogs ran happily down the towpath, sniffing at every blade of grass until Katie was yards ahead of them. Then they raced to catch up. She didn't stop at the stile but kept walking. Arthur and Buddy Boy hesitated, taking a quick look in the field to make sure Sam and Lily hadn't magically returned. Satisfied the field was empty, the dogs ran past Katie, stopping when they reached main road. Panting, they flopped down and waited. Katie checked her phone both for messages and time and whistled to the dogs to come as she turned around, heading back to the marina and Mary's Café to meet Olivia. She would be early but she needed to check the croissant and scone orders for the weekend.

Exhausted, the dogs lapped at the water bowl and, without a second look at Katie, curled up at the Dog Moorings and went to sleep.

Laughing, she pushed open the cafe door and said, "I wish I could sleep like that." Mary stood on tiptoe to peer at the sleeping dogs. "Me too." Frowning, she added, "Do you have an order today?"

"No, I'm here for lunch. I'm meeting Olivia but I'm a bit early and just wanted to check the order for tomorrow morning."

Mary picked up her order book. "18 croissants, a dozen danishes and two dozen scones. Does that sound right?"

"It does. Can you add a dozen each of your mini quiches and mini cheese scones? Dr and Mrs. Duthie are coming for drinks on the boat tomorrow."

"Oh gosh, I haven't seen them in ages. Nancy used to come by for scones regularly. They are a lovely couple." Mary nodded towards the door. "Here comes Olivia. Two chicken specials?"

"Yes, please. It's my treat today. Add lunch to my account."

"Hello, Olivia, how are you?" Katie grinned. Olivia might have come down in the world but she still had that air of class about her. The fur collar on her designer coat, she swore, was a good quality faux fur for the benefit of the 'save-the-animals' people. It looked like genuine mink to Katie. Olivia delicately removed her exquisite kid gloves one finger at a time. Removing her coat to reveal a dress more suitable for a society luncheon than a café chicken special, she sat down. The ensemble was normal for Olivia and her clothes were the only thing left from her life as an earl's wife. Katie noticed both her crocodile shoes and handbag continued to be missing. She wondered if she had sold them, knowing Basil had left her penniless.

"I am much better than yesterday. How are you? You look a bit dishevelled."

Katie wanted to laugh. Although Olivia's remark was rude, she knew she meant well and her transition to a more ordinary life was slow and difficult.

"I just returned from a long walk with the dogs. I needed to think. I've decided to make some changes to the lounge.

Brighten it up with new cushions."

"Can I help? I'm quite good with colours." Olivia's voice was unusually enthusiastic.

"I'd like that. Maybe sometime over the weekend we can talk about it?"

Mary placed two large plates on the table. "You are looking much better today, Olivia."

"Thank you," Olivia said. "I'm rather embarrassed about the other day."

Mary put her hand on Olivia's shoulder. "Goodness, don't be embarrassed. We are all friends in this village. Enjoy your lunch." Mary grinned and Katie detected a hint of sarcasm underneath the affection. Down-to-earth Mary was not as forgiving as Katie.

Curious, but not wanting to pry, Katie eyed her companion, waiting on her for the details of her meeting with John.

"I'm always amazed at how kind people are here. I don't recall ever being treated this way by anyone," Olivia said.

"Not even by Cyril?"

"Oh of course, but Cyril and I reconnected at Lavender Cottage so it comes back to you. I think it's more than a coincidence that John, your ex-husband, is my solicitor and willing to fight for me. If I hadn't met you, none of this would have happened. Thank you."

"You are welcome. I'm a mother and I can't imagine what I'd do if someone tried to take my children away. They are adults and I still miss them. Tell me, what did John and Mr. Bryant have to say?"

"There is little to add from my text message. John is a fighter. He plans to win. Mr. Bryant is not so certain. Katie, I wish you had been there to see the delight in their faces when they read Jonathan's letter. John was very kind and told me those words were Basil's, not my son's."

"I'm inclined to agree with John. I suspect Basil dictated and forced Jonathan to write it. I know it's hard but you're doing well," Katie said.

"I'm not sure I agree, given the way Jonathan has treated me lately, but it was reassuring." Olivia stared out into the marina. "It's so peaceful here. You know you gave me the courage to tell them about his abusive behaviour, including a couple of trips to the hospital, that my previous legal counsel ignored. Mr. Bryant said that he thinks my previous solicitor was coerced. They should have investigated the false accusations of infidelity but then Basil threatened he'd deny all access to the children. I agreed but he neglected to explain all the visitation conditions. I told them how worried I was about Poppy. John says he will request a visit to Poppy's school. If he agrees to accompany me, Basil can't insist on a chaperone being present. I am so happy about that. The legal team has some investigating to do and told me to be patient. John texted me this morning to say he has requested a visit to the school next Saturday and asked the headmistress if we can take both children out for lunch, assuring the school I will be chaperoned by a solicitor."

"You must be excited about that. John was a good and loving father when the kids were young. I suspect he is appalled at the way Basil treats his children. He is not only fighting for you but for your children."

"I sensed that at the meeting. What happened to you two? I'm sorry. I didn't mean to intrude."

"It's okay. It happened after the children had grown up. John had a mid-life crisis and lost his way for a while.

Unfortunately, I had trouble with forgiveness back then and we agreed to part. In the end it was quite mutual and we've both moved on. I guess I'm very lucky to have experienced two loving men, even if one didn't end well. Perhaps Cyril will be a loving experience for you." Katie stopped talking, wondering if she'd said too much.

"I'm hoping so. He really has been good to me and often when I do not deserve either his kindness or understanding. Sometimes I feel like a teenager again when I'm with Cyril. I don't think I ever stopped loving him."

Olivia's phone gave a loud horn sound. "Sorry. I have to have it loud or I don't hear it." Grabbing it from her bag, she beamed and looked at Katie. "A text from John. The meeting is confirmed for eleven next Saturday. We can take both Jonathan and Poppy for lunch."

"That is good news. I suggest you relax and enjoy this weekend with Cyril. Speaking of Cyril, it's almost two. I need to get ready for the guests and you need to meet him. Is your car here?"

"No. I left it at Lavender Cottage. Adam saw me park and took my bags to the suite. I'll walk with you and then up to Cyril's." Katie glanced down at Olivia's feet, expecting to see high heels and was surprised to see stylish flat heels. "I can't go as far as sneakers and jeans but, I agree, flats are more practical." Olivia giggled. "I must admit it is nice to walk in comfort."

Katie laughed, patting her jeans. "And jeans are comfortable too. We'll have you in designer jeans before you know it."

As they approached Lavender Cottage, Katie noticed two cars already parked on Marina Lane. "It looks as though we have some early arrivals. I'll see you later." Katie hurried through the gate and waved as Olivia walked towards Main Street.

Lydia was at the reception desk and looked up when Katie walked in. "Everything is finished," Lydia said with pride, adding, "Ms. Moreland's bags are in the Lavender Suite and Adam is showing guests to the Marina Suite." She glanced at the computer screen. "And the other guests aren't due until dinner time. Is it okay if I leave a bit early?"

"Thank you, Lydia. Go ahead. Does your mum need you?"

Lydia blushed. "No, not tonight. I have a date with Mike. He's taking me dancing."

"Off you go. Dancing sounds like fun. I'll see you in the morning."

Katie busied herself in the kitchen, preparing dinner and waiting for guests, her eye on the clock more for Piers, than guests. It was past 4:30 and he'd promised to be home an hour or more ago. She checked her mobile, nothing. Was he on his way? Why hadn't he called? No sooner were the questions out of her head than her phone pinged with a text from Piers.

On my way. Just leaving the office. A crazy day. Love you.

I love you more, she replied with a sigh.

Katie worried, knowing he'd be driving in the thick of Friday afternoon traffic, meaning a slow return to Springsville.

Revealing Moments

The last of the guests were settled in their rooms and Katie could hear happy chatter in the lounge as antique dealers, old friends and strangers, discussed the upcoming auction. Cyril was well-known for his skill and expertise, especially with rare antiques, and she suspected the excitement was about the evening's preview. The front door banged and she hoped it was Piers but as the chatter subsided she realized the guests were leaving for dinner at the pub. Lavender Cottage only served breakfast and snacks.

Adam held up a bottle of red wine. "How about a drink to cheer you up? Piers is stuck in traffic. There's nothing to worry about."

She reached for the wine. "Cheers! I know, but Piers really hates the commute in bad traffic and speak of the devil, here he is."

Piers appeared at the French doors with a scowl. Katie opened it and greeted him with a kiss, which removed the scowl. "Dare I ask, how was the drive?"

"Pretty bloody awful. There was an accident on the M25 that backed up traffic to kingdom come and I get home to find cars everywhere, including my reserved spot." Piers finally raised his head. "I'm sorry. My fault for not leaving earlier but the parking thing is annoying."

Adam spoke up. "I'll fix that for you after dinner. I think Katie is ready to serve."

"Right, yes. I'm hungry and thirsty. That wine looks good." Piers put his arms around Katie and whispered, "I'm sorry. Am I forgiven?"

"Only if you pour me another glass of wine and sit down to eat." She kissed his cheek and noticed how drawn and tired he looked. "Was it a bad day?"

"Usual really, but the surgery was full. Mostly coughs and colds and some more serious bronchitis. I was already running late and then I had to wait to get a hospital bed for a sweet old lady. She's been my patient for decades and she's very ill. I suspect flu. All indications point to a new strain of flu this season, which means the vaccinations won't be as effective. Anyway, enough about work. I am glad to be home. Katie, do you mind if I take the boat out tomorrow?"

"Did you forget the Duthies are coming tomorrow?"

"Ah yes, I forgot." Piers gave Katie a sheepish grin. "What time did you say?"

"Three at the dock. Why don't you go for a spin in the morning? Take Arthur and Buddy Boy. I'll be busy with guest breakfasts. By the time you get back, we can have lunch and you can help me get ready for Nancy and George."

"You are amazing. That sounds wonderful and after a good night's sleep I promise to be in better humour. By the way, how was your lunch with Olivia?"

"It was good. John and Mr Bryant seem positive. I do hope John isn't in over his head."

"You still have doubts?" Piers quizzed her.

"Not really and Olivia seems to trust him and that's what matters. Here, have some more wine and let's sit by the fire. Adam, will you join us?" Katie said.

"No, but thanks for asking. I'll leave you two to catch up. I'll sort the cars out and watch the game on TV."

Katie cuddled up to Piers in front of the Morning Room fire, Arthur and Buddy Boy at their feet, fast asleep. They sipped the rest of the wine, saying little while enjoying the silence and being together. Katie felt Piers relax and slowly succumb to tiredness. She leaned her head on his shoulder and closed her eyes.

Voices in the lounge disturbed her. Not sure whether it was night or day but stiff from having fallen asleep in Piers' arms, she glanced at the grandfather clock as it chimed half past ten.

"Wake up, sleepyhead. It's time for bed."

Piers stretched. "Goodness. How long were we asleep?"

"Long enough." She stood up and pulled his arm to lead him into the bedroom.

Katie quickly slammed the alarm so as not to wake Piers. He groaned and turned over. It was 6 a.m. she had work to do but Piers needed his rest.

She crept into the kitchen and gently closed the bedroom door. Arthur and Buddy Boy jumped up, tails wagging, eager to get outside. Katie opened the back door, letting a blast of cold air shoot into the kitchen. She hoped it would warm up before they set out on *Tranquil Days* this afternoon.

Adam's slippers shuffled into the room. He whispered, "Good morning. Is Piers still sleeping?"

She nodded affirmative and whispered, "I'm going to get dressed while you make the morning drinks. Can you let the dogs in?"

Katie cursed the noisy shower, hoping it hadn't woken Piers. Dressing quietly, she heard a strange whistle and turn around to see Piers sitting up, leaning against the head board with a grin from ear to ear. "Good morning! You are adorable when you creep about."

"How long have you been awake?"

"Only since you turned the shower off. Come here, I need morning kisses." Katie giggled and leaned on the bed. Piers pulled her closer and wrapped his arms around her. "I want to ravish you."

Katie laughed. "Well, ravishing will have to wait. I have a dozen breakfasts to cook." Laughing even louder at his pouting face, she added, "And, pouting won't work. As you are awake, would you go to Mary's and pick up my order?"

"Sure, I can do that but I need to be bribed with kisses." Katie gave him a peck on the cheek and left the room.

She was putting the final touches on the dining room table when Piers returned from Mary's. His mouth full of croissant, he mumbled, "Mary says the hors d'oeuvres will be ready later. I told her that was fine."

"Are you eating the guests' breakfast?" Katie scolded.

"Nope. Mary gave me an extra one in sympathy for being pushed out into the cold in my pyjamas." Piers unbuttoned his trench coat. "See!"

"Piers, you are incorrigible." She couldn't help herself and giggled at the red tartan PJs. "It's almost seven. Can you put those out on a platter and I'll start the bacon? If you want coffee, Adam just made a fresh pot."

Piers did as he was told and took his coffee into the bedroom, understanding it was better to stay out of the way. Adam and Katie prepared breakfast like an old well-oiled machine.

Showered and dressed, Piers gave Katie a peck on the cheek. "I'm heading to *Tranquil Days*. I'll take these two with me."

"I doubt you'd get out without them," Katie said as Arthur jumped at the door and Buddy Boy sat waiting patiently. Jumping was not laid-back Buddy's style. "How do they know where you're going?"

"Call it doggie sense. Arthur knows the words *Tranquil Days*. I'll see you at lunchtime. I think you have a busy morning ahead of you. There seems to be a lot of them today and very noisy," Piers said with a grin as the chatter from the dining room got louder. "Come, boys!"

Katie blew him a kiss and waved him off. She felt guilty pushing him out, although Piers was more than happy to take the boat out with just the dogs for company. He was correct about the guests being noisy and more animated than usual. Adam pushed by and placed plates of overflowing English breakfast on the table while Katie followed him with more until everyone was served, except Olivia who nibbled on a croissant. The noise subsided somewhat as the eating began. Katie approached Olivia. She always looked out of place with the mostly male dealers, large, burly men who seemed exceptionally loud today.

"Would you mind if I had my coffee in the Morning room Katie?" Olive asked.

"No not at all."

Olivia picked up her coffee and followed Katie.

"What is happening today? Everyone is excited about something," Katie asked.

"Cyril found an old bureau, which he suspects dates back to early 1800s but he doesn't know a lot about its history. However, at the preview last night, a prestigious dealer from London let it slip that it was more likely to be 1700s and hinted it possibly belonged to someone famous. When questioned further, he clamped up. When I left last night, Cyril was frantically researching and trying to reach the current owner who is obviously unaware of any famous connections."

"Wow! That sounds exciting. No wonder there is such a buzz this morning."

"The problem is it's difficult to prove the origin. Cyril is afraid the reserve is too low, given this new information. Aware he already said too much, the London dealer is staying quiet, hoping to get a bargain."

"What's Cyril going to do?" Katie asked.

"He will suggest the owner withdraw the bureau until they have more information and that will annoy the London dealer. Upsetting prestigious London dealers is not good for Cyril's business but neither is underselling a valuable and potentially famous artifact. Cyril built his business on honesty and fairness."

Katie raised an eyebrow, not in full agreement with Olivia's statement, having had several conflicts with Cyril when she first moved to Springsville. He was a pushy sales person. But after getting to know him, his pushiness had more to do with passion for the job and even Katie had to admit that he was honest and did know antiques.

"Is this dealer someone staying here?"

"Good question. I don't know and Cyril didn't mention him by name. I'll let you know if I hear more. I suspect we'll have a lively auction today. I'd better be on my way to help Cyril." Olivia smiled. "I never thought I would enjoy working but I really do. It also takes my mind off the legal case and the antique business fascinates me."

"It wouldn't have anything to do with a handsome man named Cyril?" Katie said, teasing.

"Ha, ha, maybe! I'll see you later," Olivia said, placing her handbag on her shoulder. She stood in high heels today and walked to the door with the elegance Katie admired.

The raucous guests seem to hang around drinking coffee for ages and only left when Katie reminded them the auction would be starting in less than an hour. She was anxious for them to leave so Lydia could start the clean-up and Katie could prepare for her afternoon guests.

Buddy Boy and Arthur took up their positions at the bow of *Tranquil Days,* while Katie pulled out the cushions and Piers put the wine and snacks in the little fridge. Surprised to feel warm sunshine on her back, she looked up at the slight hint of blue as the sun peaked through the clouds. It was warm for November.

"Hello!" George Duthie called as he and Nancy walked towards the boat.

"Welcome aboard!" Piers called in reply. "It has been a long time, George, and it's good to see you Nancy, as beautiful as ever. Nancy, this is my wife, Katie." He glanced at George. "I think you already met."

"We have indeed. A broken window and a nasty cut

brought us together and has reunited us, Piers. I am delighted and so is Nancy." George hesitated and Katie realized that Nancy appeared to be uncomfortable. She hoped it wasn't disapproval.

Taking a deep breath, Katie gave Piers a side glance not sure what to say. "Nancy, I am pleased to meet you. Piers tells me he and Julianne met you boating some years ago. I never met Julianne but from what I hear from Piers and other friends, she was a wonderful woman and missed by many." Katie held her breath, waiting for someone to say something and knowing that the next second or two would determine what kind of an afternoon they might have.

Nancy was shorter and a touch rounder than Katie with a pretty face framed with grey curls. She looked younger than George. Katie couldn't read her expression and then she suddenly beamed an infectious smile. "Katie, I am very happy to meet you. Piers is a wonderful man and I am so pleased he has found someone like you. It was very hard for him when Julianne passed away."

Katie had to stifle a long sigh of relief as she replied, "I know. He was grieving when we first met and we skated around each other for a long time. I came to Springsville to start a new life after an unexpected and nasty divorce. Learning to trust again was hard for both of us. Piers still has his moments and he will always love Julianne and I'm okay with that."

"I'm going to like you, Katie. I was anxious about meeting you. I guess I was thinking Piers had replaced Julianne but you are so different. Thank you putting me at ease." Nancy held the side of the boat as the it tipped when George untied the moorings. Piers gently eased the throttle as they reversed out of the dock. "Oh, I think we're on the move. This is lovely.

We had a narrowboat before we had a house. We actually lived on a boat when we were first married."

"Oh, how interesting. Have you and George been married long?" Katie asked.

"Almost forty-eight years. I was nineteen and George was twenty-two. George was still in medical school," she chuckled. "Far too young by today's standards, but we've been very happy. We have two grown up sons, the eldest a surgeon and the youngest is still trying to find himself." Nancy hesitated and Katie guessed she wasn't sure how to ask Katie about her marriage.

"I was married for thirty-five years. It was a bit of a shock when it ended but, we're friends or at least civil now. Two grown children. Our son lives in New York and manages a jazz band." Katie laughed with a knowing nod. "Ben was our free spirit and it took him a long time to find himself but he's doing well. Melanie knew what she wanted from the age of five I think. She's a scientist, a professor at Nottingham University and recently married." Katie paused. "I am grateful they get along with Piers."

"George tells me you run a B&B. That must be hard work."

"Not at all. I love it much better than a corporate job. I tried that for a while and it's definitely not for me. Running the B&B is fun and I have lots of help. We're busy this weekend because The Antique Shop has an auction today. You're a nurse?"

"Yes, I was in ICU at the Nottingham General for more years than I can count and that was exhausting. I recently took over a small nursing home. I want to retire and travel. We enjoy travelling the world on cruise ships. George keeps saying in a couple of years. He loves his work but it's getting too much for him, working alone most of the time. I'm bracing myself for the flu season. As you know, George is old-fashioned and still does house calls. He's not so young. He'll be seventy next birthday. I did manage to persuade him to hire a locum so we can take holidays but that's not enough and I worry about the long hours."

"Is that what we can expect as doctor's wives?" Katie said with a frown. "I worry about Piers, and the flu season is going to be a challenge for us too. Piers always lived close to the clinic in Nottingham. The commute to and from Springville is already a sore spot. Thank goodness for this narrowboat. He finds the boat relaxing so we use it all year, but I don't think that is enough." Katie stared into space, making light of the situation for Nancy but it actually made it worse for Katie. The situation was bleak as she acknowledged their new routine was unlikely to work long-term.

Piers and George had been in a deep conversation. George at the helm, looked as comfortable as Piers. Katie tried to listen but only caught bits about medicine and past canal trips. Swarkeston came into view and George handed the tiller back to Piers. The canal was a little wider here but still narrow and it took some skill to turn *Tranquil Days* around and begin the journey back. A comfortable silence prevailed as they returned. Nancy seemed to enjoy the peace and quiet, as did Katie after a busy day.

Once docked at the marina, they enjoyed the hors d'oeuvres and a glass of wine. Katie was amazed at how quickly they had become friends. She was really enjoying the company and so were George and Nancy, making no attempt to depart. The cool November air made Katie shiver and she wished she had invited them for dinner. It was too cold to stay outside. She gave Piers a side glance and hoped he would approve. "It's getting too cold to stay outside. Why don't you join us for some pub fare at The Boater's Inn? It's not fancy but the food is good and it's warm inside."

"I'd like that. What do you think, George?" Nancy asked.

"Well, I did say I'd check on Mrs ..." Nancy gave George a stern look. "I know, I said I'd take the day off and things have been quiet. Okay, I'll check with the answering service and if there are no urgent calls, we can stay for dinner."

Nancy and George went on to the dock and George made his phone call while Piers and Katie cleaned up. Piers hugged her and whispered, "That was a brilliant idea. I'm really enjoying catching up with George again and you look as though you're getting along with Nancy."

"I am. I was a bit worried but she's lovely. Oh look, George is giving us a thumbs up. You take them up to the pub and I'll take the dogs home and feed them. You can order me the fish and chips and a glass of white wine."

Flirting with Flu

Katie and the dogs entered Lavender Cottage by the back door. She rarely used the front entrance when there were guests. She fed the dogs and hearing chatter in the lounge, popped her head around the door and couldn't help but smile at the scene. Just how she had envisioned Lavender Cottage B&B. Several guests had settled in front of the fire, playing scrabble while others were talking or reading. The fire had burnt low and the log-box was empty of firewood. *That's unusual,* Katie thought *Adam always keeps it topped up. I wonder where he's gone.* The Morning Room log-box was full so she carried those logs into the lounge, filling up the box. First, she frowned, a little annoyed and then smiled. *He's probably engrossed in one of his football games.*

"Is there anything you need?" Katie asked.

A quiet chorus of "No thank you," replied, accompanied by contented head shakes.

"Enjoy your evening. I'll be back in a couple of hours."

Walking to the pub, Katie had a feeling of accomplishment. "Life is pretty good," she said, opening the pub door.

Maisie was just placing two steaming plates of fish and chips on the table when Katie arrived at the pub. But Piers was sitting alone.

"Where are Nancy and George?"

"I guess it's Murphy's Law. We were just about to order when George got a call from his answering service. An emergency at the nursing home where Nancy works, so they both took off. It's just you and me."

"Oh, what a shame. But it was a lovely day. Did you enjoy it?"

"It was fun and nice to have friends here in or near Springsville other than the locals." Piers chuckled. "Not that there's anything wrong with the locals. Nancy invited us for dinner. She'll give you a call."

Katie nodded, taking a sip of wine. A thought slipped into her head, although if she was honest, the thought had slipped in some time ago when she was talking to Nancy. She stared at Piers over her glass.

Piers put his head to one side. "What? You have a strange look."

"I was thinking about George and wondered if you had ever thought about practicing closer to home. I bet he'd welcome a partner."

"No, not George. He likes working solo and a country practice is not for me, Katie. Do you have any idea how hard that man works? He's never home. You think my hours are long. Even with the commute, my life is not as difficult as George's. At least I get time off. Being on call 24/7 is not for me."

"You've got a point. I just worry about the travelling. I'm afraid it will get worse as winter sets in and you get busier. Nancy was complaining about the hours so the life of a country doctor is not as idyllic as it seems. She finally persuaded George to hire a locum so they could go on holiday." Katie picked up a chip and dipped it into ketchup, nibbling it thoughtfully and judging whether to pursue the conversation or let it drop.

"I can see those wheels turning so before you say any more, I want to reiterate that I am *not,* and never will be, a country doctor. I love country living, but this is my oasis where I get away from work. I like my city practice, an efficient clinic working with Rick, my friend and partner." Piers leaned across the table and took Katie's hand. "I'll get used to the commute. We have been discussing hiring another doctor and that will free up more time to be with you. I promise things will work out."

"That does sound promising. Why didn't you tell me?" Katie felt a twinge of hurt that he hadn't include her in the discussion. She wondered if Cindy knew.

"It's not just a financial issue. We don't want another partner. Rick and I work so well together it would be hard to bring someone else in. And employing a doctor is expensive so we need to know it's financially sound."

"So, this new doctor would work the hours you and Rick scheduled for him or her. A young doctor to fill in when it's busy and a lot of after hours. I'm not sure young doctors are prepared to do that these days."

"I did it and so did Rick. It was excellent training, a bit like slave labour, but it sure taught me stuff about being a family physician that I did not learn in med school. As soon as the accountant gets back to us with positive numbers, we're going to advertise."

"I hope it works. That would take the pressure off both of you. I know Cindy is finding it difficult with two young children." Katie wanted to be supportive but, in her opinion, the current generation of young people weren't as willing to be *slaves* as Piers was twenty-five years ago. Although, Rick was much younger and he did it, so maybe it would work. Katie yawned. "Too much fresh air and possibly too much wine. I'm ready to call it a night."

"Me too. It's catching," Piers said with a yawn. "I'll pay the bill and meet you outside."

Piers put his arm around Katie's shivering shoulders. It had turned very cold in the short time they'd been in The Boater's Inn and they hurried to the warmth of home that was hauntingly quiet. The guests had all retired and there was no sign of Adam.

"Piers, do you mind knocking on Adam's door and seeing if he's okay. It's odd he's not here, closing up. I noticed he hadn't stoked the fire when I was here earlier."

Katie heard voices in Adam's room and then the door closed. There was a menacing quiet and she had the sense that something was wrong when Piers came running down the stairs.

"What is it?"

"Adam is not well. I need my bag. Can you bring a glass of water and some aspirin?"

Piers leapt up the stairs, followed by Katie. Adam was lying on his back, his face glossy with sweat and his breath wheezy between coughs. Katie took a facecloth from the bathroom and waited for Piers to finish listening to his chest and remove the thermometer before placing it on his forehead.

"Adam, can you hear me?" Piers said, staring at the thermometer. "You have a high fever and a chest infection. When did you start feeling unwell?"

Adam's reply was a whisper. "I had a sore throat yesterday but I felt okay until this afternoon. I thought I'd feel better after a nap but when I woke up, I couldn't get out of bed." He gasped for breath, coughing convulsively.

"Shush! Don't try to talk. Katie, can you fetch some pillows? We need to prop him up so he can breathe." Piers linked Adam's arm and lifted him into an upright position. "Try and relax. I want you to sit up and take these Aspirin. Can you swallow?" Adam gulped the water as he stifled coughs.

Katie returned with two big pillows and placed then behind Adam. Piers let go of his arm so he could lean back slightly. "I want you to stay in this position. How does that feel?"

"Better," he said closing his eyes. "I need to sleep."

Katie rinsed out the facecloth and mopped his face. Feeling the heat radiate from his body, she glanced at Piers. Adam fell asleep, every breath a raspy rattle.

"He has a fever. The Aspirin should bring it down and I'll give him an injection of antibiotics. We need to keep him cool." Seeing Katie's worried face, he added, "My diagnosis is flu that has settled in his chest with a bacterial infection. It could be viral bronchitis. Either one, he is very ill and I'd rather be safe with the antibiotics. I suspect he hasn't felt well for a few days. Did Adam get his flu shot?"

"I'm not sure. He didn't say. He still goes to the doctor near his son's place."

"And, you? I'm sorry, of course you had your shot. I gave it to you and you were not happy about me sticking needles in you." Piers laughed and kissed her forehead. "It's going to be a long night. Why don't you go to bed and I'll sit with Adam?"

Katie didn't argue. She was very tired. "Okay. Come and wake me in a couple hours and I'll sit with him while you sleep." Katie brushed his thick hair from his forehead, seeing the lines of an old man, not a fit fifty-year-old. Piers was tired too.

Katie hit the alarm button and glanced at the clock, 6 a.m. She stretched and felt for Piers. Her heart skipped a beat, remembering how ill Adam was last night. Piers hadn't woken her. Did that mean Adam was worse or he just didn't want to wake her? She jumped out of bed and ran up the stairs, slowly opening Adam's door, partly not to disturb them and partly afraid of what she might find. She sighed, pleased to see Adam sleeping, still raspy but breathing easier. Piers had moved to the sitting area and was flat out on the sofa, snoring. She smiled and carefully closed the door and headed to the kitchen to do the morning teas and coffees.

Picking up Adam's list, she shook her head. As sick as he was, he had still managed to make the morning list. *I think you were right, Piers. He's not been well for several days but has not told anyone. How did I miss that?*

She began to fill the trays when a noise on the verandah made her frown. It sounded windy but the noise was rhythmic. She opened the door to see the chair rocking. She scrunched her shoulders, wrapping her arms around her middle. It was cold and a white frost covered the lawn. She perched on the edge of the chair, its wooden slats cold under her thin pyjamas. She wished she'd dressed.

"Doris!"

A shaky voice, even for ghost Doris, said, "Adam came to visit last night." Katie's heart missed a beat. *Was Adam that close to death?* Her eyes filled with tears. "No tears, my dear Katie. I sent him back and he's going to be alright for a good many more years. But, you must watch him carefully. He's not good at telling anyone how he feels."

"I had no idea he wasn't well and Piers said he's been ill for a while." Katie's arms hugged tighter, her jaw trembling as she tried to stop her teeth chattering from the cold.

"Now you get inside before you catch cold. You'll need your strength for things to come."

"Things to come? Doris, what do you mean?"

"You know I can't say. Oh, and by the way, send that other fellow home to his wife. He's not long for this earth." Doris' chair stilled and Katie felt the wisp of wind as she parted. *What other one? Things to come?*

"What are you doing out here?!" Piers shouted. "Do you want pneumonia?"

"I'm sorry. Did we wake you?" Katie glanced up towards Adam's bedroom. "I'm coming in. Doris wanted to talk about Adam." Katie carefully eyed Piers. He had been witness to ghostly Doris but Katie suspected he didn't really believe in ghosts, especially one that lived, permanently, on their verandah. Skeptical or not, it was hard to deny. He had witnessed his own wife's ghostly presence but had stubbornly maintained it was a dream.

Piers scoffed, pulling her inside and enveloping her in a bear hug, kicking the door closed. "You infuriate me at times. Go and put something warm on."

"I already have something warm on. You! Can I wear you

all day?" Katie's eyes twinkled and Piers kissed her forehead.

"I like that idea but we have things to do, like guests wanting morning tea. Go! Put some warm clothes on and I'll start the trays."

Piers studied the list and finished the trays with the appropriate order of tea or coffee, adding two shortbread biscuits and a mint for each guest.

It wasn't often Piers helped with the B&B and Katie smiled. It was nice. They each picked up two trays and knocked on the doors. The trays delivered, all except one. Mr. Green didn't answer the door. Katie told Piers not to worry. Guests often changed their mind and preferred to sleep on.

"Will I make a good waiter?" Piers asked when they returned to the kitchen.

"An excellent waiter but I wouldn't give up your day job, Doctor. How is Adam this morning?"

"He's still sleeping. I gave him a sedative and he settled down. He woke a couple of times during the night coughing, mostly because he'd slipped off the pillows. I think we should call his son and let him know."

"Perhaps, but I would clear that with Adam first. Kevin and wife, Sonia, can overreact. Can you help me with breakfast this morning?" Katie giggled. "Seeing as how you did such a good job with morning teas."

"Of course. I'll check on Adam and get dressed, after I've had my caffeine fix."

Katie poured two coffees and Piers lit a fire. They sat in silence until Arthur gave a sharp bark, making them both jump and laugh. They had forgotten to let the dogs out. Piers opened the back door to wet, sleety cold. The dogs ran out and returned quickly.

"Too cold, even for the dogs. It is feeling decidedly wintery," Piers said with a shiver.

Katie nodded. "It's only four weeks to Christmas. Have you and Rick sorted a schedule for the holidays?"

"Sort of. I think it only fair to let Rick have Christmas Eve and Christmas morning, so he can be with his kids. He'll take over Christmas night and Boxing Day. I'm going to try managing the calls from home. I obviously can't do house calls but I can refer patients to the hospital if necessary. Pat said she'd help screen the calls."

"Okay, that works for me. I'm happy to have you home, even if I have to share you with the telephone. I told Melanie I would do Christmas dinner this year. I can't believe we're talking about ..." An enormous bang came from upstairs. Piers flew up the stairs to Adam's room, surprised to find him awake and frowning, having heard the noise. Seeing Piers shrug his shoulders, Katie stopped, listened and opened the door to Mr Green's room.

"Piers! Come quickly!"

Mr. Green was lying on the floor, bleeding from a cut on his head, flushed in the face and shaking.

"Katie, grab my bag from Adam's room, please. Mr. Green, my name is Dr Bannister. I'm Katie's husband and a family physician. Can you tell me what happened?"

Katie handed Piers his bag and watched as he gently lifted the man's head onto a pillow. He examined the cut and placed a piece of gauze over it, all the time soothing and reassuring the patient. "Katie, can you wrap that blanket around him?" Piers pointed to the spare blanket at the end of the bed. "We need to get him warm. And if you wouldn't mind getting some warm water and antiseptic for the cut." Katie noticed Piers fingers were already taking the man's pulse, followed by the stethoscope on his chest. She heard Piers say, "Now, let's get you back in bed.

"My heart …"

"Are you in pain?"

Mr. Green shook his head. "No, headache and dizzy."

"Your heart is fine but the symptoms indicate influenza. I'll need to put a couple of stitches in that cut. Can you tell me what happened?"

Piers looked up at Katie as she put the Dettol and a bowl of warm water on the bedside table. "Thanks. I'll be fine now. I think Mr. Green would like some privacy." He nodded towards worried faces at the open door.

"I'll deal with it. Good morning, everyone! Everything is under control. For those of you who don't know, my husband is a doctor. Mr Green had a fall but he's in good hands. Breakfast might be a few minutes late. I'll ring the bell when it's ready," Katie said, motioning for everyone to return to their rooms.

Whether it was the thought of flu germs descending on Lavender Cottage or just urgent business, the guests didn't dawdle after breakfast and, with the exception of Mr. Green, they all left.

Piers called Mr Green's wife, asking if someone could come and pick him up as he was not well enough to drive.

Mrs Green arrived an hour later with her son. Piers helped Mr Green down the stairs and to the car. Piers explained what had happened. He was most insistent that they contact their own doctor as soon as they got home and tell him to call if he required details.

"What was all that about? You look worried, Piers."

"I am. Both Adam and Mr Green have an aggressive form of influenza. Adam is going to be all right but I have a bad feeling about Mr Green. I was in two minds whether or not to call an ambulance. But he insisted he was all right to go home. He just wanted to be with his wife. I'm glad the son came too."

Katie felt a shiver go down her spine. Doris' words 'send him home to his wife, he's not long for this earth' came into her head. Mr. Green was 'the other one.'

"You did the right thing. People need to be with family when they are at the ..." She paused. "When they are not well."

Piers gave her a quizzical look. "That's an odd thing to say. Is everything alright."

"I'm fine." Katie wasn't sure she was fine. Doris' words had disturbed her, not just about 'the other one' who she was certain was Mr. Green but *things to come.* She couldn't explain it. It felt like her world had shifted. Something had changed but she had no idea what, neither did she sense if it was good, bad or perhaps a bit of both.

Flu at Lavender Cottage

❧

P iers, hugged Katie goodbye in the frosty morning dawn. It had not been an unusual and challenging weekend but strangely enjoyable as she worked beside Piers. Piers blew Katie a kiss from the car window.

"I'll see you Tuesday. Keep your eye on Adam. If you're worried, call George. I'll call tonight. I love you!" She returned the air kiss and waved as his BMW turned onto Main Street. She did not feel confident that he'd make it home on Tuesday. But, in spite of all the drama or maybe because of it, she was glad they'd had the weekend. She liked that he helped her with the B&B.

Her feet up on the footstool, Katie leaned back in her favourite chair with Buddy Boy and Arthur on her knee and sipped a quiet coffee, relishing the peacefulness. She wondered how Mr Green was doing. Adam, although still very ill was going to survive. *I'm not sure how I'm going to keep him in bed. Two more days Piers said, and if his temperature goes*

151

up, more days than that. This will be my challenge for the week.
Adam's room was above the Morning Room and, no sooner
had this last thought crossed her mind, when she heard him
moving about.

"Come on boys, we have a job to do." The dogs looked at
her as she mounted the stairs, normally out of bounds unless
Judy and her dogs were in the Daisy Den. They scampered
up, sniffing at all the strange smells. Katie knocked on Adam's
door and entered without waiting for an answer.

"What are you doing out of bed? You heard Piers. At least
two more days." Katie stared at his pale face and his heaving
chest and hoped Doris was right about him getting better. It
crossed her mind that she might have got things muddled with
the other one.

"I thought I could get up but I'm very weak. This damned
cough!"

Plumping up his pillows, Katie pulled back the covers and,
with a scowl, she pointed to the bed. "Get in! Now, would you
like some coffee? What about a boiled egg with toast?"

"Coffee sounds good. Not sure about the egg, but I might
manage toast with marmalade."

"I'll make toast for us both and bring my coffee up too. I'll
leave the dogs for company."

Adam patted the bed and both dogs did little jumping actions
with paws on the bed. He laughed as Arthur made a flying
leap and landed on Adam's legs. Poor Buddy Boy, short and
tubby, waited for Katie to pick him up.

"You two make sure he doesn't get out of bed. Oh, there's
my phone." Katie frowned at the screen. "Piers already."

"Piers," Katie said and then listened.

"Is everything okay?" Adam said.

"I think so. Kind of a mixed message. He wanted to let me know the commute was fast and uneventful this morning. I am very pleased to hear that after Friday's fiasco. But just as we had an eventful weekend with two cases of flu, so did Rick. The clinic was inundated with calls and emergency home visits. Piers says influenza is in full swing, early and aggressive. That is not good news. I'll get us the coffee and toast."

Adam could barely eat between coughing spells and one slice of toast had exhausted him. Katie fussed over him until he fell into a fitful sleep. She thought of Doris' words, questioning her wisdom and wondering how Mr Green was doing. She brushed her worrying to one side as there was work to be done.

Lydia arrived to clean the guest rooms, always a bigger job on Mondays. Dan Ingram with his son Derrick arrived at the same time to finish the windows off.

"Good morning, Dan! How's the hand, Derrick?" Katie greeted them and nodded to Lydia who ran by shyly, even blushing. She glanced from Lydia to Derrick, a smile touching her lips.

"It's much better. The doc gave me the all clear as long as I wear a glove to keep it clean. He laughed as he held his hand in the air. "I feel like I'm going to operate on someone."

"Son, you need to operate on these windows." Dan motioned to Derrick to start on the kitchen window. Speaking directly to Katie, he asked, "When did you say Adam was going to paint and decorate? Before or after Christmas?"

"Guest rooms before and downstairs after. But as the guest rooms are finished ahead of schedule. I had hoped we could get the downstairs painted before rather than after Christmas but Adam is ill in bed. He won't be doing anything for a while so it looks as though we'll have to stick to the original plan."

"Sorry to hear about Adam. There's a lot of flu going around. My wife had it and she made us go get the vaccination. I'm glad I did. I can't afford to be off work."

"Dad, I could do the painting for Ms. Bannister. It might be easier than windows." Derrick stopped prying the window frame and put down the crowbar, rubbing his hand.

"Is your hand hurting?" Dan said, with concern.

Derrick nodded. "A bit. The crowbar lodges right in the cut area when I try to lift the window frame."

"Let me do that. You can just help today. I'm fine if you think you can paint instead. Katie? I'll give you a good price and Derrick is a good painter. He'll have it done this week, well before Christmas."

"This is perfect. Derrick, are you sure about your hand?" Katie asked.

"Using rollers and brushes is no problem. It's the action of that tool digging in my hand that hurts."

"Okay! Give me an estimate and you can start whenever you're ready. But you can't paint or leave a mess Friday to Sunday. I'm booked all weekend. After that, I'm not booked until Christmas week, but that could change."

Dan gave Katie an acceptable estimate. The lounge was to be done before Friday and Katie's private area the week after.

Dual phones began ringing and Katie excused herself. More bookings on the business line and messages from Olivia and Judy.

Katie made some tea, checked on Adam, and took a break from the crazy morning. She felt better now the painting was arranged. She had worried about Adam, even before his illness. Judy had done the bulk of the painting earlier. Now she was happy to hand the job to Derrick without hurting Adam's feelings.

She was about to return her phone messages when her mobile rang.

"Olivia, hi. I was about to call you. What's up?"

"I thought you'd like to know we have a court date December 20th," Olivia said.

"Gosh, that was quick. I thought it would take months."

"Katie, there's a problem. John said Basil must have pulled a lot of strings and they are worried he's hiding something. Either that or he's banking on John not having time to prepare and messing up."

"Olivia, try not to worry. I'm sure John will ask for more man power to prepare. John is the kind of person who will use all the resources he's got and some. I can assure you he loves a challenge and it will actually help your case. John doesn't like to be used as a pawn, and I reckon he's already figured out Basil is playing games. Believe me, Olivia. Basil has met his match."

"He seemed quite nervous when I spoke to him and Mr. Bryant was not encouraging." Katie heard a quiver in Olivia voice, she was close to tears. It was unusual for John to be nervous preparing a case. Sometimes he'd be on edge as a case began. *But*, she thought, *those were the days when he was a hot lawyer. He seems to have his old fight back but I wonder. Is he ready?* "Katie, are you there?" Olivia's voice screeched down the phone.

"Yes, yes I'm here. Um … in my opinion, what you are interpreting as nervousness is John figuring out what to do next. Obviously, they have to speed up any investigating. Sit tight for a few days and make an appointment to see them."

"John already did that. I see him next Monday. I had a call from his investigator, who apologized for not meeting me in person, but said they needed to escalate. He asked me all kinds of questions."

"That's his job, Olivia. I hope you were honest with him. You know how important Basil's cruelty is to your case."

"I was, but I feel guilty. It will ruin Basil's reputation."

"Good! Olivia, stop feeling sorry for him. He's a cruel bully and deserves all he gets."

"Oh, I nearly forgot. John has made an appointment at the school for Saturday, so I won't be coming this weekend. Cyril will have to manage the auction on his own."

"Did the school accept your solicitor as a chaperone?"

"It was surprisingly easy. Mr Bryant made the appointment and the headmistress didn't even question it."

"Excellent. I'm sorry to cut you off but I really have to go. Call me when you have news and try not to worry." Katie clicked her phone off, immediately dialling Judy, which went to voicemail.

"Hello Judy, this is Katie. I guess we're playing telephone tag. I'd love to see you this weekend. Piers is on call so I could do with the company and some help. I'll expect you for dinner on Friday. Cheers!"

Friday was Adam's first day out of the house. Katie had followed Piers' instructions and Adam had not objected, happy to be out. They took a short walk to the marina and back. Upon their return, Adam sat on the verandah for a brief chat with Doris. It was too cold to stay more than a few minutes and, by the time he came inside, he was tired from the exertion, content to sit by the fire, reading.

Katie glanced at his pale, drawn face. He looked his seventy years, which was rare as Adam was always busy and active. She noticed he didn't even fuss about getting the lounge ready, content to leave it to someone else. She knew the illness had knocked him sideways but she found herself wondering if he would fully recover. He must have sensed her thoughts because he looked up and gave her a reassuring smile.

"Katie, I'm fine. I need time to recover, that's all." He bent down and patted each dog in turn. "I have good company." He paused. "If somewhat crowded." Adam was surrounded by Sam, Lily, Buddy and Arthur, all hogging the Morning Room fire. Judy had arrived early, leaving the dogs in the Morning Room and rolling up her sleeves, getting to work by stoking the lounge fire, normally Adam's job.

"I know but I can't help worrying about you. You are so pale and even today's short walk exhausted you."

"Piers said it will take a few days for the antibiotics to work and a couple of weeks to get my strength back. So, for once in my life, I'm doing as I'm told. Unless of course you want me back at work, *boss*." He said the last phrase with a twinkle in his eye.

Horrified, Katie replied, "No, definitely not. Just get better." She gave a tut at his teasing. "Oh, I hear the door. Can I get you anything before I attend to the guests?"

"I am quite content, thank you."

Judy was already taking details and Katie showed the first guests to their room. Some of the dealers were not familiar to her. Cyril's find of the antique bureau had not been owned by a 18th century author as was suggested but, none the less, it was old and unique, as Cyril had thought in the first place. However, other items from the same manor house had generated a great deal of interest, good for Cyril's business and Lavender Cottage. Katie was glad of the bookings as this was the last full house until Christmas, which housed mostly friends and family with few, if any, paying guests. January and February were notoriously slow months so the extra income in November was appreciated.

It was Sunday before Judy and Katie had any downtime to relax and enjoy their favourite exercise of walking the dogs. The chill in the air was exceptionally cold and flakes of snow settled on their coats.

"I'm not liking this snow," Judy said holding out her hand. "If you don't mind, I think I'll hit the road early. It may be nothing." She looked up at the darkening sky. "I want to check on Dad before I go home."

"It does look dark. There's a storm heading our way. I was looking forward to Piers being home tomorrow. He'll stay in town if the weather's bad."

"It will be over by then and the first fluttering won't stay around." Judy gave Katie a sympathetic look. "You miss him, don't you?"

"I do, and the commute has become such an issue between us. I'm not looking forward to winter. Anyway, I think you should try and beat the storm."

Katie stood at the garden gate and waved goodbye to Judy, feeling lonely, even despondent. There was nothing she could do about the weather or the flu epidemic. Piers had not been home all week. Both he and Rick were working flat out, but he'd promised he would be home on Monday. Now it looked as though a snow storm might prevent that. Wishing she had put her coat on, Katie wrapped her arms around her middle, walking along the garden path when she heard a car on the gravel. Wondering what Judy had forgotten, she turned, not believing her eyes, as Piers opens the car door.

"Piers, what are you doing home?" She ran back to the gate, forgetting about the cold, and jumped into his arms.

"Wow, I need to surprise you more often." Piers kissed her and hugged her so hard she could hardly breathe but it felt wonderful.

Out of breath, the two walked into the house. "Was that Judy just leaving?"

"Yes, she wanted to avoid the storm."

"That's why I'm here. The forecast warned of an early winter storm, starting tonight. Rick and I are exhausted. We hired a locum so we can have a couple of days off. I don't have to be back until Wednesday morning."

"That is the best news I've heard in a long time. Come on, let's go tell Adam. He'll be happy to see you."

"How is he?"

"Much better. He has some colour in his face and he's taking short walks on his own."

Arthur came bounding out of the Morning Room and ran circles around Piers, while Buddy sat sedately, waiting to be petted. Katie felt as though the troubles of the world had lifted from her shoulders.

"Two whole days and, for a change, I have nothing to do; no guests and no planning." Taking a second look at Piers, she realized how tired he looked and surmised it would be two days of quiet and rest for them all. She was just glad to have him home for a while.

Worries and doubts

Katie shivered in the early morning cold as she handed Piers his travel mug. She hugged him hard, sensing the last two amazing days might not be repeated for some time. Grateful the snow and sleet had come and gone, although the long-range forecast proposed a cold, snowy winter, Piers' drive into Nottingham looked clear today.

Closing the front door, Katie sighed, grinning. It had been a long time since they had spent time alone without interruption; sleeping, walking, eating and drinking wine. Katie had enjoyed cooking, most often a joint effort. Adam, tired and still recovering, had kindly stayed in his room, appearing for meals and a check-up from Doc Piers. And now she had work to do.

Delaying the decorating and stalling the final window installation by two days meant an early start and much catching up if the work was to be finished before Christmas.

She began moving the furniture away from the walls in the

160

lounge, throwing dust sheets over the furniture so Derrick could start painting. She kept an eye on the stairs, hoping not to wake Adam. It was going to be a challenge keeping him away from the work as he felt better. Piers had been adamant that he rest for at least one more week.

Dan and Derrick arrived early as promised and got to work. The final window was finished by noon and Dan left for another job, leaving Derrick to paint. Katie made lunch and noticed Adam had not only refrained from offering to help but was exceptionally quiet and retreated to his room. Katie wondered if he was having a relapse, but his cough had almost gone. She shook it off, acknowledging rest was the best cure.

A text from Olivia grabbed her attention. *'I'm at Mary's will you join me?'* Katie texted back *'Yes.'*

Delighted to have a distraction, she clipped the leashes on the dogs, equally happy to have an extra walk. Olivia hadn't told her about the school visit and, having been totally immersed in her time with Piers, she had forgotten and was eager to hear the outcome.

That's a good sign, Katie thought, as she approached Olivia, looking happy and relaxed. "Hello. So, how was the visit?"

"Overall wonderful! Poppy was happy to see me without the witch of a chaperone listening to our every word. Jonathan, not so much. A few if-looks-could-kill but at least he didn't throw insults at me. John's presence made him think twice and both children took to John. You're right, he's good with kids."

"For all his faults, John was a great father. Tell me more?"

"John explained on the drive down that he wanted to speak to the children separately, especially Jonathan, which surprised me. I thought it would be Poppy. When we arrived, the children were waiting in the entrance with Matron. She's in charge of the dormitories, a kind of house-mother. I thought it a bit odd. We usually meet in the headmaster's office but he was nowhere to be seen." Olivia shrugged her shoulders. "I had the distinct impression I was being snubbed. Matron was cordial, quite friendly actually. She kept eying John suspiciously and asked if we could talk privately. John nodded his approval and took the children for a walk in the grounds. Matron hustled me into a little reception room."

"Gosh this sounds mysterious," Katie said with a chuckle.

"I guess it does and she was nervous, closing the door and making sure we couldn't be heard. I was afraid, wondering what Basil had told the school or what tricks he was up to." Olivia paused and a smile spread across her face. "The exact opposite happened. She apologized for how the school treated me and implied she didn't believe the reasons given. She asked why John was there and I explained he was my solicitor and I decided to tell her why. She actually smiled and said, 'Good' and then went on without hesitation to talk about the children."

"It sounds as though you have an ally at last," Katie said.

"Perhaps. She is worried about the children. Jonathan is so angry he's picking fights and bullying other kids. Poppy is retreating inside herself and is so afraid to go home to the estate, she pleads with matron to keep her at school." Olivia held her breath as tears threatened.

"Why didn't she report this to the headmaster?" Katie said, feeling her anger build.

"She did and was told the children were acting out because of mistreatment by their mother. Lord Thesleton was doing an admiral job looking after their well-being under difficult circumstances. Katie, I was stunned that Basil would go that far with his lies."

"Did Matron believe the headmaster?"

"No, it appears not. I asked her to speak to John. She refused. She's afraid of losing her position."

"What happened next?"

"We drove into town for lunch. On the way to the restaurant, John walked with Poppy. Jonathan and I walked in silence at first. I was afraid he would say nasty things but he didn't. He asked how I was and when I told him I was working, assisting an auctioneer, he smiled and said 'good for you, Mum.' I saw the look of the little boy he used to be." She sniffed away tears. "It was a nice moment. We had a lovely lunch. The children chatted about school and their friends but when I asked them about home, neither of them answered. Jonathan brushed it off with a conciliatory glance towards Poppy who looked uncomfortable. Jonathan stared at me with defiance, saying they hadn't been home since the summer holidays. Which was odd, because I'm sure Basil said they were home last weekend.

"Unfortunately, that changed the tone of the meeting. John did his best to change it and he did get Jonathan laughing at his jokes but Poppy was upset. Walking back to the car, Poppy slipped her hand in mine and whispered, 'Mummy I want to live with you.' She moved closer to me and lifted her sleeve." Olivia took a deep breath, a tear slipping down her cheek. "There was a big bruise and welt around her wrist. Poppy added, 'Daddy did this last weekend. We were at home. Jonathan made me promise not to say anything.'"

"Oh Olivia, I'm so sorry. Did Poppy tell John?"

Olivia wiped her eyes nodding. "John took photos." She laughed. "I don't know how because we were walking right behind him. John has enough evidence of abusive behaviour with Poppy to make our case. He said even Jonathan is mistreated, but the child's loyalties are divided and Basil does a good job of feeding him lies. Most are ambiguous and will be difficult to dispute. Testimony from Matron would be perfect but I doubt she'll say anything."

"Overall, what is John's opinion of how it will go?"

"He's cautiously optimistic. Isn't that what solicitors always say? He's encouraged by what the children have to say but disappointed his investigator wasn't able to uncover firm evidence. He's looking for witnesses to validate any mistreatment of the children. But, like Matron, the staff are all terrified of losing their jobs."

"And John's probably worried about the time or, should I say, lack of time to prepare. Basil thinks by getting an early date, John won't have time to prepare. He has totally underestimated John, which is good for you. Try not to worry." Katie tapped Olivia's hand. "Are you staying?"

"No, I just drove here to think. I find it so peaceful by the water and I wanted to talk to you personally, not on the phone. I should get back. I have a hair appointment this afternoon and Cyril's meeting me for dinner in town."

"How are things with you and Cyril?" Katie asked.

"Good. He's a wonderful person. My life would be so different if I'd stayed with Cyril all those years ago and to have found him again is unbelievable. I don't deserve him."

"Maybe that was true at one time but I think you deserve him now. Take care. I'll see you soon."

Olivia drove off and Katie untied the dogs and walked along the towpath, thinking about Olivia. She was concerned about John. He had his work cut out. Lord Thesleton was a slimy,

164

manipulative creature and she assumed his legal team was the same. They would do anything to win. She shuddered to think he was a judge, the lives he affected and how easily he could destroy John.

She sat on the wooden step of the stile, Buddy and Arthur at her feet, giving her quizzical looks. They were probably wondering if their playmates, Sam and Lily, were going to appear. Katie patted the dogs on the head. "So, what do you think, boys? Will John play the great Lord Thesleton at his own game and win? I sure hope so but that man is evil and does not play by the rules." Katie laughed as the dogs ran off. "Ignored by my dogs. Here, boys! Time to go home."

Derrick had most of the lounge sanded and ready for the undercoat, when Katie returned. She was half expecting to see Adam helping but he was still in his room.

"Knock, knock. Can I come in?" Katie called, opening Adam's door.

"Of course. I was just reading," Adam said holding up an unopened book

"I believe you have to open the book and turn the pages to read." She grinned. "What's wrong, Adam? You don't seem yourself? Are you not feeling well? I can call Piers or Dr Duthie."

"I'm feeling much better. It's not that, although I wish I wasn't so tired. I called Kevin, hoping he would drop by. I haven't set him in almost a month. But, as usual, he doesn't have time. His wife's expecting him home. He suggested the weekend he and Sonia would come by. You know how I feel about Sonia. I know she's his wife but I can't get along with her."

"Did you tell him you're recovering from flu?"

165

"No, germophobic Sonia would use it as an excuse not to come. I feel useless, sitting here. I can hear Derrick working away. I should be doing that, or at least helping."

"Physical work is out of the question until you have your strength back. Why don't you go for a walk? It's quite nice out. I just came back from walking the dogs. If you still want something to do, you can help me in the office when you get back."

The unseasonable and threatening cold, sleety weather of late November continued into December, the sleet frequently switching to snow and the temperature dropping below freezing at night. Katie was glad of the new double-glazed windows, which she hoped would reduce the heating bill. Whether it was a bad year for flu or the unusually cold weather that was causing it to spread so rapidly was hard to tell.

Katie was happy to stay home and out of harm's way, although she'd had her flu shot. So had Adam and he still became ill. Thankfully, Adam had fully recovered and, other than a few guests like Olivia or Judy, Lavender Cottage was quiet. Even Piers had cancelled his last weekend off and stayed in town because of bad weather.

In fact, Piers had not been home for more than one night since their two day break in November. Her intellect told her staying in town when he was exhausted and faced with less than ideal road conditions, was the sensible thing to do. He'd already landed in the ditch once, unhurt but none too pleased by the experience. Why was her heart screaming warnings as paranoia crept in? Was it really the weather and the flu epidemic that stopped him coming home or was it an excuse?

Annoyed with herself for allowing old insecurities that had nothing to do with Piers to surface, she pushed them to the back of her mind.

She'd talked to Cindy, who reminded her she was a doctor's wife and this was normal. Rick was working just as hard. Cindy was frustrated too but she was more accepting. Now Katie felt guilty for expecting too much. Piers had been honest with her before they married and they both knew the commute might be difficult.

"You are pensive today," Adam said, gazing out of the French doors at his beloved rose garden that looked very sad in the frosty snow. Usually a few blooms persisted into December, but not this year.

Katie moved to Adam's side and replied, "Thinking about Piers, and feeling a bit like those poor roses, sad and bitten by this crazy winter." She sighed. "And I'm missing Piers. Am I being selfish?"

"There's nothing wrong with wanting your husband home. I thought he was expected today."

"He is. Just for tonight and back in the morning. I will take whatever I can get." She turned her attention to planning Christmas but that only reminded her of Piers' plan of being on call from Springsville. How could he manage his patients from this distance and in the middle of a flu epidemic? Piers had insisted that with Pat, his nurse, screening the calls from the answering service, he could manage Christmas Eve and Christmas Day and then Rick would take over. Katie mentally shook her head. *It will never work and this has nothing to do with my insecurities,* she mused. *This is a disaster waiting to happen. I will speak with him tonight.* She hadn't noticed Adam slip outside to inspect his rose bushes. She worried he would get

167

cold but didn't have the heart to call him in. Adam loved his roses and a few minutes wouldn't hurt. She heard the garden gate click and assumed it was Piers but Sir Walter peered round the corner. Katie opened the French doors. "Sir Walter, what a lovely surprise!"

"I came to check on this fellow," Sir Walter said, patting Adam on the back. "I thought I'd take him for a pint at the pub and maybe challenge him to a game of darts. Will you join us, Katie?"

"Thank you for the invite but I'll let you two catch up. Are you staying overnight?"

"No, Pablo will pick me up from the pub."

"Pablo?"

"My new chauffeur, from Portugal. I'll see you at Christmas. Book me in for the week."

"Okay." Katie wanted to ask about Pablo but Sir Walter wasn't always forthcoming with personal information and suddenly Piers arrived in the garden.

"Hello everyone! Sir Walter, good to see you. What is this?" He laughed. "A winter garden party?" Piers walked to Katie, kissing her cheek.

"I'm here to drag Adam to the pub. I invited Katie along, although she already refused," Sir Walter said.

"Thanks, but I'm in need of rest and time with my beautiful wife. Another time, perhaps."

Piers slipped his arms around Katie and closed the French doors behind them. Katie melted into his embrace, so pleased to see and feel him.

"Dinner smells good," Piers said, opening a bottle of wine as Katie served dinner. It wasn't until they sat across the table from each other that she saw the lines and strain in Piers' face.

She tried to hide her shock. She had never seen him so pale. He looked ill.

Piers looked up and said, "Do I look that bad?" He stretched his hand across the table and stroked the back of Katie's hand. "Don't look so …" He started coughing and had trouble catching his breath.

"Piers, you are ill. Do you have the flu?" Katie could feel the panic in her voice.

Recovering from the coughing spell, Piers squeezed her hand. "I'm fine, really. I think I got a mild dose. We all did in the office but I promise you I'm on the mend. I even had Rick check me out." He started laughing.

"Piers, this isn't funny." Katie could feel tears prickle the back of her eyes.

"Sorry! I'm laughing because it was comical seeing the stethoscope going from one to the other, me, Rick and Pat, all of us hacking away with this cough. But thankfully it is viral and will run its course." Katie was only a little reassured and wondered why she hadn't detected it. Then she realized he'd been so busy they had communicated by text or very brief phone calls.

Piers ate his dinner, at least he had an appetite but she was still worried.

"You are exhausted and you do not look well. I'm ordering the doctor to rest. Bed rest and no arguments," Katie said in her sternest voice.

"Oh, there will be no argument from me as long as I have company." His eyes twinkled as he took Katie's face in his hands and kissed her, walking backwards into the bedroom. His foot flipped the door closed with a bang, making Buddy Boy and Arthur lift their heads from sleep.

Piers' Secret Flat

P iers could still feel Katie's warmth and the softness of her skin. The fragrance of her shampoo filled his nostrils and her voice resonated as she pleaded with him to take the day off. She was right, as always. *I'm exhausted but so is Rick. I have to get back.* He coughed and put his hand to his chest. It hurt like the devil. The diagnosis was easy, pneumonia. He didn't need a stethoscope to hear his bubbly lungs. He tried to hide it from Katie, but she must have known something was wrong when the exertion of making love to his adorable Katie had almost made him pass out. At least he'd slept a few hours and he didn't feel too bad now. *I'll get some antibiotic when I get to the office.* He mentally counted the days before Christmas Eve. He had enough time for the antibiotics to work before he returned to Springsville. A few nights alone in his tiny flat and he'd be over this damned infection.

He felt his stomach tighten with guilt. He had meant to tell Katie last night but he did not want to spoil the one night they had together. Keeping his illness from her had been hard enough, although that had not really worked. She knew he was ill, just not how sick.

Piers had moved out of Rick's place two weeks ago. A patient mentioned she had a fully furnished bachelor for rent but, because it had no parking and she was picky about her tenants, she'd had trouble finding the right one. He heard his own voice saying, 'I might be interested' and the next thing he was viewing the flat. Only a two minute walk from the clinic, the parking wasn't an issue. He'd leave his car there. It was a small room with a mini kitchen, a bathroom and a couch that pulled out to a bed. A bistro table with two chairs completed it. Again, he heard his voice saying, 'I'll take it.' He sat at the little table and wrote a cheque for three month's rent and drove to Rick's to collect his things.

Rick and Cindy were kind and insisted he didn't need to move, but Piers had noticed them bickering. Much the same complaint as Katie, Rick was never home, his patients came first. He'd heard it all before. Cindy had her hands full with two young children. She didn't need a house guest and they needed their privacy. Initially, Piers had planned to stay maybe once or twice a week but recently, between flu and weather, he'd been there almost every day.

Rick helped him load the car. Piers was amazed at how much he'd accumulated in just over a year. Rick, a true friend, reiterated that Piers didn't have to move but Rick did acknowledge that the family needed their space. Piers'one request was that they keep it a secret until he'd had chance to talk to Katie. Rick reluctantly agreed while strongly advising Piers that secrets, no matter the reason, were never a good idea. He agreed, promising he would tell her.

The clinic's parking lot was empty as expected at six in the morning. Piers unlocked the main doors and went directly to the dispensary, a small locked cupboard where they kept mostly samples of drugs left by the pharmaceutical reps. He took a sheet of foil wrapped acetaminophen and searched for suitable antibiotics. Satisfied with his choice of medications, he switched on the coffee pot. Pat always prepared it before she left at night. He flung a double dose of pills in his mouth and downed them with a glass of water. The water felt good and cold inside him. He put the cold glass to his forehead as the coffee gurgled to a halt. He hesitated before pouring hot coffee but the need for caffeine won. He carried a steaming mug to his desk and flopped on to his leather chair, grateful to sit down. He closed his eyes, willing the meds to kick in. The acetaminophen, a new version of Paracetamol, was supposed to act fast. *That's what all the reps say,* he thought. Opening his eyes, he saw a list and a stack of patient files on his desk. He groaned at the length of the list; patients booked for the morning surgery. The first one in half an hour, at 7 a.m., all part of the new schedule to lighten his load and get home early. It had worked a couple of times, at first. Mostly, like this last visit to Springsville, he had less than 12 hours at home, making the working day longer and the commute harder. Even the thought of his lovely Katie in his arms didn't fully compensate for the exhaustion. But the thought of Katie brought a smile to his face. His head leaning on the chair, he allowed himself to dream a little.

"Hello!" a voice from reception called. Piers quickly put thoughts of Katie out of his mind and switched to doctor mode. Rising from his chair, he felt a little better. Perhaps the fast-acting meds were working.

He leaned around his office door. "Good morning, Mr Shaw. Please, come in." The heavy construction boots thumped unevenly over the tiled floor. The whole idea of early appointments was to allow patients like Mr Shaw to come early and avoid taking time off work. It was a great system for the patients, but it was rare the doctor could finish at three as scheduled, which made for longer, not shorter, days.

Piers sighed with relief when the intercom beeped at 8 a.m. and Pat's friendly said, "Good morning." Pat, the queen of efficiency, managed the patients, allowing the doctors to catch up with notes between appointments.

By mid-morning he was coughing again, and told Pat to hold his eleven o'clock patient and bring him a glass of cold water.

Pat handed him the water and glanced at the pills on his desk. "Doctor, do you have a headache?"

"Something like that," Piers replied. The headache sounded like a good excuse. "Give me a few minutes, please."

"Of course. Buzz me when you're ready." She hovered for a second. "Are you sure you're all right?"

"I'm fine. Is Rick in yet?"

"He'll be back at noon. He's doing hospital rounds this morning."

"How booked is he this afternoon?"

"Solid until six this evening. Why do you ask?" Pat frowned.

"Nothing in particular."

The pills had reduced his chest pain and fever but he knew it would be 24 - 48 hours before the antibiotics would relieve any of the infection. He still had patients booked and two house calls, plus it was his turn to check on the nursing home patients. He had hoped to pass the house calls to Rick but that wasn't possible.

Piers left the clinic and struggled for the rest of the afternoon, almost literally crawling to his tiny flat. He threw himself on the couch and unwrapped the ham sandwich which Pat had picked up for his lunch. He hadn't felt like eating and now his stomach was reeling with so many pills inside him. He dunked the tea bag in the paper cup full of hot water, scrunching his nose at the unappetizing offerings, and wishing he was home with Katie. He picked up his phone. She had phoned once and texted twice. He'd answered only one. He decided to text. It was easier than answering questions.

> *A very busy day. I'm tired but I am feeling better. Please don't worry, I just need a good night's sleep so I'm going to bed early. I'm on call but I am hoping to have a quiet night. Love you. I'll call in the morning.*

Katie replied immediately.

> *I can't help worrying. I've never seen you so pale as you were this morning and you need to treat that cough. Did you ask Rick to prescribe something? An early night is a good idea. I love you too. Until tomorrow. Love, Katie.*

Piers loosened his tie and pulled a large cushion behind his back. Sitting up stopped some of the coughing. He felt relieved that Katie had not asked any more questions about his cough or about where he was. She assumed he was at Rick's house. The guilt of not telling Katie about his tiny flat was eating him up but the memory of Katie's face full of hurt and anger when he first suggested it made him afraid to mention it again. He'd made it worse by actually doing it without consulting her. But he was also annoyed because Katie's reaction had nothing to do with him, and everything to do with her ex, John. If he was honest, that irked him. John had run off and bought a flashy loft condo to lead the high life and entertain flighty women. He had destroyed their marriage and hurt Katie so deeply, it took her years to get over it. He wasn't John and he did not have an ounce of infidelity in him. He'd been faithful to Julianne until the day she died and years afterwards. Katie had been the only woman he'd even allowed himself to get close to. He loved her more than he could say. He would never hurt Katie. Even the slightest comparison to John irritated him a lot.

Every day that passed he lied, well not exactly lied, maybe lied by omission, which allowed Katie to assume he was at Rick and Cindy's and every day he dug himself deeper into a hole. He was terrified he'd never be able to get out of it.

Katie's life was in Springsville at Lavender Cottage. The B&B was doing well and she was so happy. He was happy when he was there. The thought had crossed his mind for them to move closer to Nottingham, but then both would be giving up things they loved. He loved Springsville and his boat. Everything had worked fine when he travelled on weekends but now, living permanently in Springsville, it was a disaster. Yet he could not ask Katie to give up her life. It might have worked if the flu epidemic hadn't started so early. That compounded by the unusually cold weather had made things worse. He shook his head. "Who am I kidding? This is a normal doctor's life. It hasn't changed but my circumstances have." He felt his eyes water. "I don't know what to do. Please, dear God, find an answer." Exhausted, Piers fell asleep.

His phone rang persistently and vibrated on the side table. At first, Piers wondered why no one was answering the phone and then realized it was his. He opened his eyes to semi-darkness, trying to figure out where he was and why he was still dressed. The phone kept ringing. "Hello," he said, his voice croaky. He coughed and put his hand to his chest, remembering he wasn't well.

He took a shallow breath and answered again. "Dr Bannister speaking."

"Good morning, Doctor. This is Kitty from your answering service. The night nurse at Pine Tree Nursing home asked that you call as soon as possible. The number is…"

Piers cut her off. "Thank you, Kitty. I have the number." Piers clicked off his phone abruptly, no longer able to suppress the coughing. He searched his pockets for the pills and shakily poured a glass of water and downed a double dose. The coughing subsided as he leaned his head on the back of the couch, taking another shallow breath. He nodded. "I think the meds are working. I actually feel a little better." He glanced at the clock, 4:30 a.m. It was early but he'd slept for six hours, albeit awkwardly and fully dressed but, all the same, he felt rested and a little hungry. He pulled a face at the half-eaten sandwich curled in its wrapper as he waited for the nursing home to answer his call. He listened to the nurse and told her he was on his way. He splashed water on his face, brushed his teeth and tied his tie. A shower would have to wait.

Stepping into the street, he felt the cold morning air on his face. He had an urge to walk on tiptoe, afraid his footsteps would disturb the quiet. He was like Katie, loving the quietness of mornings and enjoying the walk to the clinic for his car.

Thinking of Katie brought him back to his deception and guilt, but also how much he liked the convenience of his tiny flat. He resolved to tell her next time he was home. Surely, if he explained how it eased the stress, she would understand.

The call to the nursing home had resulted in a 999 call for an ambulance. He doubted that Freda would survive, but she had rallied before. As much as he tried to stay unemotional, some of the patients touched his heart. He'd become fond of Freda. She was 99 and a half, as she kept telling everyone, and was determined to reach 100 and get her greeting from the Queen. Piers shook his head and smiled. If anyone could survive another stroke, Freda could.

On his way back to the clinic he called Katie, knowing she would be up. He imagined her curled up in her blue chair, in front of the Morning Room fire. Buddy Boy and Arthur would be on her knee and her hands wrapped around her coffee mug. As it rang three more times, he smiled, knowing the dogs would be reluctant to get down and she'd left her phone in the bedroom. He was right. A hurried sounding voice answered. "Piers, lovely to hear your voice. Just a minute. Arthur and Buddy Boy are trying to get back on my knee. I had to get up to get my phone. How are you feeling?"

Piers smiled at how predictable life could be. He missed Katie so much. "Much better today." They chatted for a while and Katie asked if he'd be home that night. He found himself hesitating because he'd promised himself, he would tell her about the flat and, yet, he wasn't ready. He wanted to take her in his arms, not argue about a silly flat. "I'll let you know. It all depends on when I finish here."

The morning patients list sat on his desk, not as long as usual. He wondered if Pat had done that deliberately. She had seemed concerned about his 'headache.' Pat was no fool and probably realized Piers was not well.

He did feel a little better but he was still sick. His chest hurt when he coughed and he was glad of the time to catch up the paperwork. Then he noticed a whole hour was blocked out 7 - 8 a.m. for Rick. *That's odd*, he thought. *I wonder what that is about.* He rubbed his chin, realizing he hadn't tidied his beard.

Introducing Dr Stephanie

R ick arrived with a Macdonald's bag full of breakfast and called Piers to join him in his office. "Here, I brought us Egg McMuffins, home fries and orange juice. Cindy was busy making the kid's lunches and I didn't like to disturb her."

"You're early. I noticed Pat had scheduled some time for us. What's up?" Piers was trying to be light but he felt apprehensive. He was the senior partner and should be calling meetings.

"First, I'm worried about you." Rick gave a laugh. "You do realize I'm a doctor and can detect when people are not well? When are you going to tell me what's wrong?"

Piers opened his mouth to say he was fine but hesitated when Rick raised an eyebrow. "Okay, I have a bit of a cold and I didn't feel great yesterday but it's better today."

Rick handed him an Egg McMuffin. "Eat! I'm not buying it. You either have flu or pneumonia and I think it's the later.

Pat saw you downing a handful of pills yesterday."

"You're right. I tried some of the new acetaminophen, which works by the way, and some antibiotics, a loading dose of both and I'm better this morning."

"Take your jacket off. Let me listen." Rick lodged the stethoscope in his ears and Piers lifted his shirt. "Um…now the back. It's pneumonia all right. How high is your fever?"

"It's down today. Believe me, Rick. I am getting better."

"How did you get this by Katie?"

"I haven't seen her. I stayed at the flat last night. I was on call."

Rick squinted. "You haven't told her about the flat, have you? Piers, you are asking for trouble."

"Let's change the subject. Why did you want to see me? It's usually me calling meetings. Is something wrong? You're not leaving or anything like that, are you?" Piers felt unreasonable panic as his unbidden words flew out of his mouth and his chest constricted, setting him off coughing.

Rick frowned as he waited for Piers to get his breath. "You should be home in bed. Take the day off."

"I can't. We are up to our eyeballs. I was at the nursing home early this morning. Freda had another stroke and the night nurse was saying they have a lot more flu cases. They're mild so far, but this strain seems very aggressive."

"We are up to our eyeballs, as you say, and that is why I asked to see you. We can't go on like this. You are sick from overwork and I could be next. We need help."

"We do. What were you thinking? Have a locum come in on a regular basis?"

"That's a possibility but I was thinking of something more permanent. Hiring a doctor. I'm not ready for another partner, though. You and I work well together." Rick sat back and ate his breakfast.

"I agree. I'm not ready for a third partner and I don't think there's enough work yet. Can we afford to employ a doctor? I'm assuming you're thinking of someone right out of internship?" Piers rubbed his stubbly chin.

"Yes, and I have someone in mind. Cindy has a distant cousin, who I met at a family dinner last weekend. She's just finished at the Grace Hospital. She's the down to earth type and not interested in a glamorous career. She's a bit idealistic, wants to help people. She asked me about family practice since it's a field of medicine that appeals to her. She's also thinking of paediatrics but isn't ready for more education. I told her she'd get all the paediatrics she needed in family practice."

"I like the idea. Let's run it by the accountant and bring her in for an interview. I'd like lots of references. Not that I don't trust your word but we need to be extra careful because she's a relative, even a distant one. Good work, Rick. I don't know why I didn't think about it."

"I'll talk to the accountant this morning and then arrange an interview with her. Stephanie Ward is her name. Do you want to come to see the accountant?"

"Can you handle it? I'd like to get a shower. I came straight here after my call from Pine Trees Nursing Home. Do you mind?"

"Not at all. I asked Pat to keep our schedules clear this morning. We might have to work late tonight, though. Are you up to it?" Rick asked, a tone of concern in his voice.

Piers nodded. "I'll feel better after a shower. The antibiotics are doing their job. I'll take it easy and let Katie know we're working late tonight. She won't be pleased but knowing we're getting more help will ease the blow."

Piers couldn't believe how tired he felt as he unlocked his tiny flat door. The meeting with Rick had depleted what little energy he had, although it was a good one. He thought about his plea to God. He wasn't a particularly religious man but maybe this was God's answer.

Right now, he felt sick. The Egg McMuffin churned in his stomach. He hadn't been entirely honest with Rick. For all his bravado, he was worried. His temperature was up again and every time he coughed, a knife sliced into his chest. *If I keep this up, I'll be in a hospital bed,* he thought as he rubbed his sweaty forehead. *I'm overreacting. Rick listened to my chest. He'd have said if it was serious. I need rest.* He downed more pills, had a cold shower and lay down on his pullout couch, which he had never actually pulled out to a bed. He wondered if that was his subconscious trying to keep his tiny flat temporary and easing his guilt. *I should call Katie and tell her I won't be home tonight. I can't. I'm too tired. Later.* He propped himself up on cushions, breathing easier, and immediately fell into a deep sleep.

"No, Katie, no!" he yelled, waking himself from a nightmare. He sat up, coughing and gasping for breath. The nightmare vision of Katie, angry as she slammed the door. Was she leaving? He didn't know, the vision blurred leaving him in a panic.

His phone rang and stopped and then rang again. He answered. "Hello!"

"Dr Bannister, where are you? I've been calling for ages. Your car is here but not you. You have an office full of patients,"

Pat scolded.

"Um … I'm at the flat. I must have dozed off."

"What flat?"

Piers realized Pat didn't know about the flat. He must think quickly. "No, not flat. I'm flat out not feeling good. I took a walk to clear my head. I'll be right there." His stomach churned again, this time not from food but guilt. Lying was not his style.

He dialled Katie's number as he walked to the office. He had to tell her.

"Katie, it's nice to hear your voice. I have something to tell you."

"You're not coming home tonight." The disappointment in her voice struck his heart. "I figured as much. I called the office when you didn't answer your phone. Pat told me she'd been told to reschedule and you were working tonight."

"Well, yes, but there's something else. I'm sorry about tonight but there is good news and a good reason."

"Really? Another excuse? Piers, I understand. I do really."

"This is a good excuse. Rick and I met this morning to discuss easing our schedules, the reason we're working tonight. Long story, but we may have found a doctor to work with us."

"That is good news but, honestly, Piers, I'll believe it when I see it. I have to go. The office phone is ringing." Katie didn't even say goodbye. He held his phone and stared at it, willing her to call back but he knew she wouldn't. She was angry and he still hadn't told her about the tiny flat. He punched the clinic door open and a sea of anxious patients stared at him.

"Sorry folks, an emergency." Piers glanced at Pat, rolling her eyes. A slight grin lifted her cheeks as she followed him into the office with a pile of files in her arm.

"Are you sure you're all right? You are as white as a sheet. It's not like you to be late for your patients."

"I'm not feeling well. A bit of a chest infection. Rick checked me out this morning. Thanks for your concern, but I'm okay. Sorry to be late. Let's get started."

Pat nodded and showed the first patient into the office.

Rick put his head round Piers' office door. "All finished? Do you feel like having dinner with me? I have some good news."

"Good idea. I must be feeling better as I'm hungry and I am definitely up for good news. Katie didn't believe me when I said you had news."

"Fish and chips and a pint at The Queens Head okay with you?" Rick asked, picking up a folder and walking out.

The pub was quiet and Piers found a secluded corner table, while Rick ordered dinner and picked up two pints of best bitter.

"I spoke with the accountant and he's comfortable with hiring a junior doctor." Rick opened the folder and handed Piers a sheet of numbers. "These are the results. He gave me a bit of a lecture about increasing the business to cover the cost but also said it would give us a tax break. I assured him we would increase our patient load." His last words hovered on the edge of the glass tankard as he took a gulp of beer.

"Wow! These numbers look better than I thought. It's no wonder we're so busy. What about this doctor? Do you think she's really interested?"

"I'm way ahead of you. I talked to her today and she is. I booked her to come for an interview the day after tomorrow.

There's one hiccup. She's committed to locum work until the new year.

"Oh. I was hoping she could help us out over the holiday but I guess we'll manage. It's only a couple more weeks. Are we getting ahead of ourselves? I'd like to see her CV." Piers rubbed his chin in thought.

"Call me efficient or what?" Rick chuckled. "I knew you weren't feeling good. I hope you don't mind. I went ahead and asked her to email her CV. It's pretty impressive. Top of her class and more locum work in family practice than I thought. Take a look."

Piers studied the pages and realized the barmaid was hovering at his shoulder with two plates of fish and chips. He picked up the CV, continuing to read as the hot food was placed on the table. The smell filling his nostrils, making him hungry.

"Thanks," Piers said without looking up. "You're right, she's ideal. A couple of excellent references." Piers pointed to one of the letters. "I know this doctor. He's a hard task master. A reference from him is like gold. I'm looking forward to meeting this young woman."

"You'll like her." Rick slapped him on the back, making him cough. "Sorry. How's the chest?"

"Feels like a knife in my chest when I cough but I'm getting better."

They ate their meal in quiet contemplation, both tired and hungry and considering how another doctor would change their lives.

"We can talk about this more tomorrow." Rick frowned towards Piers' strained and pale face. "You need to get some rest and I need to get home. Cindy will be on my back. I wonder if those two have been talking. Cindy is the same as Katie. She doesn't believe we're trying to lighten the work load." Rick leaned back, pushing his empty plate away. "I don't understand women. We do our best to provide for them and then get accused of ignoring the family. At least Cindy is happy about the prospect of Stephanie working with us." Rick gave Piers a stern look as he walked to his car. "Rest, my friend. I'll see you tomorrow morning."

Piers waved and walked to his tiny flat and called Katie as soon as he shut the door. She sounded like his loveable Katie, no longer angry, and excited about the possibility of a new doctor. She even understood he wouldn't be home because of the interview with Stephanie. Afraid she might react, he chickened out again, justifying his decision that it was better to tell her in person, although he wasn't sure about that. Something told him it might be harder. But she sounded so happy and he wanted to fall asleep with her words 'I love you' in his head. He undressed and lay on the couch in his pyjamas, debating whether to pull out the bed, but deciding he was quite comfortable on the couch.

Dr Ward's interview was booked for 7 pm in the evening, after the last patient. Pat had been told that Dr Ward might be joining the practice and had been asked to stay and meet her. Both doctors respected Pat's opinion and without actually saying it, they wanted her feedback. Dr Ward arrived early. Piers was finishing off his surgery and Rick was out on a call when she arrived. This gave Pat the opportunity to conduct her own interview. She made tea so they could chat and she gave Dr Ward a tour of the clinic. By the time Piers and Rick joined them, Stephanie and Pat were on a first name basis. Obviously, Pat had given her seal of approval.

Stephanie was tall and thin with coffee coloured skin, her father a doctor from Birmingham and her mother born in Pakistan, but raised from a baby in England. She wasn't particularly attractive with her hair pulled back into a severe bun and dressed in a grey tailored business suit and high heels. It was appropriate dress for the interview but the look didn't suit her and seemed to be at odds with her friendly, cheerful and most likely colourful personality. She had a charming smile that radiated warmth and kindness. Piers liked her immediately, instinctively understanding what Rick had seen in her at the family gathering.

After a brief interview, Rick and Piers took Stephanie Ward out for dinner and offered her the position, which she accepted with a start date of January 2nd. And, unbeknownst to Piers, Rick asked Stephanie if she would stay and work with Rick for two days before traveling south for her Christmas locum appointment. Rick had insisted that Piers take time off and go home so Katie could nurse him back to health. Piers didn't take much convincing and surprised Katie, arriving unexpectedly in the middle of the day.

Roses and Rest

Walking up Marina Lane with the dogs, Katie saw what she thought was Piers' car pull off Main Street. Arthur must have heard or sensed it long before Katie because he'd been pulling hard on the leash ever since they left the towpath. She wondered how dogs instinctively knew their masters were close by. Piers pulled into the driveway and opened the car door, an enormous grin on his face. He said, "Are you the lady of the house? I have a special delivery." He reached into the back seat and took out a bunch of red roses. "A peace offering for abandoning my beautiful wife."

"Roses! Thank you. They are gorgeous. I am not complaining but how come you are home in the middle of day?" Katie reached up to kiss him, feeling Arthur up against her legs. "Someone else is happy to see you." Arthur was on his back legs jumping against Piers and Buddy Boy sat waiting for a pat.

"Hey boys, did you miss me?" He bent down and patted both dogs. "I have some very good news." He took her in his arms, but as he pulled her close he caught his breath and bent double in a convulsive coughing fit.

Katie frowned and rubbed at his back. "Piers, you are ill. I knew it," she said with irritation. "I should have made you stay home last week. Did Rick send you home?"

"No! Well, sort of." Talking a breath with his hand on his chest, he added, "I'm okay. I had a touch of pneumonia. I'm on antibiotics and Rick took a listen to my chest and it's not serious. Nothing that two days rest with my Katie won't cure. Rick's words were 'I'm sending you home so Katie can nurse you back to health.'"

"You had better do as you're told," Katie said with stern determination, wagging her finger but teasing with a smile. "Inside. Change into something comfortable and get into bed, while I put these roses in water." Katie peered over the roses, sniffed the scent and watched Piers' expression. She realized bed might not work. "Alright, the sofa in the lounge. I'll get Adam to light a fire. We are guest free until the 23rd, although we might have Olivia as her court case starts the day after tomorrow and she needs to be among friends, with Cyril close by."

Piers gave a contented sigh as he lay down on the sofa, a real one, not a pullout couch. He quickly pushed that thought out of his head. Katie stuffed pillows under his head and covered him with a blanket. Adam poked at the logs already roaring in the fireplace and Katie gave Piers a kiss. "Now sleep! We'll talk later. I have some work to do."

Katie pulled the last batch of shortbread out of the oven, glancing at the clock. Piers had slept for four hours and she thought she heard voices. He must be awake, talking to Adam. She didn't tell him how shocked she was when he'd arrived home. His face was the colour of parchment, with bags under his eyes and his cheeks seemed hollow. His coughing was deep and she suspected painful. Had Rick really listened to his chest or was he lying? He'd obviously been ill for some time. Perhaps that explained her feeling that he was hiding something from her. The hurried texts and short, sometimes abrupt, phone calls. He had not seemed himself. She smiled. *But I really appreciated the roses.*

Katie checked the roast of lamb in the oven, Piers' favourite meal. He definitely needed fattening up. She made a pot of tea and set a tray with cups and a plate of shortbread. Pushing the door open with her back she entered the lounge to see Piers sitting up with some colour in his cheeks.

"Fresh shortbread and tea! You are looking much better. I was worried about you."

"I feel better. I needed the sleep. I think Adam had a nod off too. Um shortbread. I woke up to the smell. It always reminds me of Christmas."

"It doesn't take much for me to sleep. I nap more as I get older," Adam said, adding, "The smell of baking always reminds me of the holidays. Doris used to bake everything from porkpies to plum pudding. Christmas is less than a week away. Do you mind if I take my tea upstairs? Kevin said he'd call around five."

"No, go ahead," Katie said, happy to have some alone time with Piers.

"I have something to tell you," Piers said, watching Adam

haul himself up the stairs and surmised his arthritis was bothering him.

"You said you had good news," Katie said, sitting next to him on the sofa. "I thought the good news was getting two days off. There's more?"

"Much more! We have hired a new doctor. I know you were sceptical when I mentioned it, but it's true. A super woman, well perhaps not super woman in that sense." He paused with a chuckle. "But she's young and energetic. She finished her internship six months ago, is currently doing locum work and very excited about family practice. She's a distant cousin of Cindy's. Her father's a doctor, although I didn't ask what field of medicine and her mother's a nurse. A pretty good medical pedigree and, more to the point, she is a very nice person, well qualified and possibly partner material further down the road. We interviewed her yesterday, offered her the job and she starts January 2nd. And, she also passed the Pat test."

Katie laughed. "Well, I have a lot of respect for Pat's opinion."

"So do we. In fact, we were deliberately late so Pat could show her the clinic and by the time we were ready, Dr Ward was called Stephanie, a very good sign. Even before the interview we pretty much knew she was right for the job. And the reason I'm home is because she offered to work for a couple of days. I suspect Rick had something to do with that so I'd take some time off."

Katie leaned on Piers' shoulder letting out a long sigh of relief, first because it explained Pier's strange texts and calls and now with an extra pair of hands they would get more time together.

"I am eternally grateful for that. Can she work over Christmas?"

"Afraid not. She's committed to a locum appointment over the holidays. That's why her start date is January."

"It's going be a weird holiday." Katie loved Christmas but she couldn't shake the premonition that something would go wrong this year.

"It will be fine. I might have to field a few calls Christmas Eve and Christmas Day but I've talked to Pat and she is prepared as the dragon at the door. Only urgent calls will come my way. Stop worrying."

It only took Piers two short days to recover; with lots of sleep, Katie's company and, of course the antibiotics, he felt almost normal again and persuaded Katie to come on the boat.

Tranquil Days looked forlorn as they approached the marina. Arthur and Buddy Boy ran onto the dock but stopped as Bob had placed a tarp over the boat, which had to be removed before they could get aboard.

"Piers!" Bob called. "Give me a minute and I'll give you a hand to take the tarp off. We've had a lot of sleet and ice. I wanted to protect the deck."

"That's fine, Bob. Thanks," Piers called back as he untied the tarp. Bob joined them and folded the tarp, sticking it in his wheelbarrow to store in the shed.

Arthur jumped on board and ran to the bow as usual. Buddy Boy made a couple of comical attempts to jump but waited for Katie to lift him aboard. Piers started the engine and slowly reversed from the mooring.

Katie shivered. As much as she enjoyed the boat, it was chilly and she zipped up her jacket, pulled on mittens and wondered exactly why she was sitting in a boat, freezing in the middle of December, when they should be choosing a Christmas tree. She and Piers had done it together the last two years. But, glancing at Piers' pink smiling face, she knew why. Today the boat ride was more important than the tree. And a quick cruise to the bridge and back was what he needed before he headed back to Nottingham.

Piers left at noon as Dr Ward had a train to catch and Piers had patients waiting for him. Standing on the door step, they both glanced up at the sky. The pale winter sun had slipped behind some heavy looking clouds.

"Does that look like snow to you?" Piers said.

"It does. Perhaps we'll have a white Christmas. I hope it holds off until you get to the clinic."

"I'll be fine. I'll try to get home tomorrow night. I can't promise, but I will be home Christmas Eve. We're closing the office at noon." Piers blew her a kiss and Katie waved as he dove away. Pleased to see him healthy again, for once she didn't mind if he didn't make it home until Christmas. It was only four days away and she had a lot to do.

Lavender Cottage was getting a reputation for a cozy traditional Christmas, especially for loners like Sir Walter, Olivia and Cyril, although they were a couple now. Judy and her father and Katie's daughter Melanie and husband, Phil, Mary and Bob and even Maisie and Stevie popped by between opening and closing the pub. This year, Katie had not booked paying guests for Christmas, deciding to keep it to family and friends. As she ticked off the list in her head, she felt slightly panicked, remembering the turkey disaster of a couple of years ago. Back in her office, she called the butcher to make sure the turkey was at least thirty pounds and the pork roast was a good size. With sausage, bacon and two types of stuffing,

193

roast potatoes and several vegetables, it should be enough for twelve people, and unexpected guests. It was a small group this year. Even so, she was late with preparations. Adam had decorated the outside and the lights were up but they still didn't have a tree. The tree decorations were sitting on the lounge floor. With Piers' illness, she had neglected a lot of things. She'd have to trust Adam to get the tree this year and that made her a little sad. It had always been her and Piers.

Katie's mobile vibrated on her desk. She grabbed it as it was about jitter its way to the edge of the desk.

"Hello! Olivia, how are things going?"

"The judge adjourned for lunch. John is pleased with the progress and he likes this judge. He says he's fair. I feel so alone, but John is being very kind." The line went quiet for a couple of seconds. "Katie, I'm terrified." Olivia sounded as though she might burst into tears at any minute.

"Is there anything I can do?" Katie asked. "I'll come and sit with you if that will help."

"You are so kind, Katie, but there's nothing you can do right now. Just have my room ready at Lavender Cottage when this is over."

"Any idea when that will be?"

"We hoped today, but it looks as though it will be tomorrow. The judge has been asking for clarification regarding the arrangements at school. John thinks it has riled Basil's legal team and he suspects they might retaliate, but he doesn't know with what. The judge is being very fair and I saw his eyebrows go up a couple of times. Remember, these men in court, including the judge, are Basil's colleagues who think very highly of him. I don't trust any of them. Oh, just a minute!" Katie could hear Olivia talk to someone. "I have to go. Bye."

"Bye! Stay strong, Olivia. Everything will work out okay."

Katie punched the disconnect on the phone, hoping she was right and everything would be okay. She wasn't so sure. Lord Thesleton's legal team was one of high-powered, experienced, devious lawyers, known to stretch and twist the truth. Nothing pleased them more than digging up things people had forgotten. Again, she thought *Is John strong enough to handle this*? She sighed. *Is anyone strong enough*? Basil had managed to cover up his abuse for years and told terrible lies about Olivia and nobody questioned him. Unfortunately, Olivia had not been the pleasantest of people, milking her title and ordering people around, expecting to be, quite literally, waited on hand and foot. When Katie had first met her, she needed an entourage to tend to her needs. But, in the last year, Basil had done her a favour by divorcing her and leaving her penniless. It wasn't the nicest way to learn humility but it had worked and Olivia had changed dramatically. Cyril said she was more like the Olivia he knew in his youth, and reconnecting with Cyril had been a large part of the change. No matter what kind of person she was, no woman should have to endure violence and abuse from anyone, and certainly not a spouse. Katie suspected it was probably worse than Olivia had admitted. The injustice of taking her children away and making them believe she was a bad mother for no other reason than to be vindictive and mean, was incomprehensible to Katie. She thought of her own children. Her life had been different from Olivia's but a mother is a mother, and most mothers would lay down their life for their child. Although, given Olivia's history and her narcissistic tendencies, Katie wasn't sure how much Olivia would give up for her children. On the other hand, Katie couldn't imagine living under such difficult conditions. Certainly, Olivia had changed her attitude since John and Cyril had stepped in to help. She glanced at her phone. Speak of the devil, she thought. There was a text from Olivia.

> *I'm not sure what's happening. The judge ordered both legal teams into his chambers. Now, court is adjourned until tomorrow. Mr Bryant sent me home, saying it was just legal stuff and not to worry. Should I worry?*

Katie frowned. It wasn't unusual for this to happen but she wondered why and replied

> *No need to worry. This kind of thing happens all the time. Call me later if you are worried.*

Twisted Truths

atie woke even earlier than usual, her chest tight with apprehension and her heart seemed to be beating fast, in fight or flight mode. She stretched out on her back, her arm feeling the cool sheets on Piers' side of the bed. She wished he was there, whispering into her ear and kissing her neck. She missed him and couldn't wait for Christmas Eve when he'd be home. She was worried about the on-call arrangement but why was she so tense? Christmas was her favourite time of the year and all her favourite people would be there. "Which reminds me, I must confirm with Mary," she said to Arthur and Buddy Boy, both sitting on the bed with their heads to one side. She gave a chuckle. "Not only am I talking to the dogs but I'm half expecting them to answer." She tickled each dog behind the ear. "Well, boys, I had better get moving. There's a lot to do today and I promised to meet Melanie in Nottingham for some last minute shopping." She groaned at the thought of the crowded shops.

She really wanted to refuse but Melanie sounded excited about something; at least excitement was preferable to problems.

She checked her phone for messages, nothing. She assumed she had been right about Olivia and there was nothing to worry about. No news was good news.

Katie put the coffee on and checked her agenda. No appointments other than Melanie but she had earmarked the day to finish decorating the Christmas cake and baking the chocolate log. She still had to get a tree and decorate the lounge. She dropped two slices of bread in the toaster. Hearing Adam come into the kitchen, she poured him a coffee.

"Adam, is there any chance you could go pick up a Christmas Tree today?" Katie paused and made an apologetic face. "And decorate it? I am so behind with Christmas and we only have three days left."

"Sure. I'd be happy to. It reminds me of taking Kevin to the tree lot when he was a kid. I might need some help," Adam said, frowning. "I'll ask Bob to give me a hand and maybe he'll take me in his pickup truck."

"Perfect!" A knock on the front door made them both stare at the door. "Who could that be so early in the morning?"

Katie opened the door. "John! What are you doing here?"

"I have to talk to you. I'm sorry I didn't know who else to…" John's voice petered off.

Katie pulled the door wide open and directed John to the couch. "This must be serious. What's happened? Is it Olivia?"

"Not directly. Katie, I know I screwed up with the drugs and I put my career at risk. But thanks to you and Melanie, and Bryant giving me a second chance, I thought I was back. I felt good with everything behind me. I knew Olivia's case would be hard, a test and a chance to prove myself. I had not bargained for this."

"John, what?" Katie said, frustrated because she had no idea what he was talking about.

"The Morton-Smith legal team has brought up my time at the rehab clinic and said I should be disbarred, or words to that effect."

"Can they do that? And why would they? If they think Olivia is getting a poor legal representation, wouldn't that be to their advantage?"

"I wish I knew. The judge has to deal with the accusations before we can proceed. Katie, we were winning, I could feel it in my bones and then a bomb is dropped on us. It's as though they want to discredit me, which doesn't make sense. The judge has asked to see me this morning. I could lose my licence, my job at Bryant's and Olivia's case would be back to square one. Katie, I'm sorry to come here, but Melanie wouldn't understand."

"He's rattling your cage, John, and it's working. What does Mr Bryant have to say about it?"

"I'm not sure he knows. The judge's assistant called me directly and said it was a personal matter."

"I find that interesting and, from what I hear from Olivia, it makes a lot of sense. Lord Thesleton does not like to lose and as the evidence of his abuse is revealed he will do anything to hide it. Imagine what that will do to his reputation. Nobody likes a wife beater.

"John, since your recovery, your work has been exemplary and prior to it, you were one of the best solicitors in town." Katie gave him a warm smile.

"Even after the way I treated you, you are still my cheerleader. That's why I came to you."

Katie ignored his comment and continued. "Mr Bryant is not a stupid man and he would never have asked you to take this case if he had doubts about you." Katie drifted into thought. She had been suspicious of Bryant's motives, putting John in this position. She considered John to be too vulnerable. Staring at his worried, frightened face, she was beginning to think she had been right all along. "If there is one thing I know about you, that is your loyalty and commitment to your clients. Okay, you had a setback but the old tenacious John is still there. This might be the fight of your life as well as your client's. But you can do this. You are correct. I think this is the fight of your career and the John I know is bracing for a fight to win." Katie felt like crossing her fingers, but even with the doubt, she felt John had it in him. "Here's what I think you should do. Go and talk to Bryant. He knows your story. Ask him to accompany you to the judge's chambers. Face whatever it is head on."

"You, as usual, are right. I knew I was right coming here." He gave her a puppy-dog look. "I screwed up more than my career. I miss you, Katie."

"John, it's over. I'm married to Piers and very happy. You will find someone. Give it time. Now, get over to the office. I'm sure Bryant is always in early."

Katie had only just showered and dressed when she received a text from John.

> *Katie, I can't thank you enough. Mr Bryant very supportive and insisted on coming with me and angry at the game playing. I'll update when I can.*

She replied with a thumbs up emoji, not wanting to start

anything with John. For old time's sake she did want to support him, and wish him well, and she wanted Olivia to get her children back.

As she expected, the traffic was heavy and the roads slippery as sleet had been falling intermittently most of the morning. At least she was lucky to find a parking space as someone pulled out of the Debenhams' parking lot. Melanie had already found a table in the packed café. Irritated at having to push past people not paying attention, the Christmas spirit in full bloom, she questioned why she was there. But, seeing her daughter, she smiled. Melanie looked radiant and definitely excited about something.

Melanie stood up and hugged her mother. "I ordered chicken and chips. I hope that's okay. They are so busy, I thought it would save some time."

"Good thinking. It is crowded. Have you finished your shopping? You look…" Katie hesitated, unsure how to describe her daughter, "happy, satisfied. Whatever it is, you look lovely."

"Said like a true mother," Melanie laughed, her eyes sparkling. "How about grandmother?"

Tears filled Katie's eyes and she almost screamed in delight. As it was, heads turned as she repeated, rather loudly, "Grand-mother! When? Oh, this is a lovely surprise."

"It's early days yet but I think the end of June, which is perfect. The academic year will have finished and I'll have the summer to nurse my baby."

"You'll be entitled to maturity leave. How long does the university give you?" Katie asked, getting the distinct feeling that Melanie was not considering leave at all.

"I don't know. I haven't told them yet and there's lots of time to work all that out. I wanted you to be the first to know. Phil would have liked to be here but he had an emergency faculty meeting. It seems there is always something going wrong. He is over the moon excited about the baby."

"How are you feeling?" Katie asked with concern in her voice, but a wide grin on her face. She couldn't hide her pleasure at the news.

"Actually, I'm fine. A little bit of nausea in the mornings but no morning sickness, thank goodness. So how are you, Mum? You looked a bit frazzled when you came in."

"I was, but your news sure changed that. I'm very behind with the Christmas preparations. Nursing Piers, listening to Olivia, and now your father. I feel as though everyone wants a piece of me."

"And I drag you downtown in the Christmas rush. Sorry! I wanted to surprise you. What's wrong with Dad? Is it Olivia's case?"

"Morton-Smith, Basil's legal team, are being nasty and have implied that your father is not competent because of his history."

"That's awful. Why?"

"My thoughts are that they want the case postponed. Your father is revealing stuff about the Honourable Judge Moreland, Lord Thesleton, that he would prefer to be concealed."

"Wow! How is Dad handling it?"

"Not well, but I'm hoping with Mr Bryant's support, he'll be okay. He might like to hear from his favourite daughter and I think your baby news will cheer him immensely."

Melanie laughed. "I'm his only daughter but, yes, I will call him and get him to come over for dinner and give him the news. Mum, I need to cut lunch short as I have some last minute shopping to do. Can you join me?"

"Not today. I have so much to do at the cottage. Oh, there's my phone. It's from your father. He says, 'meeting went well. We're back in court at 2 pm.'"

"That is good news," Melanie said.

Katie nodded yes. "Will you be over Christmas Eve?"

"We will. Do you want us to come early to help?"

"No need. Come when you're ready. You need to rest young lady, and don't stay out shopping too long." Katie had her stern Mum look, which made Melanie laugh as she left.

Katie had a permanent grin as she drove back to Springsville. She instructed her phone to call Piers at the clinic. She couldn't wait to tell him he was to be a step-grandpa. Just as she expected, he was delighted.

"Does that mean I'm sleeping with a grandmother?" They laughed together.

"I guess so, as I'm sleeping with grandpa."

"Katie, this is wonderful news but I have some bad news. I can't get home until Christmas Eve. The clinic is crazy busy and there is an outbreak of gastroenteritis at Pine Trees that's not helping. We are working flat out. I haven't seen Rick in two days."

Katie thought he was joking. "Really? Don't you see him at breakfast?" She felt a sudden silence. "Cindy still makes you breakfast right?"

"Katie, I have to go. Pat just buzzed me. That is great news about Melanie and Phil. I have to get used to 'grandpa.' We'll talk about it when I get home. Love you."

"Love you more," Katie said, frowning. Cindy always

insisted they start the day with breakfast, knowing full well that they often didn't have time to eat during the day.

Adam greeted her at the door and made her close her eyes as she walked into the cottage. She smelled the pine before as she stepped over the threshold. "You can open them now."

"Oh Adam, this is beautiful." An eight-foot tree stood in the corner by the window, completely covered in white twinkling lights and icicles with contrasting and sparkling coloured baubles from Katie's box, decorations she had collected over the years. Bows of holly, heavy with red berries, cut from the holly trees outside decorated the mirror and pictures. Finally, the cottage looked like Christmas. Buddy Boy and Arthur ran to greet her, silver tinsel in their fur from investigating the bottom of the tree.

"Out of there, you two, "Katie laughed, happy that Christmas was coming together and so excited about a baby coming into the family.

"Adam, I almost forgot. Melanie is expecting a baby."

"Congratulations! Doris always wanted grandchildren but Kevin and Sonia didn't oblige. Sonia has a daughter from a previous marriage but never considered us grandparents."

"I'm sorry, Adam, that must have been disappointing. But I know Melanie will share with you. This little boy or girl will have some many grandpas, Piers, John and you. I'll leave you to it. I have some baking to do and some office work.

December 23rd and everything was ready, except for the last minute things, which could wait until later in the afternoon. Katie was exhausted but very happy. She hummed Christmas carols and decided the dogs deserved a long walk and promised herself a cup of Mary's coffee and a scone on their return. She clipped the excited dogs on their leashes. It was chilly but with a thick jacket, scarf, hat and woolly mitts, Katie was toasty warm and the dogs didn't care about the temperature as they walked along the towpath. She laughed at the dogs as they ran way ahead of her, then stopped, making sure she was still there. It was a dull day, the clouds heavy with sleet or snow. A white Christmas would be lovely, she thought, as a few flakes drifted to the ground. It appeared that Buddy Boy and Arthur had had enough walk as they turned around and ran back towards the marina. Katie wasn't sorry as her fingers were getting numb and a hot cup of coffee was calling her. She tied the dogs at the Dog Moorings. Mary was happy to see her. The café was quiet in the winter time, and even quieter close to Christmas. Most of her business at this time of the year was take out and bakery sales for parties and gatherings. The Lavender Cottage order alone kept her busy. Katie sat at the corner table, enjoying her coffee and scone. She didn't stay long. Mary was busy and it was cold for the dogs waiting outside. She bought a couple of extra scones and walked the dogs home, realizing she had not told Mary her big news. But maybe she'd let Melanie and Phil make the announcement during Christmas dinner.

Taking her jacket off and settling in the office, Katie sorted her guest list out, calculating how many meals and who was staying overnight. Olivia and Cyril had booked the Marina Suite from Christmas Eve right through to New Year's Day. Olivia had confided in Katie that she hoped the children would be able to join her for part of the holiday and the Marina Suite had a pullout couch for the kids. Sir Walter had his usual Morning Glory Room, leaving the Daisy Den for Judy.

Depending on whether her father came too, she might have to shuffle the rooms. Cindy and Rick would not be staying overnight this year. The in-laws were visiting and offered to babysit so they could enjoy Christmas Eve at Lavender Cottage. It was a cottage full of people, just the way Katie liked it. Although she couldn't put her finger on it, it felt different this year.

About to relax and put her feet up, Katie heard a knock on the front door and Olivia call, "Anyone at home?"

Katie took one look at Olivia's face and knew something had gone horribly wrong in court today. She was surprised she hadn't heard from John.

"Olivia, what happened? Is it over?"

Olivia shook her head, tears streaming down her face. Between sobs, she explained that Basil was furious because the judge had dismissed the accusations against John as unfounded.

Katie poured them both a glass of brandy and led Olivia to the sofa.

"Here, I think we need this. Take a breath and tell me what happened."

Olivia took a sip of brandy, wiped her tears and said, "Basil was with his legal team in court today. If looks could kill, I would be dead. He argued with the judge and was dangerously close to disrespecting the bench. I could see the judge was frustrated at this point. I think he gave him some latitude because they are colleagues. The legal team took over." Olivia took a trembling breath. "They questioned the legality of our visit to the school and said the information was not admissible because it was taken illegally. That was a lie. John has proof in writing that we had permission to visit. But they twisted it and at this point I don't understand anything. Nothing makes sense. I don't know if the judge believes Morton-Smith and their lies, but if he does, I will lose my children."

"Stay calm. You're getting ahead of yourself. Tell me what happened. The judge didn't make a decision then."

"He didn't look too happy. He said he couldn't make a decision yet and we're back in court in January."

"Can you see the children over Christmas?"

Olivia nodded yes with a very broad smile. "Christmas Eve. John is working out the details now." Olivia's smile disappeared. "I don't trust Basil. When he appears to be compliant and cooperative, he's up to something, and that really frightens me. Can I stay here tonight?"

"Of course. Your room is ready. Is Cyril coming?"

"Not until Christmas Eve and he can't stay if the children are here. I talked to him when I left court. He's upset and doesn't understand why I don't want to see him. I love him but he can be, shall we say, 'smothering' at times. Katie, I need to be alone."

"I understand and Cyril will too. He's worried about you. That's all."

Mixed Emotions

John didn't just call. He arrived on Katie's doorstep to give Olivia the news. Uncomfortable with his presence twice in one day, Katie questioned if John had an ulterior motive. The thought crossed her mind that he might be flirting with her. She knew him well enough to realize he had many regrets and missed her. And if she was honest, unlike herself who had moved on with a new life, John was clinging to what he had lost.

"John! What a surprise! I'm assuming you have news for Olivia." Katie opened the door wide so John could greet her without hugging or kissing her on the cheek.

"I do have some good news, which is welcome today."

"Come in. Olivia and I were just chatting."

"John, what did they say?" Olivia jumped up from the sofa, her hand on her heart.

"Mr Bryant did most of the talking and it has been agreed the children will spend Christmas Eve with you here at Lavender

Cottage. Lord Thesleton's chauffeur will drive them here at 4 p.m. and pick them up at noon on Christmas Day."

"I don't know what to say, John. Thank you, thank you," Olivia, uncharacteristically, gave John a bear hug.

Clearing his throat, and somewhat embarrassed, he said, "You are welcome but a lot of people made this happen. Mr Bryant was brilliant. His negotiation skills are second to none. The fact that you are staying here with Katie was also a factor."

"Did the judge say anything about the school?" Olivia struggled to keep her voice from panic. "They've twisted the truth of our visit to the school, haven't they?"

"Olivia, we don't know that. The judge needs to study the reports."

"I know Basil. He'll make me a liar and you too. By the time he's finished twisting and denying the information, the visit to the school won't be worth a thing. John, you can be honest with me. Believe me, Basil has done worse than twist words. Tell me what the judge said at the meeting."

"He wasn't at the meeting. This meeting was between solicitors for the purpose of working out the details of the Christmas visit." However, I did expect more of a fight about the Christmas visit and frankly expected some push back regarding supervision. The judge was satisfied with the accommodation at Lavender Cottage and it might have been that you were not alone. It's hard to say. I could be wrong, and believe me lawyers of the Morton-Smith ilk are as poker faced as you can get, but I got a sense of concern, even fear. The over confidence of when we started was not there." John smiled and patted Olivia's arm. "Just a lawyerly feeling. Stay strong, Olivia, and enjoy your children. This is the first positive step we've had in a while. Children are the greatest blessing you

can have. Treasure it. Don't abuse it like your ex-husband."
John glanced at Katie with a strange expression. "I've taken
up too much of your time. I'll see you at 4 p.m. Christmas
Eve." John raised his hand in a goodbye gesture. "I'm late for
dinner with my daughter." He looked at Katie. "She said she
has some exciting news. Katie, do you know what it is?"

"Melanie and I had lunch today, so I have an inkling but she
should tell you." Katie closed the door behind him, feeling
proud of her ex. He had done a good job for Olivia. She
wondered if his proposed visit when Olivia's kids arrived was
necessary but it would be nice to see him after he heard he
was to be a grandpa.

Christmas Eve morning was busy with last minute preparations and a certain amount of apprehension as the afternoon
unfolded. Olivia paced the lounge, peering through the front
window and waiting for the children to arrive. Adam had
taken Sir Walter to the rose garden for advice on the roses
distressed by the early cold weather and some neglect because
of Adam's illness. Even Katie felt the tension. It was mostly
waiting for the children, but Katie was waiting for Piers, who,
not surprisingly, was late.

However, it was Piers' BMW that pulled up first. He
looked tired but happy to be home. She suspected he would
have preferred a quieter welcome. She hugged him and he
responded with a tighter hug, whispering, "I'm so glad to be
home. Is it going to be this busy all Christmas?"

"I'm afraid so but right now Olivia is waiting for the children
to arrive. It's kind of tense. I could do with some help."

"And, that you shall have. But first …" He didn't finish the sentence but took Katie's hand and pulled her from the busy lounge into the empty Morning Room. Kicking the door closed with his foot, he spun her around and kissed her. She responded with every ounce of passion.

"I miss you so much. I hate being apart. I wish I could lift the clinic and plop it on Main Street so I can walk to work and spend the rest of the time with you."

Katie pulled away. "We have work to do. I wish it could happen, but we both know it is a fantasy. I'm grateful you're home. Let's enjoy Christmas!"

"You look worried? Is something wrong?" Piers put his arms around her waist, speaking into her ear, which made her shiver in delight.

Pulling away, she said with a giggle, "Stop that!" Katie thought for a moment, the giggle long gone. "I'm worried that Basil might change his mind and Olivia will be devastated. Plus, by all accounts, the boy is not exactly a pleasant child."

"You worry too much. Between us, Adam, Cyril and Rick, there will be enough father figures here tonight to cope with a spoiled ten-year-old brat."

"You're right," Katie said but she was not convinced. Jonathan Moreland was a handful. Suddenly John sprang to mind. She hadn't told Piers. "Um, you can add another to that list. John will be here."

"John! Why?"

"To be honest, I'm not sure. He said he'd be here when the children arrived. I have no idea how long he's staying."

"I suppose you invited him for dinner." Piers' voice was sharp.

"No, I did not," Katie snapped back. Her face broke into a smile. "Are you jealous?"

"Of course not." Piers blushed slightly and lightened his voice, adding, "He's not a bad fellow. It's just awkward, that's all. I hear activity. We'd better join them."

The front door was open. John had arrived and stood with Olivia at the garden gate as the black limousine pulled up. The chauffeur got out, nodded, and said, "Good afternoon, Lady Thesleton!" Katie noticed the use of Olivia's title that was no longer applied but he chose to use it out of respect. His manner had an implied understanding, possibly frustration, as he spoke, "Master Jonathan is …" He paused, raising an eyebrow, "Shall we say upset, milady?"

"I understand, Ernest. And thank you for bringing the children."

"It is my pleasure." Ernest opened the doors for the children and gathered their knapsacks, not quite sure who to hand them to. Adam stepped forward. "I'll take those for you."

The children stood by the car, looking forlorn, until Olivia opened her arms and Poppy ran to her. Jonathan stood with his arms folded in front of him, very angry.

"I am instructed to collect the children at noon tomorrow." Ernest doffed his hat and gave Olivia an understanding smile. The limousine's wheels whipped up some gravel as the large Rolls Royce attempted a three point turn in the narrow lane.

Katie had noticed how easily Olivia slipped into her ladyship role. Having gotten used to a different Olivia, it seemed odd to hear the chauffeur call her milady. She guessed Ernest had a lot of sympathy for her and, like most staff of a large manor house, he would see behind the scenes. But whether from loyalty to the family or not, she thought that might be true in the Downton Abbey era, but today it was more likely fear of losing his job. She imagined chauffeur positions were not too plentiful in 2021. Ernest would keep the secret of his lordship's abuse and say nothing. *Mores the pity,* she thought.

Olivia held Poppy's hand and gestured towards Jonathan with the other. "Come give me a hug, Jonathan." Jonathan stood, legs apart, arms still folded, his angry expression now stubborn determination. "Let's get settled. Katie has some treats for you." Jonathan stood his ground and Olivia's voice was beginning to tremble. "We could go and see the boats in marina afterwards. You like boats."

John touched her arm in sympathy and gave her a smile. "Olivia, take Poppy inside. I'll talk to Jonathan." John walked towards the boy and started talking to him. Olivia hesitated but put her arm around Poppy and went inside.

Katie had a plate of decorated gingerbread biscuits and a bottle of cream soda waiting for them. Poppy tucked in, giggling at the faces of the gingerbread men. Jonathan and John finally joined them. Katie gave John a questioning look, which was returned with a subtle nod but no words were exchanged. She handed the plate of cookies around and offered the grownups tea. At first Jonathan refused the biscuits but when the plate was left on the table he picked up the largest gingerbread and shoved it in his mouth. She felt sorry for him. He was just a sad little boy forced to grow up in a toxic environment. She had the urge to cuddle him. That was what he needed.

"Hello! Is there room for us?" Judy's voice called as Sam and Lily came bounding in through the French door. Buddy Boy and Arthur jumped up to greet them. Poppy squealed with delight at the sight of the dogs, although she did hang on to her mother, afraid to touch them.

"Judy, come in! Let me introduce you to Poppy or should I

say Penelope?" Katie directed her question to the little girl.

"No. I like Poppy. That's what Mummy calls me," Poppy said, looking up at Olivia.

"Poppy, and this young man is Jonathan. Olivia's children are staying with us tonight. And children, these fine dogs are Sam and Lily." Buddy Boy and Arthur pushed their way to the front. Katie laughed. "And these two are Buddy Boy and Arthur." Katie noticed how Jonathan relaxed and bent down to pet the dogs. Lily sidled up to him and put her paw on his arm. Jonathan looked up at Katie with the warmest smile.

"You always loved our dogs." Olivia put her hand on his shoulder. Katie almost gasped as Jonathan glared at her with hatred.

"Dogs are stupid and dirty. Father got rid of them. He shot them. I want to go home now," Jonathan kicked at Lily and folded his arms again. Surprisingly, Lily moved closer to him and licked his hand.

"Jonathan, you are being rude. You are a guest in this house. We are staying until tomorrow." Olivia spoke with the authority of a parent and Jonathan mumbled something.

"I made a gingerbread house that needs decorating," Katie said cheerfully. "Who would like to help me?"

"Me, me," Poppy said with her hand up as if she was in class. Olivia looked at her son. "Jonathan?"

"Must I?" Jonathan sighed.

"You know cake decorating isn't really a boy's thing," Piers said, raising an eyebrow towards Katie. "I have an idea. Jonathan, would you like to come see my boat and we can leave the girls to do the gingerbread house."

Jonathan replied, moderately more enthusiastic, "Thank you, sir!"

"Anyone else want to come?"

"I'd like to join you," John said.

The room went quiet and Katie held her breath. Her husband and ex-husband were about to take a distraught kid on a boat ride. She wondered who would be thrown in the canal first.

"Of course," Piers answered. "I can always use an extra pair of hands."

Arthur and Buddy Boy were already at the door, the word 'boat' familiar to them. Piers laughed. "And these two will be joining us."

"Can the retrievers come too?" Jonathan asked.

"Sorry," Piers said, eyeing Jonathan cautiously. "Sam and Lily love the water and it's almost impossible to stop them jumping in the canal. It isn't safe at night and the resulting wet-dog smell is not pleasant." Piers screwed up his nose and Jonathan actually giggled. "We'll be back in hour. If the answering service calls, text me." Katie nodded, having forgotten he was on call.

"Okay, let's get this gingerbread house decorated. Poppy, what colour should we make it?"

Poppy picked the red icing. Neither Olivia nor Judy were the artistic types and Katie suggested they retire to the lounge with a glass of wine, while Katie and Poppy worked their magic. Poppy chatted almost constantly about coming to live with her mother. She wouldn't talk about her father. Katie saw how afraid she was and changed the subject to school, which wasn't much better. She was shy and the other girls picked on her, but the house-mother they called Matron was nice. Katie wondered if that was who wrote the report for John and was the cause of the court delay.

"All finished," Katie said as Poppy put the last snowman into the icing. "We let that dry and you can have a piece after dinner."

Poppy ran off to sit with her mother and Katie started to put the food out. She traditionally had a cold dinner on Christmas Eve, but there was a lot of food.

John, Piers and Jonathan returned from the boat and Katie eyed them carefully. No one was wet and there seemed to be no black eyes. In fact, the three were chatting about wildlife. They had spotted a badger on the river bank. The terrier instinct in Arthur had made him bark. They praised Jonathan for his quick thinking in grabbing Arthur's collar before he jumped off the boat.

Katie served dinner and the meal was uneventful. Adam and Sir Walter insisted on doing the clean-up, which made Katie smile as she was sure Sir Walter had staff to do these things. But it gave the two time to chat about roses and darts. The boat ride had calmed Jonathan, although he was still hostile towards Olivia. Katie could see how much it hurt her. John had just stayed. It was hard to suggest he leave after the boat ride and much to her surprise, John and Piers were being friendly towards each other. John had winked at her a couple of times, making her uncomfortable. She wasn't sure if he was taunting her or flirting. When he kissed her cheek as he was leaving, his gratitude at being included was genuine and she decided he was just being appreciative and that seemed okay. He hadn't mentioned Melanie's baby news and she wondered if he knew but it occurred to her that was what the kiss was for.

Olivia took the children up to bed. Katie and Piers curled up in front of the fire. Judy sat, reading, the dogs were snoring at her feet. Katie leaned her head on Piers' shoulder, smiling at the dogs. Arthur snuggled up to Lily's belly and Sam lay a protective paw across Buddy Boy. All were snoring with the occasional yip or growl as they dreamed of what, no one knew. A very mixed Christmas Eve. Not what she was used to but that seemed okay too. As the fire died down, they pulled out the presents, labelled from Santa and loaded up the tree before saying sleeping good-nights and going to bed.

A Troubled Start to Christmas

Katie woke up with a start. Something slammed above her head. Piers rolled over and pushed himself up on his elbows. "What the hell was that?"

"I don't know but it came from the Marina Suite." Katie glanced at the clock. 3 a.m. Next, loud voices. There was no mistaking that Olivia and Jonathan were yelling at each other.

"Should we intervene?" Katie said. "They're going to wake everyone up."

"I'll go. The kid talked to me on the boat and he definitely has it in for his mother. I suspect he's brainwashed by his father."

Piers climbed the stairs two at a time, tapped on the door and whispered, "Is everything all right, Olivia? We heard a bang."

Olivia opened the door a crack. "We're fine. Jonathan fell out of bed. Sorry to disturb you."

"If it's crowded, Jonathan could sleep down here on the sofa."

Suddenly the door flew open and Jonathan ran down the stairs. "Olivia, you're crying. What happened?"

She shook her head and whispered, "I'm fine. My son can be difficult. If you wouldn't mind settling him on the sofa? Good night!" She closed the door and Piers heard her tell Poppy to go back to sleep and all went quiet.

Katie had gathered a pillow and blanket and Jonathan was already lying on the sofa. Hearing the commotion, Judy had appeared at the top of the stairs with Sam at her side. Lily continued down the stairs, giving Jonathan a paw and then lay beside the sofa. Jonathan reached out to pat her but did not say a word. Lily licked his hand and looked up at Judy with her head to one side, as if to say, 'I'll stay here.' Katie switched the light out and all went back to bed.

Katie lay in Piers arms, soaking up his warmth, and thinking about Olivia and Jonathan. She couldn't imagine what it was like to have your son dislike you. Basil must have said some terrible things about Olivia and, yet, Katie had the impression the boy was afraid. Not of Olivia, but what his father might do if he said or did anything kind. She could see snowflakes drifting by the window. "A white Christmas," she whispered, realizing Piers was fast asleep.

It seemed as though she had only just closed her eyes when Piers' phone rang. The screen lit up the room as he answered in a croaky voice. "Hello. Dr Bannister." He listened before saying, "Thank you, I'll call them. I have the number."

Katie switched on the light and glanced at the clock as the numbers rolled over to 04.50, not even five o'clock. Piers sat on the side of the bed, rubbing his face. Katie kissed him. "You look how I feel. What a night. Do you have to go out?"

"Maybe. I'll call first."

"I'll make some coffee while you make the call." The floor felt cold on Katie's feet as she slipped into her fluffy slippers and wrapped her housecoat around her. The kitchen seemed bright even before she put the light on. She peered through the window to a blanket of white and a misty moon reflecting the snow covered lawn. She made the coffee and opened the backdoor for Arthur and Buddy Boy who chose not to venture out as a blast of cold air greeted them. Katie laughed as they curled up in their bed and immediately went to sleep.

"You two have the right idea." Katie patted each head.

"I agree," Piers said, slipping his arms around Katie's waist. "I'd like to go back to bed."

"What about the call?"

"I spoke with the night nurse and I've adjusted the patient's medication. If that works, I won't have to visit. She'll call me back in an hour and let me know."

"Light the fire and we'll have a quiet coffee. It's too late to go back to bed."

Piers lit the fire and disappeared into the lounge. Jonathan was fast asleep and Lily was now on the couch, stretched out by his side. He crept past them and picked up one of the presents from under the tree, creeping back to the Morning Room.

"How's Jonathan?" Katie asked.

"Sleeping with Lily. He's a troubled kid, but he can't be all bad or Lily wouldn't have adopted him."

"It is sad to think his father got rid of his dog. Poor kid."

Katie put two coffees down and Piers pulled her onto his lap, kissed her and handed her the box. "Merry Christmas!"

Katie gave a chuckle and returned the kiss, handing Piers a much larger box. "Merry Christmas to you!"

"Great minds think alike." Pier kissed her again. "You first."

Katie pulled off the wrapping paper and ran her fingers over a blue velvet box and carefully opened it. "You remembered!"

"Of course, I did. How could I forget? We had a wonderful day browsing and you stopped and stared at Watts Jewellers' window. Your eyes lit up and you said, 'my grandmother had a bracelet just like that.' Then you told me it had disappeared and you couldn't find it after she died."

Katie lifted a delicate charm bracelet from the box and Piers fastened it around her wrist. Tears filled her eyes as she kissed him, so touched that he had remembered and kept it a secret for months.

"My turn." Piers lifted the box. "It's heavy and solid." He ripped the paper off to reveal an exquisite wooden box with an antique sexton inside. "Oh my goodness, where did you find this? Cyril?"

"No, I found it online. It's not antique, but a nice replica. Cyril did give his seal of approval, grudgingly I may add, and I had to listen to his opinion of the flaws of all reproductions."

Piers hugged her. "I love it. It will take pride of place on *Tranquil Days* and it works so I can play around with it. I think this is going to be a great Christmas. It has certainly started well." No sooner were the words out of his moth than his phone rang again. "I may have spoken too soon. It's the nursing home."

Katie got up to let Piers answer his call. The expression on his face told her he was going to have to make a house call. She rattled the bracelet on her wrist, grateful for his loving thought and that they had at least been able to have time together and exchange gifts. She tried not to be disappointed, assuming he would be gone most of Christmas morning.

Pulling her hat over her ears, Katie went outside to help Piers brush the snow off the car. Normally she relished snow but not today, even if it was Christmas. The roads would be slippery and Piers had to drive almost to Nottingham. He had tried to call an ambulance but A&E said they were full to the gunnels and Piers explained he just could not subject an old man to a long wait when he could treat him at the nursing home.

Opening the back door, four dogs came flying out, running and rolling through the snow. Judy was pouring coffee and Poppy was jumping up and down, wanting to know when they could open their presents.

"Good morning!" Katie said with a shiver as she hung up her jacket. "Piers has been called to the nursing home so we'll go ahead without him. Poppy, is your mummy up?"

"She's in there," Poppy pointed to the living room. "Cleaning up the mess."

"Mess!" Katie frowned, wondering what had happened. Opening the door, she gasped. Jonathan was standing in front of the Christmas tree, his arms folded. Presents had been kicked all over the lounge and Olivia was gathering ripped wrapping paper and broken boxes. She looked up at Katie, tears streaming down her face. In a halting voice between sobs, she declared, "I don't know what got into him. I am so sorry."

In the short time that Katie had been outside and the dogs had bounded into the garden, Jonathan had kicked, ripped and destroyed as many gifts as he could before Olivia stopped him.

Katie stared at Jonathan. "Why would you do this? We have been nothing but kind to you and some of those gifts Santa left for you and your sister."

Jonathan shrugged his shoulders and said, "I don't want anything. And Santa doesn't exist. Are you stupid?"

Katie heard Olivia gasp and sob, and she'd had enough. "I have had enough of your insults and bad behaviour." She grabbed his arm and dragged him into the Morning Room and through to her office, closing the door.

"Jonathan Moreland, I understand life has not been easy for you lately but everyone is doing their best. Your mother worked hard so you could spend some of Christmas with her and your sister here with friends. I don't care what you think of your mother but you will stop the insults now. She loves you more than anyone else in this world and if you think your father loves you like that, you are mistaken."

Jonathan burst into tears. "But Father told me Mother didn't deserve me and she hated me." Katie saw fear and hatred in his eyes, for whom she wasn't sure. "My mother is a whore!"

Shocked, Katie kept her cool. "Your mother is no such thing and how do you know words like that? Do you know the meaning of that word?"

"That's what father called her. He said it means she sleeps with other men. He said she stole all his money and now she's telling lies about him in that court thing."

"I can tell you for certain that your mother does not sleep with other men." Katie wondered if Basil was aware of Olivia's relationship with Cyril. The children hadn't mentioned him and Katie had suggested he not be there while the children were. "And your father took everything away from her, leaving her penniless and told a lot of lies about her. The accusations are not true. Your mother is in court because she loves you and Poppy and wants to see more of you."

"I need to be with my father. I am the heir to the title and estate." Jonathan had stopped crying and made the last statement forcefully.

"So you are and that is a heavy burden to carry. The first thing you need to learn is respect and to be responsible for others. Do you think your behaviour has been responsible or respectful since you've been here?"

Jonathan shook his head and, for the first time, Katie saw a hurt, vulnerable and very sad little boy. She put her arm around him. "Oh sweetheart, let your mother love you. Your father can teach you about being a lord and, if you want to live with him, nobody is going to stop you. But let your mother teach you to love." Surprised, Katie felt him relax and melt in her arms. She rocked him a little.

"Father will be very angry if I can't live with him and he punishes when he's angry. I need to live on the estate. I thought if I misbehaved, Mother wouldn't want me."

Katie didn't agree with his rationale but it did explain some things. "Your mother will not drag you away from the estate if you don't want to go but she would like you to visit. Can you do that?"

He pulled away from her. "I think so."

"I also think you need to apologize to her and this behaviour has to stop." Katie gave him an extremely stern look and then smiled. "Bad behaviour is unbecoming for Lord Thesleton in waiting."

He gave her a warm smile. "I like that. I like you and Dr Bannister. I like his boat."

"Well, if you behave, I am sure you can come visit and Piers will take you on the boat. Perhaps you can take your mother too. But for now, enjoy Christmas morning with us and then,

224

this afternoon, you can be with your father."

Katie took some tissues and wiped his face and ran her fingers through his hair. "There. You look very handsome, Lord Thesleton in waiting. Let's join the others."

Jonathan stepped into the kitchen hesitantly and almost bumped into his mother. He recoiled slightly and Katie heard him take a breath. "Mother, I am sorry for behaving badly." His words were stilted and lacked feeling but, Katie thought, it was a start.

"Thank you, Son. I don't understand…" Olivia saw Katie shake her head and added, "I appreciate that."

The mess in the lounge had been cleaned up and tea, coffee, shortbread and eggnog were set out on the coffee table. Katie noticed the breakfast table was set. "You have been busy bees. Thank you. Who will do the honours of passing out the presents?"

"I will," Poppy said

"I'll help," Jonathan said, smiling at his sister.

Katie checked the time as they finished breakfast. It was only 10:30 and she was already exhausted. Piers had called to say the roads were bad and he hoped he'd be home by noon. Although it was not her usual happy Christmas, the atmosphere had improved. Olivia asked what she had said to calm Jonathan. She told her they'd had a chat and to enjoy his company now and they could talk later. The last thing Katie wanted was to get into discussion involving Basil or the custody case. It was a good decision as Basil phoned Olivia, accusing her of mistreating Jonathan. It appeared the boy had called his father, demanding he send Ernest to fetch them. The kid had changed his mind after talking to Katie, but it seemed the chauffeur was on his way. Olivia had run to her room in tears yet again. Jonathan had displayed his temper, muttering something no one heard, fortunately, and Poppy was in tears because she didn't want to go back to the estate. Adam and Sir Walter had escaped to the pub, leaving Katie alone in the empty lounge, staring at the Christmas Tree and feeling as though she'd been dragged through a hedge backwards, an expression her mother used that made her smile.

The grandfather clock struck twelve times and there was still no sign of either Ernest or Piers. Katie checked the turkey which had filled the cottage with its delightful smell. She put the plum pudding in the steamer and made some snacks as dinner would be early and she refused to make lunch.

Piers and Ernest arrived at the same time and Katie heard them chatting and decided to join them.

"Ms Bannister, are the children ready? It will be a long drive back and his lordship will not be pleased if we are late."

Olivia must have heard them because she had thrown a shawl around her shoulders and was carrying a weeping little girl. "Ernest, Poppy is very upset to be going home."

Ernest tickled her chin. "I happen to know that Santa Clause has left a mountain of presents under the tree and Mrs Combs has some special treats. If you are good, I'll let you go in the kitchen to get them. How does that sound?"

"Mrs Combs is our cook," Jonathan announced. "Come on, Poppy. It will be fun. Perhaps Mrs Bannister will let you take the gingerbread house home."

"Of course. I'll fetch it for you." At this suggestion, Poppy let Ernest take her from her mother and put her in the car. Ernest took the gingerbread house and placed it on the floor on the passenger's side of the front seat.

The limousine drove off and a tearful Olivia waved as it

reached Main Street. Katie guided her into the house, trying to be sympathetic but the tears were beginning to be irritating. Piers poured everyone but himself a drink.

"Not drinking?" Katie asked

"I may have to go out again. The roads are bad. There's not much traffic but a layer of ice on the road surface. I skidded a couple of times." Piers sighed and rubbed his forehead. He looked tired. "I don't think we'll do this long distance on call thing again."

"I agree. It's not much of a Christmas with all the coming and going." Katie tried to keep the annoyance out of her voice but the thought of Piers leaving again had put her in a bad mood.

She scowled when the phone rang, thinking it might be a call for Piers. She brightened as she heard her daughter's voice. "Hello, Mum. Just letting you know we are on our way; the roads are a bit slow."

"Well, at least that's good news," Katie said. "Melanie and Phil are on their way."

"That's good but," Piers held his phone up, "the nursing home. I have to go. I'll be back before dinner."

Katie was not happy and was about to tell him so, when Adam and Sir Walter returned from the pub, quite merry. Judy teased them as they claimed only to have had a couple of beers. Mary and Bob followed together with Melanie and Phil.

Welcoming her guests made Katie feel a little more like Christmas. Cyril arrived and comforted Olivia, which stopped her crying. Katie thought the wine might have helped too. She was pleased to hear laughter and bantering as she adjusted the oven, dinner would be late.

A Rollercoaster Holiday

K atie had planned to serve Christmas dinner at three and now it was past four o'clock and Piers was not home. She texted to find out where he was. He replied he was leaving the nursing home but it would be a long drive and to start dinner. She surveyed the room. Her guests were polite, but they looked tired and hungry. Adam and Sir Walter had drunk too much without eating. She needed to get the dinner on the table.

"Piers is on his way but the roads are bad so he said to start without him." Katie felt her throat constrict. She wanted Piers to be here to carve the turkey. *Well, it can't be helped,* she thought. Taking a deep breath she added, "Melanie, give me a hand, please. Phil, perhaps you could carry the turkey in? It's too heavy for me. And, as Piers isn't here, would you do the honours of carving?"

Everyone sat around the table, all eyes on the door as Phil entered with a large golden turkey and Katie followed with numerous dishes until the table was full. The room went quiet except for the clinking of cutlery and the occasional, 'Oh this is so good.'

It always pleased Katie to see her guests enjoying an amazing meal but she not only missed Piers, but worried about the slick roads. He should have been home by now. Not able to wait any longer, she excused herself and went to text him, just as the phone lit up. Piers' voice said, "First, don't panic. I'm okay." His voice was trembling he sounded angry.

Katie could hear voices in the background. "Piers, where are you? We've started dinner without you." She was annoyed and mirrored his anger in her reply.

"Sorry! I was in a bit of an accident."

"What!" Katie almost screeched into the phone.

"I'm okay, which is more than I can say for the car. It's a bloody write-off." Piers spat the last words, took a breath and added, "I'm talking to the police now, exchanging insurances etc. Do you think Adam could come and fetch me?"

"Are you sure you're all right? No injuries or anything?"

"I'm fine and so is the other driver. We just skidded on the ice. No ambulances, but we had to call the police. Can someone pick me up? I'm really looking forward to turkey. You didn't eat it all, did you?"

Katie laughed, knowing he was trying to ease her worries. But his irritability had not escaped her. "No, lots of turkey left. Where are you? Someone will pick you up. It won't be Adam. He's been drinking."

"I'm on the Willington Road, just past Barrow, near the old vicarage."

"Okay, someone will be there shortly. Stay warm. Do you have your Parker on?"

"I'm fine. See you soon."

All eyes were on Katie as she clicked her phone off. "Piers has been in an accident. Slippery roads. He's okay but the car is a write-off. He needs someone to pick him up. Not you, Adam, you've been drinking."

"I'll go," Bob offered. "I'm not a wine drinker." He lifted his almost full glass. "I only had couple of sips, so I'm good to drive."

"Thank you, Bob, but do be careful. Piers said the roads are icy." Katie was grateful but she also felt bad because she knew Bob didn't drink wine and she had forgotten to offer him a beer. Although, under the circumstances, it had worked out well.

"My truck is heavy and has four-wheel drive so it's not a problem. Save me some pudding. I won't be long."

The rest of the table finished dinner and Katie made a plate for Piers and, with the remainder of Bob's dinner, she put it in the oven to keep warm. Everyone elected to wait until Piers and Bob returned before tucking into plum pudding. It was a welcome rest to digest the copious amounts of turkey that everyone had consumed.

Mary heard the familiar engine of Bob's truck pull into their driveway next door. "Katie, they're back."

Bob and Piers came in through the rose garden, a shortcut from Bob's driveway, laughing and rubbing their hand from the cold. Bob called, "We're back!"

Katie ran to greet and put her arms around Piers. He seemed fine. She couldn't see any cuts or bruises and he was in good spirits. "Come in! I'm so glad you're back. Bob, here's a beer.

Sorry, I forgot earlier. Piers, would you like beer or wine?"

"I'm going to have a Scotch to settle my nerves. It was quite an ordeal."

"Are you all right?" Katie gave him a worried frown.

"I couldn't be better," he said, holding up a glass half full of Scotch. "And I'll be even better after this. Merry Christmas, everyone! Now where's the turkey?"

Everyone went back to the table. More wine was poured while Bob and Piers ate dinner. Katie stood up, glass in hand and said, "I'd like to make a toast to friends and family." Glasses clinked as they repeated, "To friends and family." Katie motioned to Melanie to stand up, who, in turn, grabbed Phil's arm. Katie raised her glass again. "Congratulations to my daughter and husband and welcome to a new baby in the family." A roar of congratulations with clinking almost to the point of breaking followed.

"Congratulations to you both," Piers said.

"Would someone switch out the lights please?" Katie asked as she slipped into the kitchen. The guests drummed their fingers on the table as the lights went out. Katie carried a flaming Christmas pudding into the dining room.

It may have been a weird Christmas for Katie, but it turned out to be fun and Melanie and Phil's news was the icing on the cake. By ten o'clock, everyone had either retired or walked home. Katie and Piers put the food away and went to bed.

Katie had the sense that something was wrong. Piers had drunk far more than she had ever seen him drink. He was a pleasant drunk and laughed a lot, but underneath, something was going on. They undressed in silence and got into bed. Piers wrapped his arms around her, almost clinging as he kissed her good night.

Unable to keep quiet she said, "Piers, is everything all right? Are you worried about the car?"

"I'm fine. Very tired and I drank too much tonight. Go to sleep."

Katie lay beside him and smiled. He was already snoring. She thought he might have a thick head in the morning. He had said nothing about the accident or the car and she knew it had upset him but couldn't shake the feeling there was something else. She'd worry about that tomorrow. Having drunk several glasses of wine herself, she soon joined him in sleep.

"Would you like a cup of coffee?" Adam whispered, peering through Katie and Piers' bedroom door. "It's almost 7:30."

Katie sat up in bed. "Oh, my goodness. I slept in." She looked at Piers, still sound asleep. "Shush! I'll be right out." Katie grabbed her housecoat and tiptoed out of the bedroom.

"I can't believe I slept so long." Katie opened the dining room door to an empty table. Where is everyone?"

"All asleep, except Judy, and she's taken the dogs for a walk. Too much wine and an eventful evening."

"It sure was eventful. Not our usual Christmas. I am so glad we didn't have new guests this year. What a terrible Christmas Day!"

"It was fine. You might not have enjoyed it and poor Piers didn't, at least not until later, but everyone else did. You put on a great meal in spite of the interruptions. We had a good time, albeit we drank more than usual. Walter's still sleeping and so are Melanie and Phil. I took tea and coffee up but brought it back. No point in disturbing folks."

"Thanks for the support." Katie opened and closed the fridge door. "I'll just do a cold breakfast today. Scones and croissants with preserves, fruit and maybe some cheese. Then everyone can help themselves." Katie started plating the fruit.

"Is Piers on call today? I was wondering about his car," Adam said, nonchalantly. Katie suspected he was curious as was she.

"No, Rick took over last night and is on call today and tomorrow. Piers hasn't said anything about the accident but he doesn't have a car. He'll probably use mine."

"Did I hear my name?" A pale, sleepy man emerged from the bedroom. "Do we have any Aspirin? I've a bit of a headache."

Katie grinned. "We do. Perhaps too much whiskey last night?"

"Yep. I was upset about my car. I think it's a write-off." Piers reached for his coffee and the Aspirin and winced, putting his hand on his mid-riff. "It hurts when I move."

"Let me look." Katie lifted his T-shirt. "Oh, my goodness, you have a black and purple bruise across your torso." Katie gave him a stern look, annoyed because he'd obviously been hurt more than he was admitting. "You didn't mention if an ambulance was called. Was it?"

He looked down at his abdomen. "That's the seatbelt. Judging by that bruise, it saved my life. I'm surprised I didn't feel it last night."

"I think the whiskey numbed things," Katie said with a cheeky grin and then realized he hadn't answered her question. "Was it?"

"Was what?"

"Don't play games with me. You mentioned the police but not paramedics. When are you going to tell me what happened?" Katie words clipped as they often did when she was angry.

Pier expression was contrite. He gave a sigh. "There's not much to tell and I didn't want to upset you on Christmas Day. A car coming towards me lost control on the ice and slammed right into me. We both spun around, I don't know how many times. It's a bit of a blur. My car stopped spinning when we plunged into the ditch. It was pretty terrifying. The car following him happened to be an off-duty cop and called it in. The police were there in ten minutes and yes, an ambulance followed and a tow truck. They must use police scanners, because two appeared literally on the tail of the patrol car."

"Keep talking," Katie said. "I have to get breakfast ready."

"The police took statements, asked if we'd been drinking. The other man had and so they breathalysed both of us. I was okay but the other guy was over the limit. The paramedics checked him out and the cop put him in the back of a panda car."

"And, what about you? Did they check you over?"

"One of the paramedics recognized me from the nursing home. He checked for head injury. Asked if I wanted to go to A&E. I told him I was shaken but okay. I had already called you for a ride and both the police and paramedics where okay with me coming home. My poor car was hooked onto a tow truck and I waved goodbye to my favourite car. Like I said, not much to tell."

"From the sound of it, Piers, you are lucky to be alive. Do you think it was ice or drink that caused it," Adam asked.

"It's hard to tell. Depending on how intoxicated he was, his reactions would be slow. On a normal dry road, he might have been okay." Piers nodded towards Katie, who was carrying a platter into the dining room and whispered to Adam, "I don't want to worry Katie, but the police said I was lucky to get out

234

of the car alive, let alone unhurt. It shook me up, Adam. I saw my life pass before me. I'm still shaking."

"You need to take it easy for a couple of days. You are in shock." Adam raised an eyebrow. "Right?"

"Yes. Is the doctor getting a lecture?"

Katie answered. "He certainly is and I agree you are in shock and need rest."

The weather remained cold for most of the week between Christmas and New year but there were no incidents. Piers recovered and returned to work, driving Katie's car while the insurance decided what they would do about his. It was not repairable but the insurance company seemed reluctant to cut a cheque. Waiting for the police report was the excuse they used. Piers chose not to come home on his off-call days and because of the weather, Katie agreed. It wasn't worth the risk and she could use Adam's car in the interim.

Dr Stephanie Ward presented herself at the clinic two days earlier than expected, much to Rick and Piers' delight, especially when she offered to take the calls over New Year.

The insurance company finally cut a cheque and Piers immediately went to the car dealership to pick out a new one. Four-wheel drive was a must. It was a blue, General Motors SUV, not his beloved BMW, but it had all the bells and whistles you could want and he felt safe driving it to Springsville on New Year's Eve afternoon. Katie had planned a dinner party, partially to celebrate both Rick and Piers having time off together. A holiday celebration spent with Cindy and Rick was a rare treat. George and Nancy Duthie and Olivia and Cyril were invited. A small party by Katie's standards, but after the disastrous Christmas, she was looking forward to the more intimate gathering. It was just three couples. Adam had gone to stay with Sir Walter for New Year.

Katie assumed Piers wanted to make a dramatic entrance with his new car as he had called from Main Street. She was waiting at the gate as he drove onto Marina Lane.

Piers jumped out of car with a broad grin and said, "So, what do you think? Do you like it? It drives really well and I feel safe in it. That accident took the wind out of me." Piers put his arm around Katie.

"I love it. The colour is gorgeous and leather seats in the interior, very posh, and that new-car smell. I'm glad you like it. I think it's a safer car than the BMW. I won't worry so much when you're on the road. Now, I have work to do and you need to change. Our guest will be arriving for cocktails shortly."

Olivia and Cyril were staying at Lavender Cottage so they were the first to arrive in the lounge. Katie was putting the finishing touches to the table. She looked up to see Cyril take Olivia's hand and kiss it. She looked into his eyes, only seeing him. *Two people very much in love,* she thought with a smile. She knew how wonderful that felt. A knock on the door brought in both the Duthies and Rick and Cindy. They had met in the driveway.

Piers entertained their guests with cocktails while Katie put the finishing touches to dinner before calling everyone to the table. The first course shrimp cocktail, mostly because it was Piers' favourite, followed by roast goose, which was becoming a New Year tradition in the Bannister household. So was Katie's chocolate cheesecake.

It always pleased Katie when her guests took their time

and savoured the meal. It was close to midnight before they finished, although the last hour had been mostly conversation over coffee and liqueurs.

"It's time for champagne," Piers declared and brought out a cold bottle, untying the wire from the cork. Everyone held their breath, waiting for the pop. Pop it did; the cork flying across the room. Champagne flutes in hand, everyone began to count down, 10, 9, 8, 7, 6, 5, 4, 3, 2, Happy New Year! Each couple hugged and kissed before greeting friends with many cheers and wishes for a great year.

Piers poked the fire and threw another log on. Olivia and Cyril excused themselves and retired.

George leaned back in the big armchair, sipped his champagne and taking in the group around him. "I'm the oldest here. My future is different to yours. I should be thinking of retiring. The work is too much, but I love it. You two," George nodded towards Rick and Piers, "have your future ahead of you."

"Retirement is a good thing," his wife, Nancy, agreed. "But I'm not sure I'm ready for a full retirement. I'd just like things to slow down a bit. All doctors work too hard."

Cindy and Katie nodded in agreement. "Perhaps the New Year is a good time to make resolutions," Cindy said. "Rick and Piers, how about a resolution to spend more time with family?"

"I think we did, darling." Rick took a sip of champagne and raised his glass. "Hiring Stephanie Ward is a good start, don't you think?"

"It is and I think she is going to work out very well," Piers added.

"You have a new partner?" George asked.

"No, the practice is not quite big enough for three but too big for two, if you understand my meaning. We hired her as an employee but she is definitely partner material."

"Well done! I should have done that years ago and now I'm too set in my ways." George rubbed his chin. "An employee, you say. That might work for me too."

Nancy laughed. "I'll believe that when I see it. But I'm all for it. We need another holiday. That means a locum and they are hard to come by."

Rick stretched and yawned. "I think it's time to call it a night. I ordered a cab for 1:30. We'd better see how Dr Ward has managed in our absence."

"She's staying with you?" Katie asked. "It must be a bit crowded."

"We have plenty of room since Piers moved out." Rick frowned and glared at Cindy who had just kicked his shin. He took a breath and closed his eyes, obviously realizing what he had done.

"Moved out! Piers, what is this about?"

Piers cleared his throat and in a tight voice said, "Can we talk later?" The room went deathly silent when a sudden and loud car horn made everyone jump.

"Ah, that will be our taxi. I'll pick my car up tomorrow, Piers." Rick put his hand on Piers' shoulder and whispered, "I am so sorry. It just slipped out."

Katie smiled, holding her anger at bay as she waved goodbye to Cindy. George and Nancy were staying overnight so Katie showed them to the Rose Suite and wished them a good night.

Piers had retreated to the Morning Room, shaking. What was about to happen would ruin a wonderful evening and possibly much, much more.

The Truth Always Wins

Katie returned to the living room and briefly scanned the mess, thinking about Piers and why he'd not told her. She idly picked up glasses and put them on the table, stacked the dirty plates and coffee cups, stalling, afraid to confront Piers. It had been a wonderful evening and she didn't want to spoil it. But how could he lie to her? And where was he staying, if not at Cindy's? Her imagination ran wild? Was he escaping from her? Perhaps he didn't want to be married. Did he want to live in Nottingham or did he have another woman?

Stop speculating, Katie, and get to the truth. Taking a deep breath, she pushed the Morning Room door open, folded her arms in front of her and glared at Piers, sitting in the chair, petting Arthur on his knee.

"Please sit down and I will explain. But first, believe me, I am very sorry." Piers waited for her to sit.

"Sorry for what?" Katie snapped.

"For not telling you. Please let me explain."

"It had better be good." Her face was taught with anger and her throat burned with tears. Katie picked up Buddy Boy as he pawed her lap. He looked across at Arthur, both dogs well aware that something was wrong.

"It's hard to explain how this happened. It was so impulsive and so unlike me. I was exhausted, with the flu epidemic and the drive, in bad weather. You and I were snapping at each other. Cindy and Rick were the same, tired and frustrated with the long hours. I thought I had outstayed my welcome." He leaned towards her to take her hand and she didn't pull away. "A patient happened to mention she had a small flat for rent, but she was picky with her tenants and it didn't have parking. I don't know why, and this sounds crazy, but I heard myself saying, 'I'll take it.' I know, I should never have taken the flat without discussing it with you."

"No, you shouldn't! But I don't understand. Why didn't you discuss it with me?"

"I was afraid you'd say no. We did discuss this option and you were very upset. I recall getting an ear full about the sins of evil because your ex moved into a trendy condo."

"Yes, well, I did not want history to repeat itself. How much is this costing us?" Katie shook her head, trying to keep tears at bay. "What is it with men and flats?"

"Just three month's rent and the clinic will reimburse me. Katie, what can I say to make you understand? I just wanted somewhere to sleep when I couldn't get home. Cindy and Rick needed their space." He squeezed her hand. She didn't respond but she didn't pull away.

"When did you rent the flat?"

"The beginning of December. I told Rick and Cindy not

to say anything until I told you. Then I got pneumonia and when I was with you, I was afraid I'd spoil what time we had together. The more time that went by, the more difficult it became."

"December! You've been lying to me for a whole month?" Anger burst into Katie's voice.

"I didn't lie."

"You lied by omission, by letting me think you were at Cindy's place." Katie could feel tears creeping into the anger. She didn't want to cry. She was so angry at Piers, the deception and the hurt that she didn't want to feel. The memory of that hurt was too much.

"Where is this place?"

"It's a two minute walk from the office. One room, a microwave, kettle, coffee pot, a pullout couch and a bathroom. Not enough room to swing a cat." He tried to laugh but quickly took the grin off his face. "Katie, I know John hurt you. But I am not John. The only woman I'm interested in spending time with is you. I love you with all my heart. I only need a place to rest when I've worked a 14 or 16 hour day. I'm too tired to drive home and, frankly, when I'm that tired, I shouldn't be driving. You know that accident on Christmas Day shook me up. I would never drink and drive but is driving exhausted any different?"

She couldn't answer him. As angry as she was, she was being unfair. Piers was nothing like John, and she had seen him drive home exhausted, trying to hide it. He caught pneumonia because he was run down and there was the time he finished up in the ditch. Was that a fluke or was he tired? *Damn John! I was always a trusting person and it never occurred to me not to be, until John gave me a reason. Piers doesn't deserve my rhetoric over*

241

someone else's behaviour. Am I being dishonest?

"I hear what you're saying. I know you are nothing like John. I'm sorry if I implied you were. I am sad that you didn't feel you could talk to me. And, you're probably right, I would have been upset. But lying to me all this time. What else have you not told me?"

"Well, I had to be a bit sneaky when I bought the bracelet," he teased, waiting for her response. When she smiled, he continued. "Nothing else and I regret ever having deceived you in the first place. It's not an excuse but facing that commute was too much. I love you so much. I hate it when I upset you and I knew renting the tiny flat would do just that. I was wrong not to tell you. Can you forgive me?"

Katie wrestled with her feelings. She desperately wanted to forgive him, but the hurt was like a persistent wasp ready to sting. It was her ex that hurt her. If she had been honest with Piers, he wouldn't have been afraid to discuss it and she was as much at fault as him. And, if she was truly honest and rational, the flat in Nottingham was a good idea and solved the commute issue, which she admitted had been a massive problem from the beginning.

She smiled and squeezed his hand, leaning over to kiss him. "You are forgiven." She gave him a rather stern look. "Although you should have told me about it, I admit I am at fault too and I promise to discuss things in the future, even John, if he is getting in the way." Katie laughed. "That's a funny thing to say but I think that's what happened. Perhaps, because through Olivia and the custody battle, he has been in our life more than would be normal. I'll be glad when that's over."

"I hadn't thought about that but you're right and I have to admit, I felt a bit jealous."

"Well, don't! John is in my very distant past. There is one other thing we are both guilty of, albeit because we were trying to be kind to each other. The commute has always been an issue that we ignored so, for the record, I think the flat is a good idea."

"Really! I don't know what to say. I love you." Piers tried to pull her in his arms but the chairs made it awkward. He stood up and Arthur rolled to the floor. Buddy Boy jumped off Katie's knee and they embraced passionately. All was forgiven. The dogs sighed, curling up in their doggy-bed in the Morning Room knowing, they would not be welcome in the bedroom tonight.

New Year's Day was quiet. Piers and Katie were happy, but tired, as were their guests. George and Nancy came down for breakfast, looking relaxed and rested.

"Good morning," Katie said. "Would you like bacon and eggs?"

"Not for me," Nancy said, taking in the spread of pastries and fruit on the table. "One of Mary's scones and a nice cup of coffee is all I need. But George might like a cooked breakfast."

"If it's not too much trouble. Good morning, Katie," George said.

"Not at all. Both Piers and Cyril like an English breakfast. Bacon, eggs, sausage, tomato and few fried potatoes. I value your arteries too much to do old-fashioned fried bread."

George gave her a big grin. "I remember my dad eating that stuff every morning. No wonder he died of a heart attack. It's a good job things have changed. Where's Piers?"

"He's getting ready to take the dogs for a walk while I cook.

Would you like to join him?"

"That sounds like a splendid idea. Blow the cobwebs off." George joined Piers and they marched off with two eager dogs.

Nancy sat down at the dining room table. "I hope it's all right if I eat now."

"Of course. We don't stand on ceremony here. I'll wait before I start cooking. They will be gone for half an hour. Cyril and Olivia will be down shortly. Olivia is not a morning person. I might as well cook for everyone at the same time." Katie topped up her coffee. "Everything is ready in the kitchen so I'll join you. I am addicted to Mary's scones."

Katie enjoyed talking to Nancy. Both married to doctors, they had something in common. She appreciated having someone older and more familiar with the life and responsibilities of a GP's wife. She hated to admit it but she was being unfair to Piers and Nancy more or less confirmed it.

Breakfast was late, usually served at seven or eight it was already past ten in the morning but no one cared. They were all enjoying a pleasant time, chatting about the future and predicting what was to come in the New Year. The only person who didn't join in was Olivia.

She was anxious and tearful, worrying about the children and the upcoming judge's decision, or more questions and accusations. It seemed that Cyril was the only person who could comfort her. It had surprised Katie. She and Cyril did not always get along. He was arrogant and dismissive at times but, with Olivia, he had the patience of Job. Supporting her, even waiting on her, it was not hard to see that they were very much in love. She wondered if they would marry when the custody battle was settled. It had not escaped Katie, how careful they were, afraid Basil might make accusations of impropriety if he knew they were dating; especially as he would remember Cyril from her past.

By noon, everyone had left, leaving Piers and Katie to clean up and have a quiet afternoon.

"Katie, I have something to tell you." He gave her a warm smile. "This is in the vein of our new found 'tell all' thing."

"Goodness, I'm intrigued." Katie moved closer to him on the lounge sofa, leaning on his shoulder. She felt so safe and content. A flame burst on the log in the fireplace, throwing out some heat in contrast to the howling wind. A storm was closing in.

"George and I had a good talk when we walked the dogs this morning. Our sudden mood change last night was observed. Both he and Nancy are or were concerned about us."

"I got that impression from Nancy. We chatted while you were walking and she enlightened me on the difficulties and responsibilities of a GPs wife. I'm afraid I feel very guilty for some of the things I said."

"No need. We both made mistakes."

"So, what is this 'tell all'?" Katie asked, leaning forward and eager for the answer.

"George offered me a partnership in his practice, with the view of taking it over completely."

"Wow! He must like you a lot. Nancy told me he would never work with a partner. What did you say?"

"Not much. I was so surprised, I stared at him like an idiot. I've never thought of leaving the clinic. I'm an urban fellow. As I said before being a country doctor isn't my thing. But I thought about it and began to question my rational and realized it is the patient care that's important to me. George saw that in me before I did. He said I'd make a great country doctor because I care about my patients the same way he does. And I quote, 'Not like the city slickers who work from big clinics and treat diseases, not people.'"

"I'd agree with him but you and Rick don't work like city slickers. Are you considering George's offer?" Katie was trying to be neutral but she couldn't help thinking this might be the answer to the commute issue.

"Honestly, I don't know. George works harder than me. We know he does a lot of house calls and, when he's away, I'd be working alone 24/7. I like working with Rick. We just hired Stephanie and that will make a big difference. I don't think a rural practice is for me. The commute is an issue, but if you would give me your blessing to keep the flat, I'm sure we can make it work."

"The flat is no longer a problem. Just as long as you don't stay away too often." She put her head to one side, needing his assurance.

He kissed her cheek. "I promise only to stay when it's necessary."

"I'm sure the new doctor will ease the work load. Let's give it time and see how things work out. Now it's my turn for the 'tell all' thing. I would like you to consider George's offer. Maybe look at ways it could work, different locations, adding another doctor or setting up a clinic here, like you have in Nottingham."

"I don't know. I don't see myself as a country doctor. Setting up a clinic here maybe. But only if things don't work out in Nottingham. I promise I'll give it some thought."

"That's all I ask and, whatever you decide, I'm one hundred percent behind you." Katie crossed her fingers. She didn't know why but the country doctor option just seemed right to her. Yet it was so different to his current practice and there were many things to consider. How would Rick manage without him? That might strain the friendship. Setting up a clinic in Springsville would be a big job and risky. What were the financial implications? Was it such a good idea?

Final Decisions

The inclement weather with high winds, wet snow and below normal temperatures continued through the first week of January. Piers stayed at his tiny flat without guilt when he was on call and enjoyed the ride home in his new four-wheel-drive car, that handled the icy roads well.

Katie loved having him home more but she still worried about the commute and was convinced the local clinic was a good idea. For now, Piers seemed happy and the new doctor quickly fit into the routine. She got along with Pat, very important as Pat ruled the office, and the patients liked her. Dr Stephanie, as she liked to be called, certainly had a modern approach with the patients and they loved it, particularly the women and children. Katie liked the way she brought a fresh and cheerful atmosphere to the office. Piers smiled more and that made Katie happy. Things had certainly improved since Christmas.

The one exception was Olivia who seemed to get more anxious by the hour. Katie was pleased when she decided to return home so she could get ready to attend meetings with John. They were due back in court at the end of the week for what she hoped would be the judge's decision. The judge had asked to meet with Jonathan and Poppy in chambers without parents. John said this was a good sign. Olivia confided in Katie that she wasn't so sure, given Jonathan's hateful behaviour over Christmas. Katie agreed and understood Olivia's concern, not just because of Jonathan but whether or not Lord Thesleton had had time to coach, or brainwash, the children.

She felt sorry for Olivia, although that had not been the case when they first met. Massive changes, a bullying husband, a divorce and now poverty, had forced Olivia to be a normal person. According to Cyril, she was more like the young woman he knew years ago. But this new life was hard for her and having her children taken away was almost more than she could bear. Navigating the harsh reality of a normal world, that she did not understand, was difficult. Katie understood why she clung on to Cyril who had a similar background. She smiled to herself, acknowledging that they were two peas in pod and in love, although with all the tension Katie wondered if they realized it.

The stillness at Lavender cottage was so unusual that Katie found herself wandering from room to room. Lydia had finished the cleaning and had gone home early. There were no guests until the weekend and Adam was still at Sir Walter's place. She didn't feel like doing paperwork and closed the office door. The sun was streaming through the French doors, a rare event these days, and it felt warm. She opened them slightly and felt no cold wind.

"Okay, you two." She looked down at the dogs curled up in their daybed. "I think a long walk is in order." The word 'walk' immediately got their attention.

The muddy, slushy towpath was not easy to walk through but the dogs didn't mind. Arthur's belly seemed to drag through the slush and Buddy Boy's white curly coat appeared two tone brown. The dogs love it. Katie breathed in the fresh air and watched the sun slip behind the clouds, zipping up her jacket. She let the dogs run ahead and settled on the wooden stile to think. She giggled as she put her fist under her chin. It remained her of the famous sculpture *The Thinker* by Auguste Rodin. "What momentous thoughts will emerge?" she said, amused by her profound question. One thing she couldn't stop thinking about was Piers in practice with Dr Duthie. It seemed right but Piers had insisted he liked the urban practice. Yet he loved the country life, the people, the lifestyle. She had a vision of a small clinic that Piers could walk to everyday and honest country folks who appreciated his caring service. George Duthie was a great doctor. He and Piers got along so well and Katie really liked Nancy. She had given her some good advice. During the last conversation, she openly said she thought Piers would do well with George. Katie stood up and gave herself a shake. "Stop dreaming the impossible and appreciate what you have. Come, boys, time to go home!" The dogs came bouncing along, covered in mud. "Oh, in the tub for both of you. You're too muddy to even stop at Mary's." Patting her stomach, she added, "Which is probably a good thing after all the festive eating. I don't need another scone."

She let the dogs loose in the back garden and filled the tub with warm water. Tucking a dog under each arm she carried them to the bathroom. Neither were impressed but tolerated the scrubbing and relished the towel wrapping afterwards. Finally, Katie let them run to dry off. Then she noticed her mobile vibrating. She'd forgotten it was on silent and the house phone was flashing as well. She hit the house phone button first and heard an exasperated voice say, "Katie, this is Olivia. Where are you? You are not answering your mobile. Call me as soon as you can." She heard noise and voices in the background. She frowned and picked up her mobile to find two text messages, both just read 'Call me,' and two voicemails, all from Olivia."

"Katie, this is Olivia. Please call me as soon as you can. There has been a big development. John is on his way to pick me up. I am so scared. I must talk to you."

Katie clicked the next message, worried as Olivia sounded so distraught.

"It's me again. Where are you? The Moreland legal team called John, informing him that they had spoken to the judge and we have been called to the judge's chambers. I don't know what this means and John is being very quiet. He says he doesn't know either. I'll call the house phone. Perhaps you lost your phone or something. We are in John's car, arriving at the court house. Please call!"

Katie immediately called Olivia but only got voice email. She left a message and tried John's phone. That went straight into voicemail. She didn't leave a message, assuming they were already in the judge's chambers. Katie knew little about custody battles or the legal process so she couldn't even speculate. But, knowing Basil's disposition to bullying, she couldn't help question if he had done something devious. *No point in guessing or worrying at this point*, she thought. *I just have to wait for Olivia to call.*

Delighted with a distracting call from Judy, who she hadn't seen since Christmas, Katie settled in her blue chair with a cup of tea and listened to Judy's news. The shopping precinct project was finished and Judy booked a weekend stay before heading up north for a new project. A little light bulb flashed in Katie's head. Recalling some names, it was easy to remember who had booked during the off season as there were usually only one or two guests, mostly boat owners coming to check on their narrowboats. Katie checked the reservation calendar and grinned from ear to ear. Abe Shapiro was booked on the same weekend Judy planned to visit. Was Katie playing matchmaker? Perhaps. She had noticed how Judy and Abe had hit it off back in November and was surprised they hadn't met outside Springsville. They were both busy people so a little encouragement wouldn't hurt.

The mobile clicked as Katie typed yet another text. It was five minutes to five and no word from Olivia. She thought about calling John but changed her mind. Her mobile rang and without checking the caller, she answered, expecting to hear Olivia but it was Pat from the office.

"Hello, this is Pat calling. Dr Bannister asked me to call and let you know he has a meeting and will be late home."

"Oh. Did he say why or where? Something to do with the nursing home?"

"No, he didn't say. It sounded personal and he was in a hurry. That's why he asked me to call you. I'm assuming he was late for whatever it was. Dr Ward is on call tonight and Dr Larkin left early to pick up the kids up from school."

"Okay. Thanks for letting me know." Katie frowned. *Where would he be going? Why wouldn't he call from the car? I'm sure he didn't mention an appointment and I definitely heard him say he'd be home around five.* Katie felt uneasy. Was he hiding something? *Pat was vague but then she wouldn't know unless it was patient related and it seemed it was not.*

Buddy Boy barked, followed by Arthur, as they both ran to the front door. "Anyone home!?" Olivia called.

"Olivia, I've been trying to call you. What happened?"

"Sorry, my phone died. You will never believe what happened. I'm just bursting to tell you but I'll wait for John because I'm not certain I understand everything that happened." Her voice rose in excitement.

"John!?"

"That would be me." John walked in, looking like the cat that caught the canary or more like the Cheshire cat that caught the canary. "I did it, Katie. I'm back." He walked past Olivia and, for a moment, Katie thought he was going to kiss her and stepped back.

"I am pleased, surprised and a little confused. Is someone going to tell me what this unexpected visit is all about?"

"It is quite a story. We may need a whole pot of tea," John said.

"Come into the kitchen and take a seat." Katie pointed to the kitchen table and put the kettle on, thinking a glass of wine would be more appropriate, forgetting John did not drink since his recovery. "Start talking!"

"I'll start with the result and John can fill in the details. We have a sort of joint custody. I have full custody of Poppy and John has full custody of Jonathan. We both have unlimited visiting rights and are obliged to inform and/or discuss the children's welfare such as education, health and major changes. We each have to prove we can provide the children with a good home." Olivia beamed. "Basil has been ordered to pay a lump sum to assist me in providing adequate accommodation and substantial child support for Poppy and waived my obligation to pay child support for Jonathan."

"Wow! Olivia, congratulations! This is wonderful news. When does this take place?"

"As soon as all the paperwork is done. The children go back to school on Monday for the winter term. This will give us time to find a house and I intend to find a school close by for Poppy so she can live with me and Cyril. I don't like that school. Oh, and I have complete control when I visit. No more chaperone. The judge was appalled at that."

John added, "The judge was appalled by many of the restrictions."

Katie's forehead creased in puzzlement. Ignoring John, she raised her hand and said, "Just a second. Did you say Poppy would live with you and Cyril? Is there more news?"

Olivia giggled. Katie had never heard her giggle before and she blushed as she answered. "Cyril and I are to be married. We haven't said anything because we were afraid it would affect the custody settlement. Actually, it helped. The judge liked the idea that the children would have a stable family home. We are buying a house right here in Springsville." Olivia giggled again, her happiness quite infectious, making Katie and John smile with her. "I will be an ordinary housewife and mother."

Katie wasn't so sure about that. She had trouble imagining Olivia scrubbing floors. Perhaps Olivia's idea of an ordinary housewife might include a maid or two. "Congratulations!

My goodness, so many surprises." Katie turned to John, who had been very quiet. "And all this happened because of your legal skills; the lawyer who cares for his clients. You are correct, 'you are back.'" She was proud of him and actually felt some old warm feelings flare up. Touching his arm, she said, "Congratulations, John!" Hearing someone clear their throat, she pulled her hand away.

"Very touching," Piers whispered under his breath, but loud enough to be heard. He then raised his voice and asked, "What are we congratulating?"

"I have custody of my children and John made it happen," Olivia blurted out.

"That is something to celebrate. I am very pleased for you, Olivia." Piers gave Katie an apologetic glance as he turned to John and tersely added, "You must be pleased. I don't profess to know much about the law but I'm assuming this a victory for you."

"It is but I can't take all the credit." John spoke with confidence, ignoring Piers' sarcasm. "I had a great legal team behind me and an amazing investigator who managed to find proof of Lord Thesleton's abuse of Olivia, which was no easy task. He covered his tracks well. The clincher was the children's statements. Olivia, I haven't had a chance to tell you yet, but you should be proud of both of your children. Poppy told the judge she was frightened of her father and didn't like boarding school or living on the estate. She wanted to live with you. The judge noticed the bruise on her arm but she wouldn't outright accuse her father. The judge wisely assigned you full custody. Your son was amazing. He's going to go a long way. He said he wanted to live with his father as he was heir to the title and estate, but he didn't believe the things his father said about his mother and wanted to be able to visit her as often as he could."

The news that her son had defended her prompted Olivia to burst into happy tears. "Thank you, John. That means so much." She brushed the tears away. "You never actually told me what finally happened."

"Most of the settlement was not of the judge's making. It was Lord Thesleton."

"I don't believe you. Basil has never done anything for me," Olivia said with shock.

"I have no illusions about that, Olivia. He did it for himself. Here's what happened but none of this goes out of this room." John looked everyone in the eye. "Understood?" He waited for nods of agreement. "I have no proof, but I believe Jonathan admitted his father coerced him into writing the letter that pleaded or threatened you to stop proceedings. Reading between the lines, and after discussing things with one of my colleagues, it is quite possible that the judge gave Lord Thesleton some latitude as a professional courtesy. In other words, one judge to the other, which, of course, would be denied. There is no doubt in my mind that Lord Thesleton wanted to avoid a scandal and possibly losing his judicial appointment. The evidence of threats and lies in the wrong hands would have the paparazzi foaming at the mouth. I doubt we had enough proof to make it stick but, at the very least, the scandal would have been damaging and embarrassing. However, his legal team would advise him to cease the unreasonable vindictive demands and offer a reasonable compromise and settlement that the judge would agree to. An acceptable settlement would mitigate any further investigation."

Katie jumped up from her seat and paced the kitchen. "That is terrible. The man shouldn't be allowed on the bench. He should be exposed and pay for the way he treated Olivia."

"Calm down, Katie. I know and understand what you're saying." John used his best soothing voice. "Olivia won in more ways than one and Basil lost big time and is suffering the consequences. Olivia has custody of Poppy, visits with Jonathan and money in the bank. Basil would not dare touch or hurt the children. He knows his bullying could be his undoing. One false move and his colleagues would turn on him. Protecting an associate only goes so far. Olivia and the children have nothing to gain by fighting and everything to lose. The scandal would hurt them as much, if not more, than Lord Thesleton. Don't you think they have suffered enough? It is time for them to settle down and enjoy life as a family."

Katie nodded, feeling chastised. John was right. As much as she hated letting men like Basil get away with bullying, she did agree that the humiliation alone would be punishment for Basil. The knowledge that one wrong move might put his past at risk of exposure would make him feel the same fear and intimidation he had inflicted on others.

Katie moved towards Piers and sat next to him, giving him a kiss on the cheek, making sure that John had seen it. Piers was reassured that the only person she loved was her husband, not her ex. She may have been proud of him, but that was all. Glancing from one to the other, she was tempted to giggle as there was no doubt in her mind that both men had received the subtle message loud and clear.

"Piers, I am not sure you heard the news that Cyril and Olivia are getting married and buying a house here in Springsville."

"That is good news. When's the big day?" Piers had a

strange look about him. His words seemed almost forced and polite, but not at all happy about the room full of people. In the confusion, Katie had forgotten about Piers' mysterious personal meeting. Did Piers have news and, if so, about what? Now *she* wanted her visitors to leave.

"No date set, but it will be soon. We want to buy the house and get this legal stuff settled first. Is it okay if we book in for a couple of days?" Olivia asked. "Both of us. Cyril place above the shop is not that comfortable."

"Of course, the Lavender Suite is always ready for you," Katie replied.

"I'd like to freshen up before Cyril gets here. If you would excuse me, I'll leave you now. John, would you be a dear and fetch my bag from the car?"

Piers squeezed Katie's hand. She dared not look at him she knew he was smiling. *You can take the lady out of the manor house but not the manor house out of the lady.* Her thought almost made her burst out laughing, as John looked taken aback by the request. But he did as he was asked and returned with her leather weekend case.

"Well, I had better be on my way. Lots of paperwork to finish. Goodbye!"

Piers walked John to the door and closed it rather firmly. "I thought they would never leave. I need a drink and from the look on your face, so do you." Piers put his arm around her waist and, with the other hand, reached to the wine rack. Squeezing her, he laughed and said, "I'll have to let you go while I open the bottle."

"Bring the wine into the Morning Room, where we won't be disturbed. Do you have something to tell me?" she asked tentatively.

"I most certainly do. And, before you accuse me of being secretive, I had no choice. But you are going to love what I have to say and we have a lot of discussion ahead of us tonight." He poured two glasses of wine and placed the bottle of Merlot on the side table between them.

"I am intrigued."

"First, I have to give you an explanation. I took our 'tell all' pledge seriously. I was not being secretive but I needed to do some in-depth thinking about myself and what I wanted and why."

"This does sound serious. This isn't bad news, I hope."

He leaned over and stroked her creased forehead. "You worry too much and this is good news. Men need to get in touch with their inner feelings too, you know. "

"I know." She gave him a quizzical look. "Are you teasing me?"

"A little, except I'm being truthful. I needed to do a lot of thinking. You remember George and Nancy suggesting I join the practice and I said, no it wasn't for me? It wasn't or isn't in its current format. George has called me a couple of times and I gave him the same answer every time. I like my urban practice with a hard working partner like Rick and an excellent nurse and receptionist and now a really good new doctor."

Katie was on the edge of her seat. What was Piers saying? "I hear a 'but' coming."

"Sort of. Rick and I had our usual business meeting with the accountant, who always freaks me out with numbers. He has some concerns about the extra expense of Dr Ward."

"I thought he approved the hiring of a new doctor?"

"He did, but he also said we needed to increase our income

to support the salary. I think we glossed over that, keen to have some help. Our current situation is too many patients for two doctors, but not quite enough for three and he's right, particularly as Stephanie is fast, full of energy and easily sees more patients than either Rick or me. As much as I'm enjoying the shorter hours and a bit more time off, that doesn't pay the bills. We have to find a balance."

"What does this have to do with George?" Katie held her breath, hoping for the answer she was looking for.

"I'm sorry. I know I should have called you but it was last minute. I was delayed and late. That's why I had Pat call you about my meeting today and, obviously, I couldn't give Pat any details. George offered me the partnership again. I told him what I wanted and how I would run the practice. This time, he agreed with me. Katie, I am considering it but we have to talk."

"We sure do. What about Rick?"

"After we met with the accountant, Rick was quite upset. The money issue is important to him. He has a young family to support. I made the suggestion that if I accepted George's offer, there would be only one partner to pay, plus Stephanie's salary. She made the brilliant suggestion of hiring a nurse practitioner, which we turned down at first, but might be the answer. The idea of coming home every night and walking to the clinic is growing on me every day. I want to open a clinic here in Springsville. George likes the idea but it took some convincing. George, me and possibly a nurse practitioner. I wondered if you would be our receptionist. We could work around when you're needed at the B&B, maybe hire someone from the village part-time." Piers stopped talking and waited for Katie's response.

"Whoa, that is a lot to take in," Katie said. Her heart pounded with apprehension and excitement at the same time. What Piers had just said was what she was hoping for. Although she hadn't expected the receptionist offer. "Yes! I think it is a brilliant plan."

"Wow! I thought I'd have much more explaining to do. However, there is a 'but.' We will need to finance an office. George has some equipment but it is very outdated. We need to find office space and furnishings. I thought we could use the money from the sale of my house in Nottingham. What do you think?"

"I think that's a perfect idea. Let's do it. Old man Cuthbert's place is for sale on Main Street, next to Cyril's antique shop. It needs a lot of work but you'll have to renovate anyway."

Piers called George that night to accept the partnership with conditions, the main one being a clinic in Springsville.

Piers and Katie spent the evening making plans and lists of who to call and what to do. Exhausted from too much thinking and planning, they eventually went to bed. Katie lay in Piers' arms, so much in love, and whispered, "A new exciting adventure, Dr Bannister. We'll do this together. I love you so much."

"I love you more." Piers kissed her, knowing he was the luckiest man alive.

This brings us to the end of this book.
For more Lavender Cottage Novels
Click here https://geni.us/oMhF

Epilogue

Piers left the clinic in Nottingham in March after buying and renovating the house on Main Street. He and George opened the Springsville Medical Clinic on April 1st. Olivia and Cyril married in a small civil ceremony in February and settled into family life with Poppy and frequent visits from Jonathan.

Katie fussed over her daughter, impatient for the birth of her first grandchild, and was delighted with the friendly romance blossoming between best friend Judy and contractor Abe.

Katie and Piers settled into a new routine, more in love than ever. Piers embraced the role of country doctor. Katie loved having him home and being part of the clinic.

The Lavender Cottage Novels will always focus on Katie, the B&B guests, her friends and inhabitants of Springsville. However, future stories will also feature Dr Piers Bannister and his adventures as a country doctor. Stay tuned for the next mystery, adventure and, of course, love story.

Acknowledgements

As always there are a many people to thank for their support and encouragement getting this book to print. Thank you to the Historical Writing Ladies Group for listening to a contemporary work of fiction, which was a big stretch from our usual historical fiction. Gratitude abound for Meghan Negrijn, my official editor, who navigates the prose through, among other things, a minefield of commas and I have now been officially designated the 'Queen of Commas.' It never ceases to amaze me how many typos get through multiple readings from multiple readers. Thank you to proofreaders Mary Rothschild and Kathleen Bigras, for ferreting out the mistakes. And, my apologies for any we missed, the grammar police will nearly always find something but we did our best.

The cover design came from the author with the assistance of BookBrush.com

About the Author

Susan A. Jennings was born in Britain of a Canadian mother and British father. Both her Canadian and British heritages are often featured in her stories. She lives in Ottawa, Canada where she writes, historical fiction, women's fiction with later in life romance. She has published numerous short stories and contributed to several anthologies and dabbled a little with nonfiction. Susan is also past president of the Ottawa Independent Writers (OIW)

You can connect with me on:

🌐 https://susanajennings.com

🐦 https://sajauthor

📘 http://facebook.com/authorsusanajennings

Subscribe to my newsletter:

✉ https://geni.us/NewsfromSusan

Also by Susan A Jennings

The Sackville Hotel Trilogy
   Book 1 - The Blue Pendant
   Book 2 - Anna's Legacy
   Book 3 - Sarah's Choice
   Box Set - All three books
   Prequel – Ruins in Silk*

Sophie's War Series
   Book 1 - Prelude to Sophie's War
   Book 2 - Heart of Sophie's War
   Book 3 - In the Wake of Sophie's War (2022)
   Prequel - Ruins in Silk *
   *Leads into The Blue Pendant and Sophie's War

The Lavender Cottage Books
   Book 1 - When Love Ends Romance Begins
   Book 2 - Christmas at Lavender Cottage
   Book 3 - Believing Her Lies
   Book 4 - Second Chances

Nonfiction
   Save Some for me - A Memoir
   A Book Tracking Journal for ladies
   Forget-Me-Not A Book Tracking Journal
   A Dog with a Blog - Miss Penny Speaking

Short Stories:
  Mr. Booker's Book Shop
  The Tiny Man
  A Grave Secret
  Gillian's Ghostly Dilemma
  The Angel Card
  Little Dog Lost Reiki Found

Story Collections
  The Blue Heron Mysteries
  Contributing author to:
  The Black Lake Chronicles
  Ottawa Independent Writers' Anthologies

Printed in Great Britain
by Amazon